CROOKED HEART

CROOKED HEART

A NOVEL

Lissa Evans

HARPER

An Imprint of HarperCollins*Publishers*

CROOKED HEART. Copyright © 2015 by Lissa Evans. All rights reserved. Printed in the United States of America. No part of this book may be used or reproduced in any manner whatsoever without written permission except in the case of brief quotations embodied in critical articles and reviews. For information, address HarperCollins Publishers, 195 Broadway, New York, NY 10007.

HarperCollins books may be purchased for educational, business, or sales promotional use. For information, please e-mail the Special Markets Department at SPsales@harpercollins.com.

Published in Great Britain in 2014 by Doubleday, an imprint of Random House.

FIRST U.S. EDITION

Library of Congress Cataloging-in-Publication Data has been applied for.

ISBN: 978-0-06-236483-8

15 16 17 18 19   OFF/RRD   10 9 8 7 6 5 4 3 2 1

To Kate Anthony and Gaby Chiappe

PROLOGUE

She was losing words. At first it was quite funny. 'The box of things,' Mattie would say, waving her mauve-veined hands vaguely around the kitchen.

'The box of things for making flames. It's a song, Noel!

> *'The box of things for making flames*
> *I can't recall their bloody names.'*

Or 'that church', she'd say, standing at the top of Hampstead Heath, gazing down at the scribble of blue and grey that was London. 'The one with the dome – remind me of what it's called.'

'St Paul's Cathedral.'

'Of course it is. The architect has a bird's name. Owl . . . Ostrich . . .'

'Wren.'

'Right again, young Noel, though I can't help thinking "Sir Christopher Ostrich" has a tremendous ring to it . . .'

After a while, it stopped being funny. 'Where's my . . . my . . .' His godmother would teeter around the drawing room, slippered feet not quite keeping up with her heavy body. 'Where's that damn thing, the blue thing, goes round my shoulders, the *blue* thing . . .'

Some words would resurface after a few days; others would sink for ever. Noel started writing labels: 'SHAWL', 'WIRELESS', 'GAS MASK', 'CUTLERY DRAWER'.

'Helpful little man,' Mattie said, bending to kiss his forehead. 'Be sure to take them down before Geoffrey comes to check on me,' she added, suddenly shrewd again.

Uncle Geoffrey and Auntie Margery lived a mile away, in Kentish Town. Once a month, Uncle Geoffrey came for Sunday tea, and once a year he dropped by for Mattie's birthday, always bringing a gift that had been made either by himself or by Auntie Margery.

'There are times,' said Mattie, examining yet another cross-stitched antimacassar, 'when it's very useful to have an open fire. What is the one thing that is more important than money, Noel?'

'Taste.'

'Which is something that Geoffrey and . . .' she paused, '. . . bosoms . . .'

'Margery.'

'. . . will never have.'

At the monthly teas, Uncle Geoffrey smiled all the time and talked about his job in rate-collection, the marquetry picture frames he made in his spare time, and Auntie Margery's delicate health, which prevented her from ever leaving the house. His teeth were regular and well-spaced, like battlements. Noel liked to imagine tiny soldiers popping up between them, firing arrows across the room or pouring molten lead down Uncle Geoffrey's chin.

'And what have you been up to, young Noel?' his uncle would ask. 'Keeping busy with hobbies? Model aircraft? Stamp collecting?'

'Hobbies are for people who don't read books,' said Noel; it was one of Mattie's sayings.

After tea, Uncle Geoffrey would ask whether there was anything he could do around the house, and Mattie always found something awkward or messy – shifting furniture, oiling a door. When the blackout regulations were published, Uncle Geoffrey was set to work sticking brown paper on the door-panes and checking every shutter for soundness.

'After all,' as Mattie said, 'you are our war expert.' He had enrolled as an air-raid warden the day after Mr Chamberlain came back from Munich. He had a hat, a whistle and an armband.

'So all you need now is an air-raid!' said Mattie.

She didn't believe that there would be a war.

Mattie's house was a spacious brick box, with a fancy ironwork verandah and a garden full of azaleas. 'A Victorian gentleman's residence,' she said. 'Or, more likely, the place where a Victorian gentleman secreted his mistress. Family in Mayfair, lady friend in Hampstead. It would have been considered frightfully out of town.'

The road ran along a little crease in the fabric of the Heath, coming to a dead end at a bolt of rabbit-cropped turf; from the rear windows of the house you could see only trees.

'Who would know we were in London?' said Mattie, nearly every day.

It was a hot, slow summer. In the early morning, when it was still cool, they walked the mile to Parliament Hill and back, leaving dark tracks through the wet grass, singing songs of protest to the skylarks:

> *As we come marching, marching,*
> *We bring the greater days.*
> *The rising of the women*
> *Means the rising of the race.*
> *No more the drudge and idler,*
> *ten that toil while one reposes,*
> *But a sharing of life's glories:*

Bread and Roses!
Bread and Roses!
Our lives shall not be sweated
From birth until life closes;
Hearts starve as well as bodies;
Give us bread, but give us roses!

On the final chorus repeats, Mattie would simultaneously hum and whistle. 'A rare and underrated skill,' she'd remark, 'and one that, sadly, has never brought me the acclaim it deserves.'

During the afternoon heat, she slept in a deckchair and Noel lay on the lawn and read detective stories, noting down clues as he went along. Wood pigeons crooned in the trees.

'Who'd know,' sighed Mattie, 'who'd know we were in . . . in . . .'

In the silence that followed, Noel rolled over and looked at her. Her square, sure face was suddenly unfamiliar; her expression one he'd never seen before. It was panic, he realized. Somewhere inside herself she was teetering on a ledge.

'London,' he said, 'it's *London*.'

'Ah yes, London,' she repeated, inching back.

The mechanical digger arrived one day when they were at the library. By the time they came home, the first lorry was already roaring back past their house, leaving a frill of sand along the verges behind it.

'What are you doing?' called Mattie to the driver, but he ignored her.

They followed the gritty trail to the end of the road, and there stood the great red digger. It had already scalped the grass from fifty yards of heath, and was taking savage bites out of the sandy slope. Another lorry was waiting for a load.

'No!' shouted Mattie.

Three neighbours arrived, sweating and gesticulating, and then a fourth, grim with knowledge.

'It's official,' he said. 'I've been talking to the council. It's for sandbags, they say they're going to need thousands if bombing starts. They're grubbing up Hyde Park, too . . .'

Within the week, there were four diggers, not one, and a constant stream of lorries rattling up past the house and then grinding down again. The hole in the Heath grew daily, the cut edge a palette of yellows: ochre, mustard, butter, gold. When the wind blew, Mattie's front garden was more beach than grass. Every floor in the house crunched underfoot. Mrs Harley, the char, said the extra work was too much for her, and left.

A man came to the door, offering filled sandbags at £5 for a hundred, or empty ones for 3d each. 'And then you can do them yourself,' he said. 'Lucky for you, you're right on the spot.' Mattie closed the door in his face.

Their morning walk was changing. The detour they took to avoid the hole at the end of the road added another mile to the round trip; it was just too far for Noel, with his gammy leg, to manage comfortably, and meant he was always limping by the time they arrived home. There was a gun emplacement behind Parliament Hill now, and shelters being dug along the fields by the railway line. Mattie would stand and stare at the horizon, at the silver blimps motionless on invisible wires, and shake her head in disbelief. 'Isn't it strange,' she said, 'that there's always enough money in the coffers for war?'

During his August teatime visit, Uncle Geoffrey talked about the international situation before patting Noel on the head. 'And I wonder where this young shaver will be off to?' he said, smiling as usual.

'What d'you mean, "off to"?' asked Mattie, very sharply.

The smile wavered. 'You'll have registered him, I suppose, for evacuation?'

'No, why would I have done that?'

Geoffrey looked flustered. 'I didn't mean to annoy you, Mattie dear,' he said, advancing a hand as if to pat one of Mattie's, and then wisely withdrawing it again. 'It's just that the government . . .' With an effort, he hoisted the smile back on to his face, where it hung a little crookedly, '. . . the government considers that the best place for children, in the event of a war, is away from the areas of likely bombardment.'

'There is no war.'

'Not yet, perhaps, but I think the likelihood is—'

'And since when have I ever taken any notice of what the government says?' asked Mattie.

There was no possible reply to this. She had been gaoled five times as a suffragette; she still had the scars of handcuffs on her wrists.

'Do you want to be evacuated?' Mattie asked Noel, afterwards.

'No,' he said.

'I'm sure Roberta would have you to stay in . . . where is it that Roberta lives? Ipswich? I'm sure you'd be safe there.'

'I don't want to go anywhere,' he said. He was a little bit worried by the thought of bombs. He was far, far more worried by the fact that Mattie seemed to have forgotten that her best friend Roberta was dead. The funeral had been eighteen months ago. Mattie had worn her old sash, and a white, green and purple rosette.

Poland was being invaded and the summer holidays were almost over. On the Saturday before the start of the Michaelmas term, Noel went to the library. He had read every Lord Peter Wimsey on the shelves, and every Albert Campion. The tall librarian with the moustache suggested he tried a thriller instead of a detective story. 'You'll find Eric Ambler very good,' she said. Noel was brooding over the choice of titles when he received a blow between the shoulder blades.

'Hello, Lugs,' said Peter Wills, loudly.

Noel nodded at him, in a polite but dismissive way. Peter was in the form below him at St Cyprian's Prep – only-just-nine to Noel's nearly-ten – but Peter tended towards condescension because his father was in the army reserve. And because he had a father.

'Ready for the off?' asked Peter. 'My mother bumped into Cleggo and he says we'll be heading for Wales, worst luck. But it's near the sea, he says.'

'I've decided not to go,' said Noel. 'I'm staying in London.'

'Crikey.' Peter looked envious. 'You'll get to see all the fun then.'

'*You can imagine what a bitter blow it is to me—*' the Prime Minister was saying, as Mattie swatted the 'off' switch. 'Bugger,' she said. 'Bugger and bugger. Bloody *men*. Everything has to be solved by firing guns at each other. Bang bang you're . . . you're . . .' She paced around the dining room, pushing her hands through her hair so that it stood up in a wild crown. 'How did it come to this?' she demanded, looking at Noel.

Uncle Geoffrey, who never telephoned, rang to inform them that war had been declared, and to ask whether they needed help with the blackouts. 'Thank you, but we can manage,' said Mattie. It took them an hour, and the light was fading before they finished.

'Don't like a room without windows,' said Mattie, who rarely closed the curtains in the evening. 'Airless. Reminds me of those places. The ones with locks and so on.'

In the night, Noel woke suddenly. He lay in the stifling darkness, and listened to Mattie walking from room to room, flinging open the shutters.

The day after that, all the children disappeared, as if London had shrugged and the small people had fallen off the edge. Noel, running an errand, was stared at in the street. The baker asked why he hadn't gone with the others. 'I think you'll find that evacuation is not compulsory,' replied Noel, loftily. It was what Mattie had said to an interfering neighbour.

He took a walk up the hill to his school, and looked at the padlock and chain around the gates. 'Closed until further notice' read a sign. It hadn't occurred to him that this would happen; he'd seen himself as the sole pupil, attending exclusive lessons. The council school on Fletcher Road was shut as well, the windows boarded up.

Noel sat on a wall for a while, before going home; Mattie hated the government but she was very keen on education.

For two weeks he left the house at eight, wearing his school uniform and carrying his satchel and gas mask. After calling at the library, he took the bus to the top of Hampstead Heath, and walked to the Climbing Tree. It was an oak that had been struck by lightning three years before, and lay full length across a clearing. It was usually infested with children, but now he had the great sprawled form to himself, and he sat in the crook of a branch and read all of Eric Ambler, and then all of Sherlock Holmes. Early in the third week, he looked up to see Mattie staring at him.

'I was listening for woodpeckers,' she said, 'but instead I found a lesser-spotted truant.'

'The school's all locked up.'

'Then we shall turn our house into a school.'

For three days, she gave him proper lessons (Great Women of History, the Causes of the French Revolution) and set him essays ('Would You Rather Be Blind or Deaf?', 'What Is Freedom?', 'Should People Keep Pets?', '"All Things Are Difficult Before They Are Easy": Discuss Fuller's Aphorism'), marking his work with red ink and rolling sentences: *A splendid attempt. Your argument was presented with considerable éclat.* On the fourth morning, there was a knock at the door. It was a short man in a boiler suit and a white helmet – the Chief Warden, he said, from the East Hampstead Branch of the ARP. There had been reports of breaches of blackout regulations.

'Reports from whom?' asked Mattie, booming out the last syllable, so that it sounded like a dinner gong.

'Neighbours,' said the warden. 'Shutters open, shutters closed, lights on and off. They said it looked like signalling. Not that it was, I'm sure,' he added, hastily, seeing Mattie's expression, 'but people are entitled to be a bit anxious at the moment, aren't they, madam?'

'Miss,' corrected Mattie. 'I am not a brothel-keeper.'

'I have to warn you that the next step is a summons,' said the warden.

'D'you hear that?' asked Mattie, turning to Noel. 'This little man is threatening me with court.'

The warden flushed a dark red. 'There's no need for rude-ness,' he said. 'I'm enforcing government rules. And while I'm here, I'd like to ask whether the following have been carried out. Taping of windows. Readiness of buckets containing sand and water. Insulation of a room to be used as refuge in the event of a gas attack.'

'Are those, too, legally enforceable?' asked Mattie.

The warden shook his head.

'Then no,' said Mattie. 'Go away, little man, and interfere with someone else.'

'You do realize,' said the warden, his voice hardening, 'that the courts take blackout infringement very seriously indeed. We're not just talking about fines here; there could be a prison term.'

He left, crunching along the sandy path to the front gate. Mattie gave a little grunt and Noel looked up at her. Her face was puffy and skewed, as if the warden's last sentence had been a blow with a boxing-glove. 'Those places . . .' she said, and gripped Noel's hand. 'Never,' she said.

★

In the weeks that followed, Noel found himself thinking about Dr Long, who taught algebra and physics at St Cyprian's, and who presented each new law or principle to the class as if he were lifting a jewel out of a casket. Dr Long expected interest and asked for wonder, unlike Mr Clegg, whose Geography lessons were like a series of punishments. Thirty strokes with the principal exports of the Malay Peninsula.

'Imagine,' Dr Long had said to Noel's form last term, 'imagine Archimedes' lever. Imagine it stretching from star to star, one end nudging the base of our planet, the centre of it propped on a titanic fulcrum, and at the other end, standing on a cloud of galactic dust, a small man in a toga. He extends a hand, he places a finger on the end of the plank, he presses down . . . and our Earth goes bowling across the universe.'

One nudge and the world was changed. The warden's visit had done it; it had flicked Mattie out of her orbit and now she was spinning off on a course of her own.

She drew up a list of neighbours who might have reported her to the warden. It started off with Mr Arnott, who lived in the next villa, but then she kept adding names until everyone was on it. 'We shall no longer speak to them,' she said to Noel. 'In fact,' she added, 'I should prefer not to see them at all.'

Now, when they went out for their morning walk, Noel had to go to the front gate and check that the road was empty before Mattie would leave the house. Though they weren't really 'morning walks' any more; Mattie wasn't sleeping well, and woke late, so it was almost lunchtime before they were cresting Parliament Hill. The lessons were replaced by occasional questions: thirty-five multiplied by fifteen, the Roman invasion, the life-cycle of the honey bee. Once Mattie woke him at dawn, and asked him to name three British scientists. 'Newton, Boyle, Darwin,' he said, yawning, while a wren shouted in the ivy outside.

The days became untethered. Mealtimes slid around or disappeared altogether. Noel ate mainly biscuits for three days, and then found a cookery book. The recipes were wonderfully satisfying; it was like doing an equation, in which the correct answer was edible.

'Very good indeed,' said Mattie, of the blackberry pie that he made with fruit picked on the Heath, but she ate only a mouthful or two. For the whole of Noel's life with her, she had been quite large – stout and solid, like a tree-stump, but now she was dwindling. Her stockings drooped. She had no time to eat, she said; there were too many things she needed to do.

One morning, he came downstairs to find that all the helpful labels he'd written had been crossed out. He was standing with '~~CUTLERY DRAWER~~' in his hand when Mattie came into the kitchen.

'Someone's been breaking in and writing messages,' she said. 'I shall have to have a new lock installed on the . . . the object for opening.'

When Uncle Geoffrey rang the doorbell on the following Sunday, Mattie stayed seated, finger marking a place in her book. Noel stood up, and she shook her head at him.

The bell jangled twice more, and then they heard the gate creak.

'There,' said Mattie, looking pleased.

'I just need the WC,' said Noel, and ran upstairs. He peered out through the round spyhole window on the landing and saw Uncle Geoffrey still standing in the lane, looking unhappily back at the house. Noel ducked down, counted to a hundred and looked again. Geoffrey had gone.

'Why didn't we want him to come in?' he asked Mattie, that evening.

'Who?'

'Uncle Geoffrey.'

'They all know each other,' she said. 'Wardens. All authority is linked, Angus, that's how the world is run. Independence is one's only hope. You must promise me one thing.'

'What?'

'To never tell anybody anything.'

'All right,' he said. 'You called me Angus,' he added, after a moment.

'I did not.' She spoke with absolute certainty.

That was the first time he really felt afraid; soon, he began to carry the feeling around with him, a cold scarf wrapped around his neck, a stomach full of tadpoles.

The autumn was warm and dry. Noel raked and burned leaves while Mattie did other things. He wasn't sure what. The two of them had started to revolve in different directions, moving into alignment only three or four times a day, at meals, or in the drawing room where Mattie would delve around in the desk, rearranging papers, while Noel sat in the window seat and read all of Edgar Wallace and then all of Dashiell Hammett. Sometimes he sat and watched the lorries lurching along the track.

They had no more visitors, apart from delivery boys, and the postman, and once a woman who was collecting for the North West London Branch of the Army Comforts Fund. Noel watched from the drawing-room window as she sprinted away up the lane, Mattie shouting after her. Uncle Geoffrey made no further appearances, and neither did the local warden. Noel would walk round the outside of the house every evening, making sure that no chinks of light were visible.

Winter seemed to start suddenly. He woke one morning, and saw his own breath. The scuttle in the kitchen was empty, and he went outside to the bunker and raised the heavy sliding door. A cascade of small coals tumbled out, and then a slither of paper. Letters, open and crumpled. A thick sheaf of forms, torn in half. He crouched and fingered them, and saw his own name under the smears of black. Gathering the whole lot up, he took them to the summerhouse.

It was in a corner of the garden: a fretwork chalet, built on a turntable so that it could revolve to chase the sun. At some point it had rusted and stuck, facing east, and then ivy had crept across the roof so that now it was just a green hillock, rarely used. The wood of the front rail was silky with age. Noel knelt on the cold boards of the porch, and spread out the papers:

A letter from Mr Clegg, the headmaster of St Cyprian's, suggesting that Noel should join them in Llandeilo:

> . . . *unless, of course, you have made other arrangements for his education, in which case perhaps you would be kind enough to let our bursar know as soon as possible, and to settle your outstanding account accordingly. Places at St Cyprian's are greatly sought after, especially in light of the current international situation, and I think you may find that your godson's capricious approach to study, coupled with his reluctance to participate in team activities may not be catered for with the same degree of tolerance at other educational establishments . . .*

National registration forms, dated 7th September:

> *There is a legal requirement for you to furnish such details as are requested on the following pages. Without this information, we will be unable to issue the ration book that you will need for basic food purchases, or the national identity card, which it will be necessary for you to present whenever requested by authority. Please use black ink. Erroneous or deliberately misleading information will result in prosecution.*

Two letters from Uncle Geoffrey and Auntie Margery:

25th September 1939
Dear Mattie,
Geoffrey called on Sunday, as per usual, but perhaps you were out. On the other hand, perhaps you were feeling 'under the weather' and had rather not receive visitors. Geoffrey thought he saw Noel, but perhaps he was mistaken.
Should he call next Sunday instead?
Yours affectionately,
Geoffrey and Margery Overs

9th October 1939
Dear Mattie,
Just a little note. We tried to telephone you, but there must have been some fault on the line since you were unable to hear our voices.
Is all well with you and young Noel? Shall Geoffrey call on the usual Sunday this month? We imagine there may be some little jobs around your house needing attention, and it's always Geoffrey's pleasure to help out.
Yours affectionately,
Geoffrey and Margery Overs

Geoffrey and Margery always said 'we' for everything, as if fused together like Chang and Eng. He imagined their ears jointly pressed to the telephone. He had witnessed that call, he realized – Mattie listening silently for a few seconds before replacing the receiver.

His hands were black. He filled the scuttle and dragged it back to the kitchen and when the range was lit, he burned the papers one by one, keeping only the letter from the National Registration Office. He would write to the office, he decided, asking for another set of forms, and when those arrived he could fill them in himself.

He washed his hands, and made some porridge. Mattie was awake; he could hear her talking to herself. She'd been doing that, off and on, for days now – odd, chipped remarks, without obvious context, as if she were reading a newspaper article, and throwing out comments. 'Never asked permission,' he heard her say, from halfway down the stairs, 'just went full speed ahead. It's a bit thick, if you ask me.' He heard her slippers slapping down another three steps, and then pausing. 'I *told* you it damned well wasn't,' she said. The footsteps began again, but this time heading back up towards her bedroom.

Noel looked at the spoonful of porridge he was holding. It was wobbling, and he realized that his hand was shaking. He put the spoon down and knitted his fingers together. It must be awfully cold, he thought, to make him shiver like that.

He found a pair of mittens and a scarf in the boot-room, and then, because it seemed silly to dress so warmly and stay in, he went out. He had an urge to go somewhere quite far away, and he hopped on the 136, going down Pond Street, and stayed on it until it rounded the corner at the North Side of Regent's Park. As soon as he got off, he could hear the gibbons hooting.

It was at least six months since he'd last been to the zoo, and it was a shrunken, toothless version of its old self. The pandas and elephants had been moved outside London, the aquariums closed, the reptile house emptied of poisonous snakes. He asked a keeper what had happened to them, and the man – the sort who thought himself funny – took out a handkerchief, placed it over his own nose and mouth, and feigned death throes. 'Had to do it,' said the man. 'Once Hitler starts, it'll only take the one bomb and Camden High Street'll be crawling with rattlers.'

The remaining insects in the insect house were mostly ants and beetles. Noel stood in front of the glass box that had once held black widow spiders. 'My tutor at Somerville looked just like that,' Mattie had remarked, when they'd been here in early spring. 'Spindly little arms and legs, and a great round body. Devoured her husband directly after the wedding, apparently.'

He went to the café and ate a teacake, and then spent a

quarter of an hour tailing a group of Canadian airmen, marvelling at how many times they swore and then calculating an average per minute (twenty-three).

'Hey, kid,' said one of them, eventually, 'fuck off or we'll throw you in with the fucking chimps. You've got the ears for it.'

There was no bus coming. He started to walk back across Primrose Hill, and rapidly wished that he hadn't. At the zoo, the only children had been toddlers with nursemaids, but out here there were packs of boys, dangling from trees, playing football, jeering at the ladies digging allotments on the south slope. One group was engaged in a spitting competition, with a woman's bottom as the target. As Noel passed by, one of the spitters detached himself, and swung into step beside him.

'Hello,' said the boy. He had a scab on his lip; the greeting was not a friendly one. 'Where are you going?' asked the boy.

'Home,' said Noel.

'Where's that, then?'

'Relatively nearby,' said Noel. If he walked any faster, he would begin to limp. He kept his pace steady.

'Why aren't you evacuated?' asked the boy.

'Why aren't you?' asked Noel, bravely.

'Went. Came back,' said the boy, laconically. 'Stinks in the country. No flicks, no chippie and they shit in a *hole* in the *ground*. Give us a bob or I'll kill you.'

'No,' said Noel.

'Tanner.'

'No. I don't have any money.'

'Liar.' Almost casually, the boy extended a foot and tripped him up. 'Two bob, now, for lying,' he said.

Noel dug around in his pocket and found three sixpences. 'There,' he said, throwing them over his shoulder, and then trying to scramble up quickly. The boy stamped a plimsoll on Noel's hand, and strolled over to pick up the money. He examined the coins carefully. 'Go on, then,' he said, glancing back, 'get off home to Mummy.'

There were still three halfpennies left in the other pocket – enough for the bus – but Noel somehow found himself in the Woolworth's at Camden Town, buying a bag of cinder toffee and a skein of liquorice laces. He ate a whole lace and two lumps of toffee at the same time, and felt his mouth fill up with sweet glue.

On the way home, he happened to pass along Mafeking Road where Uncle Geoffrey and Auntie Margery lived in the basement flat of number 23. He had only been there a couple of times. 'A rabbit hutch,' Mattie had commented, after one of the visits, 'and far too tidy. One should have *large, light* rooms with comfortable clutter. Remember that, Noel.' He peered down through the railings at the whitened step, and the china rabbit beside the front door.

They weren't really his aunt and uncle; Geoffrey was Mattie's nearest relative, a first cousin once removed, and no relation at all to Noel. 'A recent literary analogy,' Mattie had remarked, not all that long ago, 'compared one's family to an octopus – a *dear* octopus, from whose tentacles we never quite escape, but I'd say Geoffrey and Margery are more like a couple of barnacles, welded to the hull of the ancestral vessel. Whereas you, Noel, are my cabin boy, and shall some day replace me as captain.' He'd loved that image: Mattie and Noel, on a little wooden ship like the *Santa Maria* – a carved nutshell, intricate and rounded, scudding across the ocean with pennants fluttering. Though with such a small crew, you'd have to hope for fine weather.

He loitered by the railings until the sweets were finished, tipping his head back and eating the liquorice laces as if they were spaghetti. Then he crumpled the bag and threw it down into the area, so that it no longer looked quite so neat. It took him an hour to walk the rest of the way.

The house was frozen, the road outside filled with growling lorries. Mattie's bedroom door was closed, but when he pressed his ear against it, he thought he could hear snoring.

He went downstairs again and knelt to open the range, and the low sun poured in through the kitchen window. Suddenly every item was doused in orange light and it was as if he were seeing the room for the first time in weeks: the crusted dishes filling the sink and draining board, the hillocks of bric-a-brac on the table, chairs, dresser, sideboard and windowsill, the drifts of shoes and books, unwashed stockings, apple cores, hair grips, used matches and crumpled newspapers on a floor that was as sandy as Broadstairs beach. And through the open door, the slovenly tide flowing on into the drawing room, with a place for nothing and nothing in its place, a clutter no longer comfortable but choking.

'My idea,' said Mattie's voice, coming down the stairs. She was still in her striped dressing gown, but was wearing galoshes and holding a torch. 'And it was in the cupboard in the room there,' she said. 'They'd hidden it, of course. The bread is quite dreadful, they must be adding that particular dust, wood dust you know, I said to the boy, that was what happened in the Great War although I don't think he believed me. How was your day?'

'Oh,' said Noel, realizing belatedly that she'd lobbed him a question. 'I went to the zoo.'

'Splendid. Toast, I think.'

She cut a couple of slices from the loaf that had been delivered that afternoon, and then seemed to lose interest, leaving it unbuttered on the bread board. 'Can't see a bloody thing,' she said. 'O radiant dark, O darkly fostered ray.'

'I'd better do the blackouts,' said Noel.

When he came back downstairs, she'd gone. The front door was wide open, moving slightly in the wind.

He went outside and looked up and down the road. The light

had dropped from the sky, leaving only a grey band along the western edge. A single lorry, the last of the day, was heading downhill towards Hampstead, its shaded lights smudging the ground as it bucked between the ruts. Noel waited till the sound had dwindled into the twilight, and then he called Mattie's name. There was no reply. Fear began to slide across his skin like a thin film of ice.

He walked along the road a hundred yards or so and then tripped on a bluish shadow, a ridge masquerading as a hole, and grazed his knee. He hobbled back to the house and spent fifteen minutes trying to find another torch, raking through drawers full of rubbish and dead moths, before snatching up the old garden lantern and a stub of candle. It was probably illegal, but he lit it anyway. By the time he left the house again, darkness had fallen.

Apart from the circle of candlelight, he could see nothing at all. London might as well have disappeared. He walked cautiously, swinging the lantern, half-hoping that someone would notice and come rushing out to tell him off, but there was no noise apart from his own footsteps. Once he saw a fox, poised in the long grass; on the next swing of the light, it was gone.

Where the track met the tarmacadamed road down to Hampstead, he stopped. A motor car, barely visible, swished past. The lantern light began to flicker; it wouldn't be long before it went out altogether. He had no idea what to do. Should he ring the police? But Mattie hated the police, she would never forgive him. Should he knock on a neighbour's door? But then whoever it was would come round to the house, and see what it looked like and that would be the end of him and Mattie; he knew that people weren't supposed to live the way that they were living now; there would be letters written and decisions made.

He turned back. Perhaps he could just tidy downstairs, in the places that a visitor might see. Though in any case, even if he summoned help, how could anyone search for Mattie when you weren't allowed to use a torch unless it was covered with two layers of tissue paper and pointed only at your own feet? Perhaps a dog could find her; a bloodhound. Except he wasn't sure if any dogs were left in London. He hadn't seen any for weeks; the Heath was full of rabbits now, the swathes of coarse grass cropped like a bowling green. And where had Mattie gone?

His body felt loose, unstrung, as if terror were cutting the cords that held it all together. He had never spent an evening without her, not since he was four. He could remember arriving at the house for the first time. 'Would you believe that I don't have a single toy?' she'd asked, and had given him a fossil of an ammonite to play with. It had looked like a large grey pebble, the size of a hot-cross bun, and then he had lifted the top half like a lid and seen the ridged and shining curl from ages past, a hundred million years ago.

The candle lasted until he reached the front gate, and then he walked to the door with arms outstretched, like a child play-ing blind man's bluff. He had hoped that Mattie might be back, but she wasn't.

Her beaver-fur coat was hanging over the banister, and he put it on and sat halfway up the stairs, under the landing window. He could see the front door from there, and hear any noise from the back. After a while, he went and fetched the ammonite from his bedroom. At first it was like ice in his hands, but he tucked it under the fur and by the time he awoke it was quite warm.

His neck felt stiff, and pale yellow light was leaking around the shutters. He walked downstairs like an old man. Mattie wasn't home yet, and he opened the front door and went to look for her.

PART ONE

1

Hitler was thumbing his nose from just across the Channel, and London had decided to move the children out again, all the ones who had come back and all the ones who had never gone. This time Noel was going with them; once again, he hadn't been consulted. Margery had packed his suitcase and Geoffrey had walked him round to Rhyll Street Junior School, like a prisoner under escort. Not that he'd had any thought of escape: being sent away with a classful of children he hated was still an improvement on life in 23B Mafeking Road.

When the whistle blew at St Pancras, he watched the guard slide backwards. The train moved from under the blacked-out roof and sunshine slapped him in the face. He wrote: *I am sitting next to Harvey Madeley. His backside is so enormous that he is wearing his father's trousers cut down into shorts.*

'Here we all are,' said Mr Waring, entering the compartment. 'The Rhyll Street Fifth Column. And young Noel with his pencil and paper. A child amang ye taking notes.'

'Where are we going, sir?' asked someone.

'All very hush-hush,' said Mr Waring. 'I have not been party to the plans.'

'Is it Wales?'

'Let us hope not.'

'They don't speak English in Wales,' said one of the Ferris twins.

The only discernible difference between the Ferris twins, wrote Noel, *is that one of them is even more cretinous than the other.*

'They eat squirrels in Wales,' said the other Ferris twin.

'I won't go anywhere with cows again,' said Alice Beddows. 'In Dorset I could see a cow out of *every* window. And I could *smell* a cow out of every window.'

'Corned beef,' said Roy Pursey, peering into the brown paper bag that the WVS woman had given him.

'Don't open those bags yet,' ordered Mr Waring. Everyone but Noel immediately opened their bags.

'The items those contain are for your foster mothers, not for consuming on the journey,' said Mr Waring, but Roy Pursey had already started to turn the key on the tin of corned beef. Noel watched as a thin pink wound began to gape around the top of the tin.

'Biscuits!' shouted Harvey Madeley.

'When we find ourselves at midnight, progressing at a walking pace up the north-west coast of Scotland,' said Mr Waring, 'you may come to regret your current greed.' He leaned back in his seat and opened a book.

Outside, London moved past very slowly. Most of the view was of backyards and washing lines, though if Noel squashed his cheek against the window, he could see enough of the sky to spot the odd barrage balloon.

'I need to go to the WC,' said Shirley Green.

'In Dorset,' said one of the Ferris twins, 'they only had an outside lav. That's why we came home. We wrote to our mum and she came and got us. She said if we'd stayed we'd have got typhoid. Mr Waring?'

'Hmm?'

'We're only allowed to go somewhere with an inside lav. Our mum said that we—'

'There wasn't even *electricity* where I was,' said Roy Pursey, interrupting. 'They used flipping candles.'

'Detention,' said Mr Waring.

'We're not at school, sir.'

'Nevertheless, my first act when we resume lessons will be to place you in detention for use of bad language.'

The train passed over a bridge and Noel glimpsed a lorry-load of soldiers on the road beneath. If Hitler invaded, as he probably would, then the next time he came to London, the streets might be full of Nazis. Everyone would have to learn German. Uncle Geoffrey, as a member of the Conservative Party, would be lined up against a wall and shot.

'What are you smirking about?' asked Roy Pursey.

'Nothing,' said Noel.

'What's in the notebook?'

'Nothing,' said Noel, again. Roy snatched it and squinted at the rows of symbols.

'It's gobbledegook,' he said.

Noel took it back, quietly satisfied. It was a very simple code called 'Pigpen' and he had just written *Roy Pursey is the most ignorant and unpleasant boy in Rhyll Street Junior School.*

The train gathered speed through the suburbs. Noel wrote down a list of other people who ought to be lined up against a wall and shot. The next time that he glanced out of the window, he saw a field, with a goat.

'It's a cow!' shouted a Ferris twin.

'And there's a horse getting on top of another horse,' said Shirley Green. 'Right on top of it. Why's it doing that, Mr Waring?'

'If a train travels at an average speed of forty-five miles per hour for three and a half hours,' said Mr Waring, 'and then an average speed of twenty-two miles an hour for five and a quarter hours, what distance would it have covered?'

Noel wrote *two hundred and seventy-three miles* in his notebook and then stared out at the mild, flat countryside. The train was beginning to slow again.

'Are we there yet?' asked one of the Ferris twins.

'We've only just left London, Doreen,' said Mr Waring.

The train slowed still further. Red-brick villas appeared outside the window.

'It's a town,' said Roy Pursey. There was a spire visible above the rooftops.

'City,' corrected Mr Waring. 'It's St Albans.'

'You're not supposed to tell anyone, sir,' said Roy Pursey. 'A spy might be listening.'

'And which of your comrades do you suspect of being in the pay of the Third Reich?'

'It's not me,' said Harvey Madeley.

'A classic double-bluff,' said Mr Waring. 'Harvey's your spy.'

Roy shook his head and looked pointedly at Noel. 'No, sir. It would be someone who started coming to our school out of nowhere six months ago, and who never speaks and when he does it's posh and who writes everything down.'

'We're stopping at a *station*,' said Doreen Ferris, excitedly. 'We're here!'

A big woman with a green hat and yellow teeth smiled brightly at them through the window.

'Hello, little Londoners,' she shouted. 'Welcome to safety.'

★

Vee paused with a plate in her hand, and stared out of the kitchen window as the children straggled past.

'Vaccies,' she said. 'Did I tell you, I saw them in town this morning? They were sending them into the Mason's Hall and that councillor with all the yellow hair who was so bloody— so rude to me last week, he was standing by the door, patting their heads as they went up the steps. Anything to get his picture in the paper.' And nits, with any luck.

The children had been fresh off the train, then, excited and shrill; now only a very few were left unclaimed. Vee watched them trudge along the lane. One of them was yawning, another scowling, a third stopped mid-stride and sneezed messily. The Seven Dwarfs, she thought – there was even a jug-eared simpleton, limping along in the rear. Only the billeting officer, thirty years too old and a yard too wide for Snow White, spoiled the illusion.

'She'll be trying Green End Cottages next,' said Vee. 'Irene Fletcher took three last year but they've all gone back to London. Not that I blame them – give me a choice between Irene Fletcher and a bomb and I know which I'd go for.'

From behind her rose a hum of eerie sweetness, like a musical saw, and Vee turned to see her mother at the table, pen poised above a half-written letter, her face tilted towards the wireless. She was wearing headphones, the wire drooping at knee-height across the kitchen.

'Singing along, are you?' asked Vee. 'That's nice.'

She turned back to the sink, spirits only briefly buoyed by the sight of the old dear enjoying herself. She was feeling irritated, and she knew why.

There were one or two people that Vee tried very hard not to think about: that blond councillor for a start, who'd been stopping people in the street, asking them to sign up for National Savings Week, and who had shouted out to Vee in front of everybody that she was being unpatriotic when she ran across Holywell Hill in order to avoid him. *Savings*. She could almost have laughed.

And that foreman at the Ballito factory, who made her wince with rage and humiliation every time she pictured him. And her current landlord, Mr Croxton of Croxton Scrap Metals, with his nasty comments ('Can you inform your lump of a son, Mrs Sedge, that the words "regular patrol of the premises" don't mean "sit on your arse for ten hours"'). And Ezra Rigg, who called himself a rates collector but was just a bully boy, plain and simple, and Vic Allerby and his 'nice little jobs' as if she might actually enjoy shredding her fingers on cut-price fancy work, and Mrs Pilcher, who'd told Vee the bare-faced lie that she only needed some 'light cleaning' four times a week, and Mr Farrell the butcher ('I am not a charity, Mrs Sedge'), and that customer at the scarves counter of Harpenden Woolworth's who just couldn't bring herself to mind her own business, and of course Irene Fletcher at Green End cottages. And now Irene had spilled into her thoughts and was fizzing away like a pinch of liver salts.

They'd bumped into each other on the platform at St Albans City station, the previous Thursday. 'Ooh, fancy seeing you here again,' Irene had said to her. 'Back to visit your Uncle Clive in hospital, are you?' Which was the excuse Vee had given when they'd met the week before, though she'd actually been on her way to Luton to see whether it might be the place to carry out a little money-spinning idea she'd had. 'And don't you look smart,' Irene had added, fixing her with eyes like steel press-studs. 'Lucky old Uncle Clive, that's what I say. What did you tell me was wrong with him?'

'Ulcers.'

'Oh, not a bladder stone like last week then?'

'All sorts,' Vee had said, rather wildly. When the train had arrived, she'd locked herself in the third-class lavatory and stayed there all the way to Luton. And once there, she'd still felt so shaken that she'd ended up taking a nip at the Bird in Hand, opposite the station. Which had meant that she hadn't been in a fit state of mind to carry out her plan of knocking on doors to ask for contributions, and the whole morning had been wasted.

The only comfort was that Irene had obviously jumped to the wrong conclusion, and had assumed that Vee was off to meet a man. Which wasn't illegal, after all. It could have been someone quite respectable, or even a soldier. So there was nothing to worry about on that score.

Perhaps, though, she ought to learn from the encounter and start making notes when she talked to people. She could keep an old envelope and a pencil in her bag:

Uncle Clive, bladder stone, Ward 4, Luton General Hospital. Told to Irene F., 14th June 1940.

That would do. And, while she thought of it:

I've always loved small dogs. Had a brown-and-white Jack Russell terrier called 'Happy' when I was a girl. Told to Mrs Fillimore, 20th June.

And, come to mention it:

Was at school with a girl who lives in California now, called Eileen, she married a salesman and did very well for herself, and she sends us parcels with more silk scarves than we know what to do with. Told to policewoman with red hair after Woolworth's incident. Second half of May.

And:

Have bilious stomach, can't come to the door, we've all come down with it, will pay it off next week. Note left on door for Ezra Rigg, 22nd June.

An exercise book, rather than an envelope, perhaps.

Her mother was humming again, a different tune this time. 'Gold and Silver Waltz,' said Vee. 'Is that right, Mum? Gold and Silver Waltz?'

There was no response. The previous letter had been folded and stuck in an envelope, and her mother had started on another, her pen sprinting across the paper. In spite of her double vision, she had lovely handwriting, put Vee's own to shame.

'Who's that one to, Mum?' she asked. In lieu of an answer, she peered at the addresses on the envelopes. It was the usual mixture of domestic and official – Cousin Harold, ex-neighbour Phyllis Gladney, the Archbishop of Canterbury, President Roosevelt. Harold's envelope was the thickest; he had a vixen of a wife, and a daughter who'd run off to live with a Scotchman, and was much in need of the words of encouragement and Christian comfort her mother offered.

'Cup of tea, Mum? Piece of toast?'

Her mother looked up and nodded. As Vee lit the grill, the electric clock made a noise like a cup hit with a teaspoon; half past five. It was nearly time to wake Donald for work.

Her son was lying with the eiderdown over his face when she went into the room. She laid the tray on the bedside table, and opened the curtains.

'It's a lovely evening,' she said. 'Proper summer.' The low sun had gilded the edge of a pile of hub caps in the yard below, and turned a dented zinc bath into a crimson shell. 'And I've made you a nice rarebit,' she added. 'Oh, and you've got three letters.'

Donald drew the quilt from his face and reached out a hand. Vee had checked the postmarks earlier, and they were the usual puzzling collection; one from Wembley, another from Luton, a third from Leicester. Two were cheap yellow envelopes, one was expensive, the paper as thick as card. All had masculine handwriting.

'Friends of yours?' she asked, brightly.

Donald said nothing, but gestured for the tray, and she waited for him to sit up before placing it on his lap. It often took him a few minutes after waking before he could speak. He'd been that way since childhood, and year after year she'd chivvied and nagged him, thinking it was just laziness, and then he'd gone for his call-up medical and the doctor had found a heart murmur. It was a leaky valve, he'd said, and every beat sent some of the blood back the wrong way, so that Donald wasn't getting the goodness out of it that he ought to be. He'd been born that way, probably. Every heartbeat, thought Vee, for nineteen years . . .

Donald had been brave about it, had only remarked that he knew now why he was so tired all the time, but the guilt that Vee felt was so awful that it seemed to call for some type of Biblical atonement: rending of garments, beating of breasts, the cleaving of something-or-other in twain. The best she could do was to give him her egg and cheese ration, for strength, and her chocolate, for love.

'How are you feeling this evening, Donny?' she asked, after he laid down his knife and fork, and was dabbing at the remaining crumbs with a finger.

'Not so bad, Mum. Bit tired.'

He looked quite like his father when he smiled. More well-built, of course, and with thicker hair. And he was trying to grow a moustache, she noticed. Earlier in the year he'd grown a beard, but had shaved it off. And last month he'd changed his parting again. He'd spent a lot of time, lately, looking in the mirror. There was a girl somewhere, Vee thought.

'I'm making a nice pie for your supper,' she said. 'Mince.' Donald was busy opening one of his letters. She glimpsed a scant half-page of writing, and a puzzling string of numbers, before he looked up and caught her eye.

'I'll just go and get your snack ready, then,' she said, and he nodded. He was reaching for his pocket diary when she left the room.

Five minutes later, putting Donald's sandwiches into a tin, Vee glanced out of the window. The view – one of only two good things about the flat – was of fields of green barley, and the meandering grass-edged course of Pollard Lane. The surface was unmetalled, a mire in winter and a ribbon of dust in summer, but from the kitchen you could see fifty yards along it, in either direction. It was a view that allowed unwelcome visitors to be spotted early on and ensured that neighbours could be avoided or deliberately encountered, depending on circumstance. The only visible building was Mrs Fillimore's slate-roofed farmhouse, but Green End Cottages and their nosy occupants were only just around the corner, the smoke from the chimneys hanging permanently above a clump of elders.

For a moment Vee thought that the lane was empty, and then she spotted Mrs Fillimore out on her constitutional, hauling her little black dog behind her. Vee watched the woman for a while, noting, with disbelief, the vigour of her walk. Eighty-seven. Mrs Fillimore was *eighty-seven*. How long was she going to go on for? When would it all end? Threescore years and ten, it said in Psalm 90, 'and if by reason of strength they be fourscore years, yet is their strength labour and sorrow'. Well phooey to that. In December, shortly after they'd moved into the flat, Vee had discovered Mrs Fillimore lying in a heap on the lane, seemingly breathing her last. The doctor had shaken his head. The vicar had been summoned. A bed had been found at the cottage hospital. Then Mrs Fillimore had rallied and made a recovery that the doctor called 'temporary' and Vee had paid a visit to the offices of Firebrand Insurance, and taken out a life policy on her neighbour. It was only a shilling a week and all fully legal; the man at the office hadn't even raised an eyebrow.

Since then she'd popped in regularly to see how the old so-and-so was doing, and every single time, Mrs Fillimore had found a task for her ('You won't mind giving Binky-Boy his worming tablets, will you? I know how much you love pets . . .') and on every visit she'd looked in better health and spirits.

That was what happened when you tried to do something

straight: the world simply laughed at you. Like the job she'd taken in the packing room of Ballito Hosiery just after the war started: 'You'll love it here, we're one big family, all our girls have a grand time' – fifty minutes' walk each way, standing for the whole shift, no time to get to the shops, no air with all the windows boarded up for blackout, bloody great boxes to lift. After a fortnight, her legs felt as if she'd borrowed them from her mother, and she took one day off, *one* day, and had turned up on the dot the next morning only to be told she'd been sacked ('The point is, Mrs Sedge, you're either a member of our Ballito family, or you're not'). On her way out of the factory she'd stumbled across one or two items of water-damaged stock that were going to be discarded anyway, and had just popped them in her bag, and the next thing she knew, the foreman was threatening to call the police.

In the end, she'd persuaded him not to. Ugly, stringy little man. Hairy too.

It wasn't something she liked to remember.

Outside, Mrs Fillimore performed a smart about-turn, and dragged her dog back to the farmhouse. Briefly, the lane was empty again, and then there was the sound of a slamming door, and Mr Croxton walked into the middle of the lane, looked directly up at Vee, and mouthed 'He is late.' For added emphasis, he held up the keys to the yard, and gave them a shake.

Vee nodded and smiled, and held up five fingers.

Mr Croxton shook his head and held up a single finger.

'Donny!' called Vee.

Mr Croxton continued looking at her, lips pursed, and then slowly lowered his gaze and disappeared again beneath the window lintel.

'Donny!' called Vee again, trying to sound bright and careless. 'Time for work.'

★

It wasn't a nice flat, nor even a convenient one: a quarter of a mile from the nearest shop, draughty, dusty, overlooking the scrapyard, subject to deafening clangs all day and the rustle of mice all night. It wasn't really a flat at all, for that matter, just a long, thin space above the workshop, roughly partitioned, one room opening out of another, the kitchen so-called only because it happened to have a sink in it. Even the staircase that led to ground-level was a botched afterthought, each stair of a different height, so that every descent was a series of jolts and surprises. The advantage – the sole advantage, apart from the view of the lane – was that it came rent-free.

Vee had spotted the advertisement in the *Herts Advertiser*: *Night watchman needed at St Albans place of business, duties include guarding premises and vermin control. Accommodation included*, and she'd telephoned Mr Croxton to make enquiries. 'He's a good steady boy,' she'd said to Mr Croxton, 'doesn't drink, hardly even smokes. He likes his crosswords.'

It had come at a useful time, three weeks after Donald had handed in his notice at the shoe shop – the bending was giving him terrible palpitations – and only a couple of days after Woolworth's in Harpenden had asked Vee to leave (on the word of one customer, just *one*), and Vee had been beginning to panic about the arrears on the cottage they'd been living in.

Manna, she'd thought, when Mr Croxton had told her about the flat. Manna. And for the first few months that they'd lived there, the simple joy of not having to find a weekly ten shillings had been as good as a holiday (not that she'd ever had a holiday); anyhow, she'd felt almost carefree, like the lighter-than-air dancing girl in the Ballito hosiery advertisement.

She'd even had a dream, one night, that she was on the swingboats with Donald's father, eating a toffee apple, and that was unusual, since her dreams were nearly always about money: finding it, dropping it, winning it, spending it, losing it. Losing it, mainly.

★

'You calling, Ma?' asked Donald, coming into the kitchen, buttoning his shirt.

'Mr Croxton,' she said, apologetically.

He nodded and sat down at the table, nudging the teapot with his cup. She'd have preferred him to hurry down to work, but he wasn't the hurrying sort, nor the sort to get riled by Mr Croxton and his perpetual watch-tapping. He'd been a sleepy baby, a contented toddler, a placid schoolboy, and Vee had seen enough of other peoples' troubles (not to mention bruises) to bless his even temper. He was never bitter, punchy or sharp. Or pushy, or nervy, or talkative. Nothing like her at all, in fact. It made it difficult to know, sometimes, what he was thinking.

She poured him another cupful.

'Can you do me a clean shirt for tomorrow?' he asked.

'Going out for the day?'

He nodded.

'Anywhere special?'

He shook his head, smiling easily. Vee could feel the usual questions piling up behind her teeth. These day trips had started a few months ago, not long after the frightening medical. Donald never said where he was going, or where he'd been, or what he'd done, though Vee had come across train tickets to Birmingham and Cheadle and Brixton in his trouser pockets. Sometimes, the next day, he'd slip her some money, a couple of pounds or so; she wondered whether he might be going to the races. Maybe he had a *system*. She didn't want to pry. Whatever he was doing, when he went out, he tended to arrive back a bit late for work.

She hovered beside the table, one eye on the clock, unable to sit down for the tension of watching Donald drink his tea in tiny, appreciative sips, but then, at last, he was done. She gave him a kiss and handed over his snack and then watched out of the window as he emerged into the yard and took the keys from Mr Croxton. She couldn't see the latter's face but she could tell from the jut of his backside that he was furious. Last week he'd threatened to re-advertise the job. 'You're going to have to give me a bloody good reason why I shouldn't,' he'd said to Vee.

She was still hoping that it wouldn't come to that.

She'd just started pushing half an onion and the heel of a loaf into the mincer, when the evacuees came back along the lane. Only two left now: a great lump of a girl who looked as if she'd eat you out of house and home, and the limping creature with the ears. Who on earth would want to look after a crippled evacuee, she wondered. You'd not only have to feed them, and deal with the lice and the London cheek, but you'd be forever at the doctor, going back and forth and—

An idea rolled into her head, fully formed, like a marble. Vee paused for a second or two, to think about it, and then snatched off her apron and tied on a headscarf.

'I've got to pop out, Mum,' she said. 'Won't be long. Back soon.'

It was a beautiful evening, balmy, the sky a washed-out pink like a faded eiderdown. It didn't take long for her to catch them up.

Noel stood by the side of the lane, next to Ada, and watched the billeting officer talk to the scrawny woman in the headscarf. He was so tired that his eyes kept closing and then jerking open again, so that the scene jumped forward like a damaged film.

'. . . and you get ten and sixpence a week,' he heard the billeting officer say. 'More if he's a bed-wetter.'

'*She* looks nice,' said Ada, hopefully. She had said this about every housewife they'd seen that day, and they'd probably seen a hundred. After a morning in the Masons' Hall, during which the smaller and prettier children had been picked off, a crocodile of the plain and badly dressed had been marched from door to door in a widening spiral, gradually leaving the centre of the town behind.

'This is Noel,' said the billeting officer, beckoning him forwards. 'And Noel, this is Mrs Sedge, who has very kindly, *very* kindly agreed to take you in. I shall drop by in a day or two, Mrs Sedge, to see how Noel's getting on. Will you make sure he writes the postcard to his parents, giving his new address? It's already franked.'

'She looks nice,' said Ada again.

'And there isn't just a chance you could also see your way to taking . . . ?' The billeting officer nodded over at Ada.

'No,' said Vee, quickly.

'I quite understand. Off you go now, Noel. He's a quiet little chap, Mrs Sedge.'

Noel picked up his suitcase.

'I'll carry that,' said Vee, taking it from him. 'Weighs a ton,' she added. 'What've you got in here? Bricks?'

She walked fast, and Noel limped alongside her. Ada was wrong, he thought; she didn't look particularly nice. She had sharp, worried features and she kept moving her head around, keeping a watch on everything, like a magpie hanging around a picnic.

'Here we are,' she said, stopping outside a shabby building that Noel had passed twice before. 'Up the steps we go.'

He stumbled three times on the stairs.

'Oops-a-daisy,' said Vee. 'Not too good on your pins, are you?' She sounded almost pleased. 'In here,' she said. 'Mum, look who I've brought.'

The older woman took off a pair of headphones, gave Noel a plaintive stare, then propped up a small slate, and chalked a question mark on it.

'It's an evacuee, Mum. Sit yourself down,' she said to Noel. She untied her headscarf and fluffed her curly, dark hair. 'You want some bread and marge?'

He nodded.

'Write your postcard, then,' she said.

He lowered himself on to a stool and sat there, rubbing his knees awkwardly. The room was cramped and comfortless, the bare floorboards patched with a couple of balding rugs. Vee's mother was sitting in the only armchair, a crocheted shawl round her shoulders, small cushions tucked behind her back and under her elbows, her slippered feet resting on a folded blanket. There was a cup of tea on the table in front of her, and a handkerchief, a slate and a piece of chalk, a copy of the *Radio Times* and a packet of Parma Violets. As he watched, Vee's mother took one of the latter and popped it in her mouth. She didn't look very much like her daughter; she was tiny, with sweet, rounded features, and fine brown hair pulled into a bun. A scar, like a delicate white thread, ran right across her forehead, just below the hairline.

'Here you are,' said Vee, holding out a plate to Noel. 'Not written it yet?' she added.

'I don't have a pen,' he said.

Posh, she thought. A posh voice. She brought him a pencil.

'And where's the card?'

Reluctantly, he nodded at the suitcase. She knelt swiftly – she seemed to do everything at speed – and flipped the catches. The postcard lay on top.

'My stars,' she said, staring at the other contents. 'What's that?'

'An ammonite.'

'Your mum packed a *rock* for you? And what's that?'

'A coat.'

She rubbed the fur between her fingers. 'Beaver. Feel the weight of it.' Without asking, she pushed the coat aside, stacked his bedroom slippers on top of it, glanced at the cover of *The Roman Hat Mystery* by Ellery Queen, opened the notebook and riffled through the pages, pounced on his ration book, and then raked quickly through the shorts, shirt and underwear that he'd stuffed at the bottom of the case. 'That's all your clothes?' she asked.

He nodded. He'd thrown all the others under the bed at Mafeking Road, to make room for Mattie's coat.

'And what's in here?' she asked, reaching for the brown paper bag he'd been given at Charing Cross. He watched her open it. For a second or two, her expression softened. 'You eat up,' she said, taking the bag over to the kitchen cupboard.

Reverently, she placed the contents on the top shelf: corned beef; shortbread; two cans of milk; a quarter-pound of chocolate. She could give Donald a couple of squares in his snack-box every day this week, as a treat. It might make up for the fact that Noel would have to sleep in Donald's room – in Donald's bed, actually, since there wasn't a spare. Though that could work out nicely, since Donald only slept there during the day. Less nicely, of course, if the boy was one of those bed-wetters.

If that were the case, then she'd have to try and get a camp bed from somewhere. And then there'd be all those extra sheets to wash and dry. And of course, with one extra in the flat there'd be more cooking, more shopping, more ironing, more water to heat and carry, more clothes to mend, and shoes to buy, not to mention visits from prying parents . . .

She had the familiar sensation of the ground crumbling beneath her, as if she were standing on a sandcastle. It always happened like this: a fresh idea, a few seconds – or even hours – of happy triumph, and then, *whoosh*, in would come the tide. Next thing she knew, she'd be neck-deep in consequences and drawbacks.

The boy was sitting with the postcard in front of him, the pencil untouched.

'It's care of Sedge, Croxton's Scrap Metal, Pollard Lane, St

Albans,' she said. He didn't move and it occurred to her that he wasn't writing it down because he didn't know how to; his notebook had been full of scribbles and silly patterns.

'Give it to me,' she said, and eased it out of his hands. She wrote the address.

'Any message?' she asked. He shook his head. She added

AM STAYING WITH A VERY NICE LADY AND HER KIND FAMILY. I WISH WE COULD GIVE THEM A PRESENT TO SAY THANK YOU, SUCH AS TINNED GOODS OR EVEN A POSTAL ORDER JUST TO TIDE HER OVER UNTIL THE GOVERNMENT ALLOWANCE COMES.

'And where do you live?' she asked, turning the card over. He said nothing.

'With your mum and dad, is it?'

He stayed silent. He was a plain child, his face not quite symmetrical, his ears just asking to be gripped between finger and thumb by a passing bully.

'We have to send it,' she said, 'or I expect there'll be trouble.'

'Dr M. Simpkin, "Green Shutters", Vale of Health, Hampstead, London,' he said, quickly.

'Who's that then? Your dad? Your grandpa?'

'Godmother.'

'So where's your mum and dad?'

He closed his mouth firmly, like someone shutting a sash window. There was, she realized, a piece of string around his neck. She leaned forward and pulled on it and a brown label emerged from the neck of his shirt. He made a grab for it.

'Noel Bostock,' she read out loud, fending his hand away. She turned it over. 'C/o Mr and Mrs G. Overs, 23B Mafeking Road, Kentish Town, London. Who are they, then?'

He shrugged. Then, without warning, he pulled the label off so violently that he left a red mark round his neck.

'That was a silly thing to do, wasn't it?' asked Vee. 'Now sit there like a good boy. I've got things to do.'

She made a pot of tea, and then put up the blackouts and got out the flowers that she had to finish for Vic Allerby for Tuesday: three hundred violets for the hat trade, or what remained of it. Green gauze leaves, purple crêpe petals, yellow felt centres, with a ribbon-wrapped wire for the stem. Each one took her a shade under ninety seconds to complete.

Noel sat and watched her fingers stitching the leaves to the petals, pushing the wire through the centre, giving the end a twist, sticking on the yellow anthers with a dab of glue and then tacking the completed flower to a length of brown cloth. She kept her eyes on the work, but she seemed to be having a long, soundless conversation with somebody, her mouth moving, her expression changing with the rapidity of a flicker book. The only noise in the room was the squeak of Arthur Askey from the headphones, and the occasional sigh from Vee's mother, as her pen looped across a sheet of writing paper. She wrote in a hand so regular that he could read it upside down. She appeared to be writing to the Prime Minister, though this was clearly impossible. After a while he laid his chin on his hands and went to sleep.

Dear Mr Churchill,

As I wrote to Mr Chamberlain in April, you never know just what's round the corner. As I hope Mr Chamberlain told you I've been corresponding with him for many years, and his secretary wrote a very nice reply in 1935 to say that he's always happy to know what the Ordinary Folk of England are saying. As a Mother and Grandmother, as well as a Christian who has laboured under a cruel affliction for many years, I feel its my duty to pass on the fruits of my contemplations.

1. *The bread is very bad. It has bits that keep being caught under my upper plate, I think there might be dirt in the flour. Also, you can't slice it thinly it's like sawing a log, everyone says this. Our minister (Methodist) kindly visited me at home this week and a piece of crust caught in his throat and he might have died if my daughter hadn't hit him on the back with a shoe. On the wireless they talk about morale and I think soft white rolls would do more for morale than all the National Anthems of the Allies put together. They play them week in, week out on the wireless and the Dutch one sounds like a funeral.*

2. *Never mind about the French, no one here is surprised. They'd have been surprised if the French had stayed and fought, that would've been a surprise all right.*

3. *There are many people Making Hay in this war and downstairs from us they are selling stolen things I heard them talking about silver-plated spoons just yesterday. It's the blackout makes thieving easy and I think*

you ought to know that the specials aren't any good they'll take anyone in the police nowadays. My friend from chapel's husband is a special and he cant even bend one of his knees and he's been deaf in one ear since Arras I should think thieves probably just laugh at him. About the spoons, I mention no names but it's a scrap metal firm half a mile south-west of St Albans. Also there are Irish people in and out of there all the time.

4. We had a pamphlet brought to us by the postman about what to do if a Parachutist Should Come to Our Door and of course I read it and the advice was mostly to stay put and be calm, quick and exact when I'd have thought that dropping heavy things (like an iron) out of the window on their heads would be more useful, or boiling water. Also my cousin Harold suggested putting needles in bread rolls on the road to cause punctures and this would be another reason for having soft white rolls, you couldn't push needles in the bread we have nowadays, they'd bend (a little joke).

Well, if you don't mind I'll leave you with a poem that was in 'People's Friend' in the spring.

When all the world is sad and grey
And all your hope seems far away
Look up and see the sky so blue
And know that joy is there for you.

Yours faithfully
Flora Sedge

2

Noel had occasionally been into a church, but never one made of tin. The outside was painted pale green and there were no pews inside, only rush-bottomed chairs. The sole decoration (unless you counted the jar of ox-eye daisies on the altar) was an embroidered banner that read *Fight the Good Fight of Faith*.

'The Iron Duke . . .' said Mr Waring, his voice beginning to fray as he stretched it over the rows of juniors. 'The Iron Duke was a nickname for which famous nineteenth-century military figure?'

'Colonel Bogey!' shouted Roy Pursey.

'And are there any serious suggestions?'

Someone blew a raspberry.

'Arthur Wellesley, first Duke of Wellington,' said Mr Waring, 'one of the subjects of our lesson this morning. Does everyone have a slate?'

There was no paper, there were no pencils. The slates had been found in the Sunday School cupboard, and three pieces of chalk had been cut into slivers using Mr Waring's penknife.

'Tomorrow, or the next day,' said Mr Waring, 'I am assured that we shall be found more suitable accommodation, but in the meantime I would like you to list *twenty* eminent Victorians, men *or* women who contributed to the public good during the reign of Queen Victoria, 1837 to 1901. Anyone who writes

"Jack the Ripper" will be required to compose a three-page essay on the subject of "public good". You have ten minutes to compile this list, and during these ten minutes I would like absolute silence.'

Above the gruesome scrape of chalk, Miss Lane could be heard reading out a story about kittens to a semicircle of seven-year-olds over by the open front doors. And in the cloakroom, the infants were singing 'Ten Green Bottles', except they had started with one hundred bottles rather than ten. The song had been going on half an hour, and they had still only reached twenty-two.

Noel picked up his flake of chalk and wrote *Gnrvjtjm Okrlyouojup*. It was a simple slip code, once down the alphabet for letter one, twice for letter two and so on, but it made *Florence Nightingale* look like a Norse God.

He crushed the chalk between his fingers and dusted his hands. He didn't want to compile a list of eminent Victorians. He didn't want to be sitting here, in this hot metal box. He didn't want to be anywhere; the world felt like a horsehair vest that he couldn't remove. He opened his notebook and wrote down the names of his classmates, and then appended a suitable punishment to each.

Roy Pursey. Liver pecked out by eagle.
Harvey Madeley. Locked into an oubliette and forced to drink
    own urine.
The Ferris Twins. Lavatory cleaners.

'I have just been informed,' said Mr Waring, staring at a note in his hand, 'that since these premises are used for first-aid training on Monday afternoons, our lessons will be terminated at midday. All right, all right . . .' He acknowledged the ragged cheer with an upraised hand. 'Carry on with your work.'

★

Eggs, potatoes, Sanatogen, thought Vee, who had forgotten her shopping list. *People's Friend*, fish, flour, purple thread, torch batteries (not that anyone would have any), Milk of Magnesia. She stopped by the gates of Firebrand Insurance, and pressed her fist into her breastbone. The route from Pollard Lane to the shops was all uphill, a solid quarter-mile, and she tried to save a bus fare by walking one way, but recently she'd been getting heartburn, and it always caught her just where the hill was steepest. She'd first suffered from it when she was carrying Donald, and the pain and the foul taste in her mouth always made her feel seventeen again.

These days it was caused by worry, unmerited and continual. She waited until the pain had subsided a little and then carried on up the hill. Parma Violets. Writing paper.

She saw Noel before he saw her. He was standing outside the window of the arcade sweetshop, staring at the jar of liquorice laces.

'Not in school?' she asked, and she had to say it twice more, and add his name, before he turned round stiffly, like a little old man.

'They're using the church for something else this afternoon,' he said.

'Which church?'

'Where we're having lessons. The green one. Made of tin.'

'That's not a church, that's the Baptist chapel,' said Vee, slightly shocked. 'Don't you know the difference?'

He shrugged.

'Well, you can help me with some shopping,' she said, and handed him her basket, before remembering that she was supposed to be cultivating his role as an invalid. She snatched it back and he gaped at her like a bullfrog.

'Come along then,' she said.

He said nothing in the long queue at the fishmonger, and

nothing at the chemist, even when Mr Harper shuffled forward and offered him a horehound lozenge.

'Say thank you,' said Vee, nudging him. She mouthed '*simple*' at Mr Harper, and then realized that Noel was watching her. She stretched her mouth into a smile. 'Come along then,' she said.

The stationer's. The hardware shop. The greengrocer. The poulterer. The haberdasher. Last of all, as a little treat for herself, the cosmetic counter at Woolworth's. Vee dithered between two lipsticks of a similar shade, finally plumping for Burnt Sugar. When she turned around, Noel had gone. She spotted him eventually, standing beside the pick-and-mix counter, his face flattened against the glass.

'D'you want some sweets?' she asked. 'Choose something, then.'

'Treacle toffees,' he said.

'*Please*,' she added.

'Please.'

She bought him two ounces, and he crammed three toffees into his mouth at once, his whole face working as he tried to chew. People nudged each other as he passed.

Near the bus stop, someone called to Vee, and she looked round to see Mrs Pilcher, wearing a green uniform and standing behind a trestle table piled with saucepans and colanders.

'We're collecting aluminium. Have you anything to help our brave pilots?' she asked, as if Vee might be hiding a double boiler inside her corsets. 'Not to worry,' she added, when Vee shook her head, 'you can give to the Scouts when they call. Or bring them round to me, I'm assembling quite a collection in the back parlour, in fact I think we'll have to start moving them into one of the sheds when you come. Who's the poor little chap?' she added, lowering her voice.

'An evacuee I've taken in,' said Vee. 'Thought I'd do my bit.'

Mrs Pilcher nodded approvingly. 'Inasmuch as ye have done it unto one of the least of these my brethren, ye have done it unto me. Is he Methodist?'

'I don't know,' said Vee.

There was a sucking noise, as Noel opened his mouth. 'Atheist,' he said, thickly.

Mrs Pilcher drew in her breath sharply.

'See you tomorrow, Mrs Pilcher,' said Vee. She took Noel by the arm and steered him twenty yards along the road, before pushing him into the doorway of the ironmonger.

'What did you say that for?' she asked, giving his shoulder a shake.

He looked at her, silently. A thin thread of brown dribble had escaped from one corner of his mouth.

'Mrs Pilcher is a lady I work for. You can't say things like that to her. Wipe your mouth.'

He dragged a knuckle across his face.

'I only got the job with her because we both go to Bethesda. That's chapel, before you ask, and her husband is the minister. The *minister*. Come along.'

She set off walking again, not looking behind her, assuming that the boy would follow.

So tomorrow, then, she could look forward to a morning of lugging saucepans around. Mrs Pilcher's definition of 'light cleaning' was infinitely elastic. 'You don't mind, do you, dear Mrs Sedge,' she'd say, revealing some new task better suited to a navvy. What was rich was that at last year's Harvest Supper, the Reverend Pilcher had written New Testament quotes on to strips of greaseproof paper, and Mrs Pilcher had baked them into savoury rolls, and Vee's had been, 'Consider the lilies of the field; they toil not neither do they spin.'

She had a sudden vision of Mrs Pilcher's expression on hearing the word 'atheist', and a bubble of laughter rose unbidden in her throat. She swallowed it and looked around. Noel was plodding twenty yards behind her, his jaw moving slowly. She watched his feet in their good, expensive sandals, and then she frowned.

'You're not limping,' she said, when he'd caught up.

He wiped his mouth again.

'I only limp when I'm tired,' he said.

'Why's that then?'

'I had polio.'

'Did you? When?'

'I don't know. I was a baby.'

'Do you ever need to see the doctor about it? Or go to the hospital?'

He shook his head, and prised another toffee from the bag, his face still distorted by the ones in his mouth.

They walked side by side to the bus stop.

'Would it hurt you to talk a bit more?' asked Vee, after the silence had stretched to five minutes. He didn't reply. The bus rounded the corner and Vee stooped to pick up her basket.

She liked a chat. The way things were at home, she usually ended up scrabbling around inside her own head, spooning up thoughts, like the Chinks eating live monkey brains. Donald's father had been a talker, full of fun and jokes, it was why she'd tumbled for him in the first place, though he'd stopped being fun after she'd fallen pregnant. He'd gone and married his boss's daughter, Jenny Fleckney, a girl half a head taller than himself, and now they had four tall daughters of their own. They looked like a circus act when they were out together. Harry Pedder and the Five Giraffes.

'We get off here,' she said, nudging Noel as the curved roof of Fleckney's Garage came into view. When she'd moved into the flat above the scrap-metal yard it had come as a shock to realize how close it was to Harry's work. For two decades she'd scarcely glimpsed him, and now she saw him nearly every time she got off the bus. He was there now, crouched by a dented baker's van, a smear of oil across his high forehead. He looked up as she passed, and his gaze bounced off her like an India-rubber ball.

'Come along,' said Vee to Noel. 'Finished your toffees?'

'Yes.'

'Did no one ever teach you to say thank you?'

'Thank you.'

'You might try and sound as if you meant it.' When they got to Pollard Lane, she handed him the basket. She had welts across her fingers from the weight of it.

'You'll have to write home for wellingtons,' she said, 'it's like porridge along here when it rains, I spend half my time scraping mud—' and then she heard the motorbike, and she seized Noel by the upper arm and pulled him across the ditch and into the spinney beside the road. He stumbled as he came, and dropped the basket; she heard something break. Ezra Rigg spluttered past, leaning over the handlebars like a racer. Vee waited until the sound had faded, and then she jerked the basket upright. The Milk of Magnesia had smashed all over everything, the coley was filled with glass splinters, the flour ruined, the whole week's egg ration gone in a blink. Her hand reached out and smacked Noel across the face.

His head jerked back but he made no noise.

Half the potatoes had rolled into the litter at the bottom of the ditch. Vee picked out as many as she could find, and found the batteries (thank God) pressed into the mud. 'What else was in there?' she asked, her voice shrill with guilt.

'Purple thread. Parma Violets,' said Noel, lips barely moving.

'Help me find them, then.'

There was a welt on his cheek. She had never hit Donald, not once, not even the time he'd accidentally set the house on fire. When the Parma Violets turned up, under a tangle of ivy, she tore the packet open and gave one to Noel. 'And a couple for later,' she said. He took them without meeting her eye.

'That man on the motorcycle,' she said, crossing the ditch and waiting for him to follow, 'is a rates collector, which means he goes round frightening people, nagging at them, saying they'll go to prison and so on, if they don't pay money that they don't have, and it's a scandal, and he gets paid a good wage by the council for doing it, too, and if you ask me, it's pure wickedness.'

'My uncle works for the rates,' said Noel.

'Does he? Well . . .' she groped around for a mollifying statement. 'There's good and bad all over,' she said, lamely. 'I expect your uncle's kind to you.'

'No,' said Noel. 'I hate him.'

At Croxton's, a lorryload of scrap was being unloaded, and the yard was full of gypsy types. Vee ducked past the office and hurried towards the door of the flat, but Croxton had spotted her.

'Letter came for you,' he called, and she had to turn back. He held out the envelope and then, as she reached for it, lifted his arm away and left her flailing at air. 'Hand-delivered,' he said, studying the address. 'I hope it's not what I think it is, Mrs Sedge. I like to keep on good terms with the council. I like to keep things straight.' He lowered it slowly into her grasp and as he did so there was an enormous metallic crash from the yard, and Vee jumped a foot. Croxton didn't move, just studied her with eyes that were the yellowish grey of bottled whelks.

She opened the envelope at the top of the stairs, and it was a summons, non-payment of rates, arrears amounting to eight pounds, eighteen and sixpence. Full restitution before 31st July or an appearance before the Justices on 15th August.

There was a noise behind her and she looked round and saw Noel coming up the stairs. She'd forgotten, for the moment, that he even existed. The light from the window fell across the side of his face, and she could see the bruise that she'd left beneath his eye. It was finger-shaped. It wouldn't do for a teacher to see it.

LISSA EVANS

'How do you fancy a day trip tomorrow?' she asked, the idea bobbing up like a duck in a hip bath.

'What?'

'Well, not a day trip,' she amended, remembering her obligations. 'I have to do Mrs Pilcher first. But after lunch. And you could take the morning off school. I expect you could do with a rest.'

He didn't argue.

'And I'll put some arnica on that,' she said. 'It'll soon fade.'

3

Donald woke him, shaking his shoulder until Noel opened his eyes.

'Up,' said Donald, quietly. 'Now.'

Noel scrambled out of bed and heard the mattress groan as Donald eased himself beneath the blankets. He was a large man, fat in a smooth, firm way, like a sea lion or a walrus.

'Pass me that, would you?' he said, nodding at the cup of tea he'd left on the tallboy.

Noel brought it over.

'And the cigarettes,' added Donald. 'D'you know how to light one?'

'No.'

'Put one in your mouth, strike a match, hold it to the end of the fag, breathe in.'

He watched critically for a while and then shook his head. 'Give it to me,' he said. 'And if you're going to heave, do it out the window.'

Noel lifted the sash. The world outside moved gently. His legs seemed to be made of string.

'When you're ready,' said Donald, 'bring over that shaving mirror.'

Noel watched him examining his reflection, twisting his head from side to side to see the jawline and running a finger along the line of hair above his upper lip. 'That'll do nicely,' said

Donald, complacently. He lifted his top lip to stare at his teeth, and then laid the mirror down. 'Get dressed and out, then,' he said. 'And bring me a cup of tea at eleven. Two sugars.'

There was no one in the kitchen. Noel had heard Vee washing dishes earlier, but she had gone now, leaving a scattering of hair grips on the table, and a note for her mother.

NOT BACK UNTIL LATE AFTERNOON. FOR LUNCH THERE IS PIECE OF PIE AND REMAINS OF BLAMMONGE IN DISH ON TOP SHELF. NEW WRITING PAPER FOR YOU ON SIDEBOARD, FORGOT YOUR HAND CREAM, SORRY, WILL GET LATER. VIC ALLERBY SAID HE'D CALL THIS AFTERNOON, HAVE LEFT FLOWERS IN BOX ON TABLE, TELL HIM NOT ENOUGH FELT FOR LAST TWENTY VIOLETS, NOT MY FAULT. DONNY HAS APOINTMENT THIS AFTERNOON, ASKED TO BE WOKEN AT 11. LOVE YOUR VEE.

Noel opened cupboard doors until he found the blancmange. There was quite a lot in the bowl, so he took a spoon and ate a half-inch all around the circumference, neatening the edges as he went. Then he broke off a square of the chocolate that was on the same shelf, and screwed a wet finger into the bag of sugar.

His cheekbone still hurt. He touched it, tentatively, and then pressed harder, enjoying the pain. She could hit him again, if it meant he got a morning off school. He put on the kettle, and walked idly around the room. There was nothing to look at, or to read. The furniture was new and cheap, or old and broken, the ornaments pale with age: a box covered in seashells, a yellow pincushion with the words 'THERE'S NO PLACE LIKE HOME' picked out in maroon beads. You could break everything in the place and it wouldn't be worth sixpence. He pulled all the beads off the 'H' in Home, and dropped them behind the sideboard, and then he made some tea.

'Mother doesn't get up till later on,' Vee had said. He went and sat on the old woman's chair, wrote 'BOLLOCKS' on her slate, rubbed it out again and tried on the headphones. The wireless fizzed and boomed as it warmed up, and then, from far away, an unctuous voice began talking about prunes. He tipped the chair back and put his feet on the table. Vee had told him that her mother, Mrs Sedge, hadn't been able to speak since she'd fainted and hit her head nineteen years ago, after receiving a nasty shock. It suddenly struck him as very odd that Vee was also called 'Mrs Sedge'. Could the older Mrs Sedge be Vee's mother-in-law, rather than her mother? But then, why not say so? 'This is my mother,' Vee had announced, in that urgent, high-pitched voice.

He turned the question over in his head, looking for possible solutions.

The lecture on prunes ended and the news began. Noel took off the headphones and the tally of Messerschmitt losses was replaced with the noise of splintering wood. He wandered over to the back window. Outside, it was a clear day, and the air was full of swallows. A man was breaking up a piano with a sledge-hammer, and a postwoman was crossing the yard.

He knew things; he wasn't ignorant. Mattie had always liked the word 'frank'. 'To be frank, Noel . . .' she'd say, when he asked a difficult or awkward question. 'To be frank, Noel, I'd say that "Vee" probably stands for "Vera", and "Mrs" almost certainly stands for "Miss".'

There was a knock at the door of the flat, and he went downstairs. The postwoman handed him a bundle of letters. There were six for 'Mrs Flora Sedge', three for Fat Donald and one for Vee, in Geoffrey's handwriting.

You could learn a lot from reading detective fiction; Noel had never steamed open an envelope before, but it was quite easy, the gum separating into viscous strands as he eased up the flap.

> *Dear Mrs Sedge,*
> *We are so pleased that you have been kind enough to offer Noel a 'home away from home', and I'm sure he will be extremely happy and of course safe with you. We have had two alerts already this week, both false alarms, but that won't be the case for much longer, we fear.*
>
> *As I hope Noel has told you, he has been living with us since his godmother sadly passed on last December. As her cousins we stepped forward 'into the breach', which of course we were delighted to do, although since we are not yet his legal guardians, having another mouth to feed (and body to clothe!) has placed quite a financial burden upon us, though one which, of course, we are more than happy to shoulder. Mrs Overs is in poor health and unable to travel, however I will endeavour to come and visit Noel, though since civil defence duties take up so much of my time when not at work, it may be several weeks before . . .*

And on and on, diddly dee diddly dah, as Mattie would say. There was another small sheet of paper in the envelope, folded in half, his own name written on the outside.

He opened it at arm's length, as if lighting a firework.

> *Dear Noel,*
> *Just a 'p.s.' to say that we have received an overdue note from Queen's Crescent Library for 'The Roman Hat Mystery' by Ellery Queen. Is it possible that you took it with you when you were evacuated? If so, could you return it, as we may otherwise be fined.*
> *Yours affectionately*
> *Auntie Margery and Uncle Geoffrey*

The writing paper seemed to exude a faint smell of furniture polish, the same smell that had pervaded his aunt and uncle's flat. Every surface there had been utterly clean, every loose object put away, so that if Noel left a book on his bed in the morning, it was re-shelved by the time he came in from school. A pencil on the floor, a notebook on the windowsill, a comb, a comic – even a fingernail clipping, left deliberately as a test – were whisked out of view, as if Auntie Margery were trying to pretend that Noel wasn't there at all. He'd started to wonder whether that were actually the case, if he was really, truly living in the flat, or whether it was a dream of some kind. There had seemed no reason for the three of them to be in the same place; they were like random items found together in a junk shop: two gloves and a spigot, a fez and two spoons.

The school he'd been sent to was full of children who tried to walk straight through him and one morning it had occurred to him that he might actually be invisible. He'd stepped into the path of a cyclist, just to check; there'd been a scream of brakes and the bicycle had slewed sideways and thrown its rider into the gutter.

'You really must try and be more observant, Noel,' Uncle Geoffrey had said.

It was after that that Noel had made the decision to stop talking. He would speak (he'd decided) in the event of a fire or a bomb, but most other things could be covered by a nod, a shake of the head or a shrug. He had also discovered that if he pretended to go to his room, and then hid under the coat rack in the little entrance porch to the flat and covered himself with the folds of Uncle Geoffrey's warden's greatcoat, then he could hear everything that went on.

When the evacuation order came from the school, Auntie Margery had said, 'Oh thank God, Geoffrey, because with the best will in the world I truly can't bear another day of being stared at by that child.'

In the frowsty clutter of Vee's kitchen, Noel looked at the

letters again. He could almost see Uncle Geoffrey's smile, lingering like the Cheshire Cat's above the paper.

. . . since we are not yet his legal guardians . . .

He twisted the envelope and its contents into tapers, and burned them in the sink. Then he took the pad of writing paper that Vee had bought for her mother. It was not hard to imitate Vee's uneven capitals and telegraphic style.

DEAR MR AND MRS OVERS
I AM VERY GLAD TO TAKE NOEL. HE IS SETTLING HERE AND AT SCHOOL VERY NICELY. DON'T WORRY ABOUT VISITING BECAUSE I THINK IT WOULD UNSETTLE HIM AT THE MOMENT SO NO NEED TO COME ALL THIS WAY. MAYBE NEARER XMAS. HE SENDS YOU HIS LOVE AND HOPES YOU ARE WELL.
HOPING THIS FINDS YOU WELL AS IT LEAVES ME
MRS V SEDGE

He posted it on the way to meet Vee, using a stamp that he found in the kitchen drawer. As it disappeared into the postbox he heard himself laugh. It was an odd sound, unpractised and staccato.

By the time Vee finished at Mrs Pilcher's ('Just one more little job, Mrs Sedge, it won't take a moment') it was twenty past one. She found Noel waiting exactly where she'd asked him to wait, on a bench at the south side of the abbey, beside the memorial to the Great War. He didn't move or speak as she approached, only watched her with that flat, judgemental gaze. *Thou God, seest me,* she thought; it had been the text on the wall in the outside lav when she was a girl, and it always made her think of carbolic, and drains.

'Did you wake Donald up?' she asked, and he nodded.

'And did he say where he was going?' she asked. He shook his head. The fingermark on his cheek had faded to a shapeless blotch.

She took a ginger snap out of her bag and held it out to him. 'Mrs Pilcher baked these, you can have one. Only you need to limp,' she said. Noel stared at her, open-mouthed. 'Because of your bad leg,' she added. 'And if I talk to anyone you're not to say anything at all. Understand?' He nodded, and inserted the biscuit without thanks.

'Come along, then,' she said.

He limped steadily. On the Watford platform at Abbey station, they bumped into Mrs Farrell, the butcher's wife, and Vee was able to say, as planned, 'I'm just taking my little evacuee to his hospital appointment to have a leg iron fitted. Have to look after their health, don't we?' and Mrs Farrell had acknowledged Vee with a tiny, icy nod, which at least better than her usual habit of cutting her dead.

'I have to do something in Watford,' Vee said to Noel, as they stood together in the train corridor. The carriages were full of soldiers, as usual. 'Business. Door to door.'

Watford was big enough, she'd decided. There'd be no danger of meeting anyone she knew. She was wearing her good slate-grey coat and a hat that nearly matched, and a gilt pin she'd found on the pavement outside chapel one Sunday morning. It had a dot of red enamel in the centre, and looked vaguely official if you didn't peer too closely.

Noel didn't ask any questions, and when they got off the train, twenty minutes later, he hobbled after her without reminder.

It was as they walked out of the station that she began to get nervous. Ideas fluttered through her head. She thought about trying the row of houses opposite the entrance, and then decided that they were too public. She thought about taking a bus to the bigger houses in the suburbs. She walked past a row of shops, turned into the first street she came to, caught the eye of an old lady who was washing her windows, hesitated, started to search around in her bag for the collecting box and then lost her nerve and did a quick about-turn, treading on Noel's foot in the process.

'Out of the *way*,' she said, and then 'sorry'. Her heart was stuttering like a road-drill. She stopped by a draper's to catch her breath, and eyed the display of silk-effect blouses in the window. The pink one was the colour of calamine lotion. She could feel Noel looking at her and she began to wish she hadn't brought him; the intensity of his stare was giving her the jitters. Until she knew what she was doing, until she'd got the *hang* of it, she'd rather not have a witness.

At the corner of the next street, she pointed to a low wall.

'Sit there till I come back.' He sat, his gaze still upon her, and she turned and walked rapidly away.

There was no one in at the first house, and at the second, the door was answered by a child.

'Is your mother in, dear?' asked Vee. The girl disappeared without a word, leaving the door ajar. Vee took the collecting box out of her bag. It was borrowed from the Sunday School cupboard at Bethesda; she'd covered up the writing on the side with a picture of an aeroplane that she'd cut out of an illustrated paper.

'Yes?' said the woman, not opening the door further, but sliding sideways into the gap. She was a shrunken little thing – Vee's age, but with a withered, papery complexion. From within the house came a steady shrieking.

'Spitfire Fund,' said Vee, giving the box a silent shake. It came to her, too late, that she should have primed it with a few coppers.

The woman nodded, and closed the door. Vee waited, uneasily. A minute went by. Should she stay? Should she try next door? Should she *run*? It wasn't the sort of house that would have a telephone, but might the child have climbed over the back wall, and be racing to call the police? She was just turning to leave when the door reopened to reveal the girl with her fist outstretched.

'Mum says to give you this,' she said, and dropped a sixpence into the slot.

The door closed again.

The rattle of silver on wood seemed to linger in the air; Vee thought she had never heard a sweeter sound. Sixpence. *Sixpence*. The ease of it – she had knocked on a door and a child had given her money. It had the jingling simplicity of a nursery rhyme. She seemed to float along the pavement towards the next house.

'Spitfire Fund,' she said to the woman who answered the door.

'What's happened to Edna?' asked the woman.

'Who?'

'Edna Cleverley who does the Spitfire collection.'

'Hurt her foot,' said Vee, randomly.

'How?'

She hesitated. 'Tripped over a dog?'

The woman frowned. 'She doesn't have a dog.'

Leave now, ordered a voice in Vee's head. 'Next door's dog,' she heard herself saying.

'The collie?'

'That's right.' A miracle. Vee smiled breezily and rattled the box.

The woman shook her head. 'I gave something last month,' she said, and closed the door with a hint of a slam.

Vee glanced in the direction of Noel. He was staring directly at her. She skipped a couple of houses, for no reason other than nerves, and swung the knocker of the third.

Another child answered, a thick-set boy this time, with pink cheeks and a scornful mouth.

'Spitfire Fund,' said Vee.

'That's not a Spitfire.'

'What isn't?'

'On the box. It's a Wellington.'

'Is it?' She peered at the picture. 'Well, it doesn't matter.'

'I'd like to see you try to fight a Messerschmitt with a Wellington,' he said. 'It'd matter then all right.'

She gave the box a shake.

'Haven't collected much, have you?' he asked. 'What you got in there, a button?'

'Can I speak to your mother?'

'She's not in.'

'Why aren't you at school?'

'None of your business.'

'You've got a cheek, speaking to me like that.'

'You gonna stop me?'

'Somebody damn well ought to.'

The boy turned his head. 'Dad!' he shouted, up the hall. Vee started to walk very quickly back along the road, her best shoes rubbing.

'Come *on*,' she called to Noel before she reached him. She dared a look back before she turned the corner and the boy was gone, the door closed; he'd been codding her. She sat on the wall to catch her breath.

Noel had already stood up, and remained standing as Vee slipped off a shoe and rubbed her heel. Distantly, a church clock struck the half hour. The last time she'd been in Watford, there'd been plenty of motor traffic, but nowadays the roads were nearly all empty, and it was as quiet as a village. She could hear someone scrubbing a pavement. And sparrows bickering. And a man shouting, 'Oi, you! You on the wall there! Did you just swear at my boy?'

She rammed the shoe back on, and started running. She could hear Noel peg-legging along behind her. A bus was coming up the road and she reached the stop and waved a hand,

and scrambled on board while it was still moving and Noel jumped up beside her, limp momentarily forgotten. There was the faintest flush of pink in his cheeks.

'I need to try another place,' said Vee.

She took a seat, and peered between the strips of grimy tape on the window. Larger houses, she thought: the sort of places where the kiddies would be away at boarding school.

It was important to have a *plan*.

When they got off the bus again seven stops later, Vee took a newspaper out of her bag. 'Here,' she said. 'Mrs Pilcher gave me last week's *Advertiser*. There's a Children's Corner in it, competitions and suchlike. You can read it while you're waiting.' She nodded at the bench beside the bus stop. After a long moment, Noel reached out his hand for the paper. He watched Vee walk away along Linden Avenue, grey coat, grey hat, her head twitching to and fro as she inspected the houses on either side of the road. The first time he'd ever seen her he'd thought of a magpie, but now she seemed more like a pigeon, drab and directionless, pecking at anything that looked as if it might be edible. At one point, she paused to crane over a laurel hedge; at another she started to open a gate, and then closed it again hastily. It was obvious that she was doing something that she ought not to be doing. He felt a little tug of curiosity; it had been a long time since he'd last felt that.

Vee dwindled into the distance.

The front page of the *Herts Advertiser* was all fine print; scores of tiny advertisements for accommodation, lodgers, help wanted. *Lady Fremantle recommends her useful maid; good needle-woman, fond of dogs.*

He turned the pages, his gaze bumping across the columns, snagging the odd line: *A fine of 5s was imposed on Alfred Field of 27, Cravells Road, Harpenden, at St Albans Divisional Sessions on Saturday, for driving a horse and cart without front lights.* Reading felt effortful. It was odd to think that for years he had sucked up print without thinking. Since leaving Mattie's house, he hadn't finished a book. He couldn't follow a plot any more, the meaning seemed to bypass his brain, or else stuck to it briefly and then fell off when he turned the page, like an inadequately licked stamp.

Children's Corner. How to make a useful and decorative letter rack. Take an old picture frame, approximately 12" by 8". You will also need scissors, drawing pins, an old newspaper, poster paints, glue or paste, a brush, a pot of clear varnish . . .

Without books, he'd had no way of making the time pass quickly. The hours at his aunt and uncle's house had stretched like knicker elastic. He had done mental arithmetic, or played ludo against himself, rotating the board between each go. And he had written a diary in code, updating it every quarter of an hour. 9.15 *Auntie Margery is making an apple pie.* 9.30 *Auntie Margery is sweeping the kitchen floor.* 9.45 *Auntie Margery is washing dishcloths.* 10.00 *Auntie Margery has just looked up at me and sighed.* Uncle Geoffrey had removed the diary, and given him a wall-map instead, with a box of red glass-headed pins, so he could mark the advance of the British Expeditionary Force in Europe. And then Germany had invaded Belgium and France and all the pins had gone tinkling back into the box again.

The sum of £96 4s 1d was raised as a result of the house-to-house collection taken recently in aid of Red Cross Parcels for British Prisoners of War. Mrs Freda Lambert, chairman of the Harpenden and District Branch of the Red Cross, stated, 'We have been delighted by the unstinting generosity shown by Harpenden householders towards such a worthy cause.'

Noel read the paragraph a second time. He felt as if someone had just reached into his head and given his brain a sharp pinch. Holmes would have put down his violin at this point; Sam Spade would have reached for his gun. Noel snapped the paper shut and looked along the road. A hundred yards away, Vee was talking to someone, her head bobbing nervously.

She could hardly believe it. Here she was, at the swanky end of Watford, standing outside a house that had to be worth hundreds of pounds, and the owner had not only refused to hand over a single penny, but had actually followed her up the garden path and on to the pavement and was giving her a lecture on communism. She couldn't grasp the half of what he was saying. He had a long face with a mouth like a letter box, and leaflets kept shooting out of it. Ribbentrop–Molotov Pact. Imperialism on Both Sides. The Worker Betrayed. Words rattled past her ears. He was scarcely looking at her; it was as if she were the front row of a vast audience.

She edged away, lowering the collecting box. A few coins slithered around inside – three or four bob at most, a rotten profit for a whole afternoon. Take out the cost of the train and the bus, and the strain on her nerves, and it wasn't worth it. Another plan kaput.

The mouth carried on moving. Struggle on Two Fronts. Spectre of Capitalism. Government Lackeys. Something moved beside her, and she turned to see Noel, blank-faced at her elbow.

'Oh, it's my little lad,' she said, gratefully. 'He's been waiting for me like ever such a good boy. I'd better take him home to his tea, hadn't I?'

'And when they come and march him off to the front, perhaps you'll reconsider,' said the man. 'With the financial support of people like yourself, the capitalist-engineered armed conflict will be eternal.'

'Yes,' said Noel, 'isn't it strange that there's always enough money in the coffers for a war?'

In the pause that followed, Vee seized the boy's hand and dragged him away along the road.

'I think that chap had a screw loose,' she remarked, as they waited for the bus, 'though he's right that the war's a racket, they're all on the make. That's what Donald says as well. Sir Winston Chiseller, he calls him.'

Noel was looking at the collecting box in her hand. The picture of the aeroplane was starting to peel off, the words *Heathen Mission* clearly visible beneath.

'How much did you collect?' he asked.

'What?' Vee twisted round to look at him.

'How much money did you actually get?'

'Never you mind.' She put the box in her bag. 'Here's the bus coming,' she said, brightly, 'we'll soon be home.'

Noel spoke again. 'Because the house-to-house collection for Red Cross Parcels in Harpenden raised over ninety-six pounds.'

'*How* much?' She turned, her arm still stuck out to signal the bus.

'Ninety-six pounds, four shillings and a penny.'

'*Ninety-six!*'

'I expect they had quite a few collectors though, not just one.'

'Yes, but even so, that's a . . . a . . .' With an effort, Vee remembered what she ought to be saying. 'There are a lot of people collecting for Spitfires as well,' she said. 'Lots and lots of us.'

Noel slid her a look; she busied herself, sorting out change for the conductor, trying to stave off panic. He'd guessed what she was doing, she could see it in his eyes. She didn't know how she could ever have thought him simple; he was the opposite – he was like one of those fancy knots, all loops, no ends. And he'll tell, she thought. That's what children do, unless they're given a reason not to.

'I expect you'd like more sweeties,' she said. 'Shall we stop off at Woolies on the way home?'

He said nothing.

'Or some pocket money?' she suggested. 'A little bit of pocket money?'

He shook his head.

'Well, what then?' she hissed, close to his ear. And then, when he didn't speak, she let out a sigh like a deflating tyre. 'All right, all right,' she said, bitterly. 'First thing when we get to St Albans, we go to the Town Hall and give the money to the fund. *Won't* all those councillors be pleased?'

'No,' said Noel. 'I don't want any more Spitfires. There shouldn't even be a war, I don't believe in it, I don't care if we lose.'

Vee found herself feeling shocked. Even if you knew all the politicians were out for themselves, you had to want England to win, didn't you?

'Perhaps I ought to give them a bit,' she said. She tried to imagine herself going up to a collecting box and actually putting money in. And being thanked, like Lady Bountiful. She'd just nod and not say anything; you wouldn't want to show off.

'No, don't give them *anything*,' said Noel. Mattie would never have given a penny.

'So what do you want, then?' asked Vee again. 'You must want something.'

On the train journey back, he turned her query over in his mind, examining it, as if it were a puzzle to which he'd once known the solution. Since that frozen December morning when he had found Mattie on the Heath, her face a mask of putty, her feet cobalt, he had only *not* wanted things. It hadn't occurred to him that anyone might ever ask him that question again.

Little brain-teaser for you, young Noel: what exactly would you like? Inside his head, the old life seem to expand, squashing the present into a thin rind. When Mattie had hugged him, it had felt like being enfolded in a mattress. He could see her heavy-featured face and hear the vigour of her voice. *What shall we do today? Go and visit poor old Rameses II at the British Museum, see if he's managed to unwrap himself yet, and then lunch at the University Club? Or would you prefer Lyons? Yes, better puddings there, I always think. Incidentally, did I ever tell you about Roberta in the British Museum, chaining herself to Laocoön and His Sons? Which London statues would you most like to have in the garden? Oh those are splendid choices, absolutely splendid – we shall have Nelson in the front garden, and Boadicea in the back, and on fine days I shall hang the tea towels from her chariot wheels . . .*

He had never been bored with Mattie, never, never, never and now he was bored all the time, *all the time*; it was unbearable, like following mile after mile of grey string, with nothing at the end of it but a grim, distant, adult version of himself.

'Here we are,' said Vee, 'chop chop.'

He followed her out of the station. 'I want to do it too,' he said.

'Do what?'

'Collect money, the way you're doing.'

'No,' she said. A woman with a yellow headscarf was passing, and Vee nodded and called out 'Hello, Mrs de Souza', and the woman with the headscarf seemed not to hear her at all but went sailing straight past.

'That's Mrs de Souza,' said Vee. 'Her husband owns the shoe shop where my son used to work. They sell brogues for nearly ten pounds there, the leather's like satin. She's a snooty type.'

'I want to help.'

'No.'

'Why not?'

'It'd be wrong.'

'So how come *you're* doing it?'

'You're supposed to be limping.' She looked up at the abbey clock. 'We're late, I need to be getting Donald's tea ready.'

She started to walk faster. She was feeling rather frightened. It was like the verse in Hosea: she'd sown the wind and was reaping the whirlwind. She could almost feel the devil snapping at her heels.

'I shall tell if you *don't* let me,' said Noel. 'I shall tell that you've been soliciting donations under false pretences.' They were just passing the blue lamp of the police station. He stopped walking, and made a feint for the door.

'No,' said Vee. They looked at each other. 'They'd never believe a kiddie,' she said.

Noel reached for the door-knob.

'All right, all right, all *right!*' Her voice was loud enough to turn heads on the other side of the street. She forced herself to start walking, her legs shaky.

'In any case, I wasn't going to do it again,' she said.

'Why not?'

'It's not as easy as you'd think.'

She risked a glance at him. He was walking beside her, his stride matching hers.

'All things are difficult before they are easy,' said Noel.

4

In the cubicle of the gents toilet at Leicester station, Donald re-read the letter and then took a hand mirror out of his pocket. He combed his hair, and gave his teeth a wipe with a scrap of paper. Then he ran a finger over his moustache. He'd only had a month to grow it, and it wasn't half bad – it suited him, in fact, made him look very much like Robert Donat in *The Thirty-Nine Steps*. Pity he'd have to shave it off again next week.

Outside the cubicle, the man who'd been retching into the urinal shuffled away. Donald heard the exterior door open and then close again. For a moment, the only noise was the trickle of water.

'What's the matter?' he asked, out loud. 'A heart murmur? What's that when it's at home?'

He looked into the mirror again, and tried out an anxious expression; he found he could make his chin wobble if he really put his mind to it. 'Oh, Christ Almighty,' he said, his voice cracking. 'Am I going to die?' No, he thought: too much. You didn't want to overplay.

Exiting the station, he bought a copy of the *Daily Express* and stood with his back to the war memorial. Immediately, a chap wearing too much hair-oil detached himself from the queue outside a tobacconist and walked straight towards him. Donald met him halfway.

'Fielding, is it?'

The man nodded. 'Pint?' he asked. 'We've got time.'

'I'd like my money first,' said Donald. 'And what happened to your moustache? You said you had a moustache.'

'My girl didn't like it.'

'I've been growing it specially,' said Donald. 'I should charge you extra.'

Fielding shrugged. 'Didn't cost you, did it? Come through here.' He jerked his head towards an alley between adjacent shops.

Donald took his time counting the cash, enjoying the feel of the notes. He hadn't known how much to ask for, the first time; he'd thought that thirty sounded a good whack, and then he'd seen the leap of relief on his first client's face, and had begun to know his own worth. Eighty-five was his rate now, and he was thinking of upping it again.

'All right,' he said, stowing the wad away in an inside pocket.

'A pint?' asked Fielding again. He was obviously the nervy type. He chose a crowded little pub across the road from the station, and led Donald into the snug.

'I'll take a brandy,' said Donald.

Fielding winced. 'Have a heart,' he said, 'after what I've just handed over?'

Donald shrugged. He didn't like brandy anyway; it was the principle of the thing: beer for friends, brandy for business. Not that he liked beer much either. He'd been thinking lately about trying wine. He'd go into a restaurant some time, and give it a go. White. Red. French names.

'Got you a port,' said Fielding, returning from the bar, his own pint already a third gone.

'Is it far to get there?' asked Donald.

Fielding shook his head. 'Round the corner. You know, I was expecting a sickly looking bloke. Want a tab?'

Donald took a Woodbine, though lately he'd found he was

losing his taste for cigarettes. Cigars, he thought. I'm probably a cigar man. I should get a humidor.

'I expect you want to know why I'm dodging out?' asked Fielding. 'I'm not a coward or nothing.'

Donald smelled the drink and put it back on the table. 'I don't have to know,' he said. 'It's none of my business.'

'It's my girl,' said Fielding. He checked over his shoulder. 'You wouldn't believe it if you saw her, she's a dream. You know Rita Hayworth? Rita Hayworth'd look like a fucking *bulldog* next to my Joan. And you know what, she loves me, she's all over me.' He paused to sup his beer. 'But girls like that,' he said, 'they get their heads turned, don't they? I go away, some flash geezer comes up and buys her a fur coat and next thing I know it's "Dear Phil, I'm tired of waiting for you, I want someone who'll look after me proper." I can't take the risk.' He finished his pint and eyed the empty glass with contempt. 'Piss,' he said. 'Might as well hold it under the tap. You got a girl?'

'Not at present,' said Donald.

'When I first saw her, I thought someone'd tapped me on the head with a sledgehammer, I swear to God. I was at the Tivoli, and I turned round and there was Joan, and I looked back at the tart I'd come with and I might as well've been dancing with a fucking chair, so I said to her, I said . . .'

Donald stopped listening. He didn't like swearing, never had, it was like someone waving a muddy fist in your face. Fielding's girl, Joan, was clearly no good, and it was obvious that Fielding was going to get the shove sooner or later, once she'd picked his wallet. It was amazing that Fielding hadn't twigged this, but like most people, he hadn't taken the trouble to actually study the way the world worked. Donald had. Snide types in the past might have accused him of sitting around not doing much, but he'd been observing the whole time; his eyes were like spy cameras, whizz snap, missing nothing. And then afterwards, lying in bed (not sleeping, *thinking*), he'd analyse the pictures and tease out the patterns. For a start he'd seen that most blokes were fools with women: they bounced around like billiard balls, one kiss and into the pocket. They didn't realize that there was never any sense in rushing. His mother was always rushing, it made him tired just watching her, like seeing a fly bang itself against a pane of glass, over and over again. And it never got her anywhere, did it? Whereas he was on the up. He had bided his time and then a window had sweetly opened.

Fielding was still talking: '. . . bought her a ring with a diamond cluster and stuck it under me tongue, and said, "Kiss me, baby" and she said, "Ooh you shouldn't of." Nine carat, I had to pay a pony.'

'You got the papers?' asked Donald.

Fielding felt in his pocket, and handed over the letter and his identity card. 'We better get going, I s'pose,' he said, and started to gnaw at a nail. 'What else do you need to know about me? Dad's name? School and that?'

Donald shook his head. 'They never ask. Sometimes they want to know what job you do – look at your hands, test your muscles, that sort of thing.'

Fielding held out his palms, pink and unmarked.

'Bookie's runner,' he said.

'Are you?' Donald felt mild interest. He'd never been to the races, wasn't interested in horseflesh, or betting, but in newsreels he'd seen the winner's enclosure, champagne foaming, ladies with haircuts that cost a tenner, so much class you could *smell* it. 'Where do you work?'

'All over, travelling all the time,' said Fielding. 'The bookie's me uncle, see, he's going to sign me over the business one of these days.'

'Racing still going on, is it? With the war and everything?'

'You *bet*.' Fielding sniggered at his own joke and lit another cigarette. 'They've chopped it back, only six courses open, half a day a week, but that just means the stakes are higher, don't it?

Another reason not to join Fred Karno's Army. Come on, then.'

They walked through hazy sunlight towards the drill hall. A street away, Fielding hung back. 'I'll be in there,' he said, nodding towards a pub. Donald joined the queue of men snaking from the entrance. There was the usual smell of anxiety, the usual jokes and rumours.

'I heard if you slip a tenner to the head doctor, he'll get you a desk job.'

'I heard if you slip him a length, he'll get you into the WRENS.'

There was a burst of laughter.

'I got flat feet,' said a chap who looked half-witted. 'They won't put me in the army, will they?'

'RAF,' said the sharpie who'd made the crack about the WRENS. 'They get all the blokes with flat feet together, and send them off to tread down the lumps on the runways.'

'Serious, though,' said the half-wit, worriedly. 'Do you think they'll pass me fit?'

A discussion began, and then an argument.

'I tell you, you gotta be using a bloody white stick before they let you off for eyesight.'

'Flat feet, though—'

'My brother, right, my own brother got 'is medical discharge for a fucking ingrowing *toe*nail so don't go telling me I don't know what I'm talking about.'

'But my flat feet, right—'

Donald unfolded the *Express* and began to glance at the headlines. He felt entirely calm, much as he had at his very first medical board. That day had been glorious; it hung in his memory like a silken banner. All his life, he'd been waiting for the moment when he'd be lifted out of the mire. What he'd been born into was all wrong for him – the makeshift shabbiness, cheap cuts of meat and darned sheets, the daily muddle – he belonged to a higher class of existence and he'd always *known* this, absolutely, as if he'd carried a fairytale birth-mark on his shoulder in the shape of a crown. The only thing that had ever made his existence bearable was the utter certainty that at some point things would change. That day in Bedford, as he'd progressed round the draughty interior of the Town Hall having his ears probed, his belly prodded, his privates fingered, he'd sensed, somehow, that his moment was coming. As if he'd heard a distant trumpet call.

'Ah. Now . . .' the doctor had said, his stethoscope pressed against Donald's chest, 'has anyone ever told you that you have a heart murmur?' Another quack had come over, and they'd listened and nodded, and marked him Unfit for Service, and then Donald had had to take a letter to a hospital specialist, who had given the verdict, in writing, of Congenital Pulmonary Regurgitation. It was something to do with the blood vessels to the lungs and it was, said the specialist, unusual, untreatable and unlikely to cause symptoms for many years.

Unusual.

Untreatable.

Unlikely to cause symptoms for many years.

The description had seemed to float up like a triple fanfare, three gifts on a golden tray, a trio of gilded doves. Donald Sedge would be excused drudgery. Donald Sedge would not be square-bashing with the rank and file. Donald Sedge was a rarity, ill yet well, fragile yet robust, officially possessed of a heart unlike others. 'Now don't worry, Mr Sedge,' the doctor had said, mistaking euphoria for terror. And miracle had succeeded miracle because that very afternoon, Donald had been hailed by the chap who'd been standing behind him at the Bedford medical. He'd let out a slow whistle when he heard about the murmur. '*You're* quids in,' he'd said. 'Some blokes'd pay through the nose to have you stand in for them.' Donald had wisely kept his mouth shut, only shaken his head disapprovingly, but word had got out, and only two days later someone had turned up at Croxton's yard with an offer. The first of many.

In the beginning, he'd put the money in a shoebox under the bed. That was full now, and the overflow was going into an old Gladstone bag. It sat on top of his wardrobe, pregnant, waiting for the hour.

The queue started to move.

'What if I say I'm a conchie?' asked Flat-Foot, panicking.

'They'll take you out the back and shoot you,' said the man behind him. "Ere, what's the difference between an egg, a hen and Hitler? An egg wants sucking, a hen wants plucking and Hitler wants—' He gave a leer and waited for laughter.

'If you were a real conchie, you wouldn't even come to the medical,' said a prim-looking boy with spectacles. 'And anyway, Hitler *does* want fucking, doesn't he?' Coming from his tidy little mouth, the phrase sounded extraordinarily filthy and there was a cackle from someone in the line. The boy flushed. 'Well,' he said, defensively, 'I think he needs to be stopped, and I don't see why I should leave it to other people. And I can't be the only one here who thinks that.' He looked around, jerking his gaze from one man to another.

'No, you're not the only one,' said Donald, quietly. All eyes turned toward him. He said not a word more, just folded his arms. There was a moment of respectful silence, and then a man with a clipboard appeared between the double doors and shouted 'Next twenty,' and the line shuffled forward. The prim boy gave Donald a little nod. I could give lessons, thought Donald. I'm good at this.

It was a slow afternoon, one queue and then another, read the top line, close your eyes and raise your finger when you hear a noise, can you feel this pin jabbing into your leg? I'm doing this for the first time, Donald kept reminding himself; mustn't look as if I know what's coming. Touch your toes, cough, walk along this line.

The chest doctor was a short man, with hair like the bristles of a scrubbing brush and flaking skin. 'Breathe in,' he said, 'breathe out, say ninety-nine.' The cup of the stethoscope hopped across Donald's back. 'Now turn,' said the doctor. Donald revolved. His moment was coming; he kept his face impassive. The doctor's hand, as rough as a washerwoman's, pressed the stethoscope into the soft flesh below his left nipple. There was a fractional pause and then a crash from the other end of the room, followed by a volley of shouts.

'Christ!' said the doctor, departing at a loping run towards a prone figure. It was the half-wit, who appeared to have fainted, striking his head on a table on the way down. There was a quantity of blood.

The stethoscope lay coiled on the floor where the doctor had dropped it and Donald stooped to pick it up. Could you listen to your own heart? He looked at the clots of wax on the earpieces and decided against it, on the grounds of hygiene. The man who'd fainted was sitting on the chair with a cloth to his head.

'All right,' said the doctor, returning, 'where were we?' He took the proffered stethoscope, glanced at Donald and then wrote something on the card. 'Right, Mr Fielding, you're all done,' he said. 'Take this to the office. And try to lay off the cream buns, or you're going to find basic training a nasty old shock.'

Donald stared. The doctor waggled the card impatiently. 'Take it, man.'

'But you haven't done my heart,' said Donald.

'What?'

'You didn't listen to my heart.'

The doctor looked at him as if he were a lunatic. 'Your heart,' he said, 'is *there*.' He jabbed a finger at the left side of Donald's chest. 'Where on earth did you think it was?'

'No, I mean you didn't listen to it properly.'

'I didn't what?'

The doctor's voice wasn't loud, but his tone turned every head within earshot.

Donald struggled to think; sweat had broken out across his back. 'I mean . . . you'd only just started listening when that bloke fell over. You didn't listen for very long. Just for a second or two.' The smell of his own armpits rose like the morning dew. 'I thought you needed to do it for a bit longer, like.'

'Take the card, Mr Fielding,' said the doctor.

One more try, thought Donald.

'My dad had a bad heart,' he said. 'He dropped stone dead when he was twenty-five. And I've been feeling a bit queer lately.'

'Really? I'm so sorry to hear that. Try drinking less beer and getting off your colossal arse occasionally. Next!'

Laughter rolled across the room. Donald gripped the card between damp fingers, and walked towards the desk at the end. His pulse was racing so fast that it seemed to stumble over itself. What if he were actually to drop dead from the shock of passing his medical, that would be rich, wouldn't it?

'He didn't listen to my heart,' he said to the clerk. 'I'm not fit.'

Without speaking, the man took the card, peered at the notes and then embarked on some very slow typing, ash from his cigarette dropping on to the keys.

'The doctor didn't do it properly,' said Donald. 'I'm not right, I know I'm not.'

'You and the rest of the bloody world,' said the clerk. 'You don't know what unfit *is*. See this?' He leaned forward and hauled down one of his lower eyelids to expose a moist crescent the colour of spam. 'Anaemic. They still passed me B1, the stinking bastards, so don't talk to me about not being fit.' He poked at a few more keys, and then tossed the card on to a pile. 'You're all done,' the clerk added. 'A2. You'll get a letter about when and where to report.'

Outside, Donald went and stood in the shadow of a wall and tried to calm himself. It was hotter than when he'd gone in, and breezeless; he felt as if he could slice the air like a block of cheese. Every minute or so, another man would exit glumly from the drill hall; the pub opposite was a roar of voices, all outrage and bravado.

He saw Fielding before Fielding saw him, he saw him crossing the road, the greasy little head looking up at the drill hall and then down at his watch. Donald placed a hand over his breast pocket and felt the bundle of notes, solid beneath his palm. He had earned it, hadn't he? It wasn't his fault that the doctor hadn't done his job. He stepped out of the shadows.

'Jesus, you were bleedin' hours,' said Fielding. He jerked his head towards a side street and they rounded the corner. 'Everything all right?' he hissed. 'They failed you?'

'Didn't go to plan,' said Donald.

'What?'

'Doctor didn't examine me properly.'

Fielding's face seemed to ice over. Donald found himself talking faster.

'He hardly listened to my chest. He had to go and pick up this bloke who fainted. And then he just wrote on my card. He didn't even—'

'You mean you passed the medical?'

'I kept asking him to have a listen but—'

'You fucking *passed*? Give me my money,' said Fielding.

'But it wasn't my fault—'

One of Fielding's hands shot out and pinned Donald's neck against the wall, while the other expertly ransacked his jacket and removed the bundle of notes.

'You fat fucker,' said Fielding, letting go. Donald crouched down, purple commas punctuating his vision, his windpipe feeling as if someone had shoved a flue-brush down it.

'Lucky for you it's all there,' said Fielding, somewhere above him. 'You lousy cheating bastard, I could have you razored, I know chaps what would turn your face to fucking rags for a fiver. I've had blokes with their legs broke for less than what you've done, I've had . . .' the words dissolved into gasps. Donald blinked up through the drifting shapes. Fielding was weeping. 'My Joanie,' he said, 'how am I ever going to leave my Joanie?' He pushed the notes into his trouser pocket, turned to go and then, almost as an afterthought, swung back and kneed Donald in the face.

Donald lay and watched the shoes disappear around the corner. A ribbon of blood slid across the pavement. After the first blast of pain had eased, he lifted a hand and began, delicately, to explore the new shape of his nose.

5

'Hitler's invading tomorrow,' whispered Harvey Madeley during register.

'You said that last week,' said one of the Ferris twins, 'and then he never.'

'He was supposed to, but it rained. My uncle told me, and he's in the RAF and he knows.'

'So why couldn't Hitler do it in the rain?'

''Cos his tanks are made of cardboard,' hissed Roy Pursey from the row behind.

'No—'

'And he'd promised all the Nazis an ice cream when they reached London.'

'*When* you're ready,' called Mr Waring, smacking the board with a ruler. Dust bloomed upward. 'May I remind you that there are only three days left of the current term, and I would rather they were not utterly wasted. It would be a hollow victory indeed for the Allies if, at the end of their endeavours, none of the rising generation could multiply, parse, punctuate or even spell the word "victory". Madeley, spell the word "victory".'

'V I C K—'

'Spelling test,' said Mr Waring. 'Who has a pencil?'

Roughly half the class raised a hand.

'Pass them to the first four rows. First four rows pass your

English primer, if you possess one, to the back of the class. Back of the class turn to "A Spring Day" on page thirty-seven and begin silent reading. Pay particular attention to adverbs.'

There was a clatter of desktops. They were no longer being taught in the tin chapel, but in a proper classroom in St Mark's Church of England Primary. The evacuees attended in the morning and the local children in the afternoon, the daily cross-playground transition a blur of spit and fisticuffs. Roy Pursey had stuck a pen in the arm of a farm-worker's son who had called him a nit-brained Cockney bed-pisser, and had received ten strokes of the cane from the headmistress, a woman who looked as if she made a living bending railings in a circus. Roy had claimed, unconvincingly, that it hadn't hurt a bit.

'Democracy,' said Mr Waring, in his dictation voice. 'De-mo-cra-see.'

Noel glanced at 'A Spring Day', judged it unreadable (. . . *and as sweet vernal zephyrs dance betwixt blackthorn and rustling rowan, that roguish fellow, the robin, tilts a curious head o'er the lea* . . .), and sat with his eyes fixed on the wall-clock. An odd, unfamiliar feeling uncurled within him: for the first time in nearly a year, he was actually looking forward to something.

'Fascism,' said Mr Waring. 'Fash-ism.'

Research, he'd decided, was the key. Vee had failed to plan sufficiently; she was a stranger to lists, a martyr to panic and whim. *By failing to prepare, you are preparing to fail*, as Mattie had liked to quote, and Noel had spent the last two afternoons in the newspaper room in St Albans Public Library, listing (in code) every cause for which house-to-house collections had been made, and comparing the resulting revenues. Lord Baldwin's Fund for German Refugees had done spectacularly badly in Hertfordshire, as had the Civil Service Distress Fund. Anything with 'Soldiers' or 'Lads' in the title had fared better; 'Benevolent' was another winner, ditto 'Comforts', while the word 'Orphans' had released a cascade of small change into the collecting boxes of Harpenden. Local names also seemed to hit the spot: The South Mimms Parochial Church Blackout Fund had raised a surprising amount, given its narrow appeal.

'Tyranny,' said Mr Waring. 'Ti-ra-nee.'

Noel had also spent some time deliberating where the collection should take place. There was something peculiarly memorable about Vee; she seemed to move like the actors in silent films, all jerks and freezes. They needed to go somewhere where there was no possibility of her being recognized or recalled, a place where strangers were not unusual and where neighbours didn't necessarily compare notes. After a great deal of thought, and a thorough perusal of local train routes, he had decided on the North London suburb of Cricklewood. 'That's a long way,' Vee had said, fretfully, but she hadn't objected – had, in fact, seemed relieved to be told rather than asked.

She'd been in a sort of daze since Donald had arrived home after his unlucky stumble over a sandbag, his shirt soaked with blood. Instead of going to work he had gone to bed with a wet cloth over his face. Mr Croxton had banged on the door at seven o'clock, and when Vee hadn't answered, he'd stood outside in the road and shouted that he had had enough, he'd have got more work out of a dead Wop and he was sacking Donald and giving three days' notice on the flat. Vee had run downstairs then, and had stayed away for some time, returning with a stain on her apron, and the news that the notice had been extended to a fortnight. She had then cried, briefly and violently, before starting work on a pile of hatbands.

'Liberation,' said Mr Waring. 'Lib-er—' He let out a long sigh as the horrible clamour of an iron triangle filled the air.

'Air-raid, sir!' shouted Harvey Madeley.

Outside in the corridor, someone began to swing a wooden rattle.

'Air-raid, sir, with gas!'

'Thank you, Madeley. Pencils down, close your books. Proceed without undue panic to the shelter.'

As the class stampeded for the door, Mr Waring stooped to pick up a primer that had been knocked to the ground.

'Still here, Bostock?' he asked, straightening up. 'You need to hurry.'

'It's only a drill, sir,' said Noel. It was a daily occurrence. The headmistress would at this moment be standing beside the playground shelter, a stopwatch in her mighty fist; the current record was a minute and thirty-two seconds.

'It won't always be a drill, you know. The ports are already getting it.'

Noel shrugged, uncomfortably. He didn't like to talk about the war as if it were actually happening; it felt like a betrayal of Mattie.

'Not', added Mr Waring, 'that St Albans will be particularly high on the list of future targets for the Luftwaffe, hence our sojourn here. Do you have your gas mask?'

Noel nodded, shielding the top of the case with his hand, to conceal the handle of the collecting box.

'Cut along then. I shall follow after inspecting the classroom thoroughly for stray incendiaries.' Mr Waring glanced around ostentatiously and then sat on the edge of the desk and began to fill his pipe.

Later that day, as Vee and Noel left Cricklewood station, there was a sound overhead like ripping cloth, and an aeroplane crossed eastward, followed by a second, and then a third, and though Noel had never consciously learned their names, he knew by now that they were Spitfires, in the same way that he knew that when a bird hung trembling in the air it was a kestrel. A lacy trail unravelled slowly in the sky behind them.

'I don't know . . .' said Vee, for the umpteenth time. She appeared to be sleepwalking, her face the colour of an unwashed pillowcase, her eyes half-closed. She had slept for nearly the whole of the short journey, while Noel had studied the map that he'd discreetly ripped out of the street-atlas in the library.

'I didn't ought to have left Donny in the state he's in,' she said. 'Anyhow, I should be out looking for new lodgings. And then there's those hatbands . . .' A hundred and fifty of them to make by Friday, khaki and maroon, ugly colours. 'It's the military look,' Vic Allerby had said, delivering the ribbon. 'Ladies don't want flowers no more, they want to look like they're in the bloody army.' She'd worked on them through the night, but her hands had refused to memorize the folds and tucks, so she'd had to concentrate on each one as if it were the first. By sun-up, she'd still only finished fifty-eight and in the primrose light she'd seen the sweat-marks her fingers had left on the ribbon. She'd have to dust them with baking soda, and then brush them so they looked like new or she wouldn't get paid. She had lined up that particular worry in front of all the others; it was small, *manageable* even, as opposed to the bloated impossibilities of the summons and the eviction.

'We'll start along here,' said Noel, and Vee followed him like a dragged sack.

The street was lined with tall, shabby houses.

He'd come here with Mattie, two years ago. They'd been visiting a friend of hers, a woman always referred to as 'poor old Alice', who lived in a single room on the top floor of number three. Noel remembered the cluster of bell-pushes beside the door, and the odd feel of an interior that was both full and peculiarly empty, its inhabitants rustling behind closed doors. At the time, he'd been working his way through Agatha Christie, and as Mattie and Alice had sat drinking their milkless tea, and reminiscing in a rapid, slangy shorthand – 'Livvy Kerr wasn't quite the thing, was she?', 'Gung-ho but lacking in fibre, had the screaming ab-dabs when they locked the cell door' – he had imagined setting a crime novel here: *Murder on the Fourth Floor*, with a visiting boy detective who'd have to interview the finite number of suspects before fingering the occupant who had crushed Alice's skull with a half-size marble bust of Mary Wollstonecraft.

The doorbell had rung halfway through the afternoon, and poor old Alice had hurried down to answer it. 'A fellow selling brushes,' she'd said, returning. And then, one by one, in a series of muffled brays and buzzes, the salesman had rung all the other bells in the house. 'Second floor back's the one he wants,' Alice had said. 'Her son hawks almanacs, she never says no to a salesman.' Six inhabitants; six chances in every house.

Another aeroplane passed eastward: blunter, more lumbering than the Spitfires.

'They say Hitler's going to invade today,' said Vee, vaguely. Someone in a shop had said it; they were dropping Nazis dressed as vicars, you had to look out for a man of the cloth who couldn't say his 'w's. Thy vill be done.

'Here,' said Noel, nodding at the next house along from Alice's, 'we'll begin here', and he took the collecting box out of his gas-mask case. He had glued a square of card to the front of it, and then made a stencil and inked the lettering himself.

Vee glanced over her shoulder.

'It's a busy road,' she said.

'That's good.'

'Is it?'

'Better than an empty one. Hiding in plain sight is a recognized form of camouflage.' He looked at Vee in her charcoal coat. The whites of her eyes were a raw pink.

'Here,' he said, giving her the box to hold.

'What do I say?' she asked, in a sudden panic.

'Just say what we're collecting for.'

He reached upward and pressed the bottom bell.

They waited for what seemed like a long time, and then footsteps scraped along the passage. The door opened, and a one-eyed man blinked down at them, a scar raking his face from empty socket to chin.

'Yes?'

Vee jumped, and there was a rattle from the box; Noel had primed it with a shilling in coppers.

'Dunkirk Widows and Orphans, Cricklewood District,' she said, in a yelp.

The man let out a sigh, and reached into his pocket. He took out a shilling and slotted it in, then extended a palm and patted Noel heavily on the head. 'Good lad,' he said. It wasn't until the door closed again, that Vee realized she'd been holding her breath.

'Another one?' she asked.

'Wait a moment.' Noel counted to ten, and then pressed a second bell. This time the footsteps were brisk. A young woman answered the door, pert-faced, curly-haired, her mouth pursed as if to receive a kiss, her stomach tautly rounded beneath a flowered apron.

'Yes?'

'Dunkirk Widows and Orphans, Cricklewood District.'

For a moment her expression was unchanged, and then the lips trembled. She put a hand to her mouth to still them. 'I'll fetch my purse,' she said, between her fingers.

She gave a handful of coppers, and then called them back and added a sixpence. 'I'm sorry for your loss,' she said, before closing the door.

Vee looked at Noel; she felt slightly breathless. 'Another one?'

Without answering, he rang the top bell. They waited a long, long time. Vee tilted the box and listened to the slither of the money. 'Do you think . . . ?' she began, and then straightened up as she heard footsteps.

'Can I help you?' It was an elderly man, with wire-rimmed

spectacles and a wheeze, and a book in one hand, his place marked with a thumb.

'Dunkirk Widows and Orphans, Cricklewood District.'

The man looked from Vee to Noel and back again.

'Is this your son?' he asked.

'Yes,' said Vee, uncertainly.

'Why isn't he at school?' His question was plaintive rather than accusatory.

'It's after lunch.'

'I'm afraid I don't understand.'

'They don't go there after lunch.'

'Why ever not?'

Despite the mildness of his gaze, Vee began to feel flustered. 'Because the school's all full of evacuees and there's no room. Not for everyone. So all the evacuees, they just go in the morning.'

'Afternoon,' interrupted Noel. 'My mother means the afternoon. And the original pupils, including myself, attend only in the morning.'

'Yes,' said Vee. 'That's what I meant.'

'Hence my presence here,' added Noel.

'Bob's your uncle!' said Vee, brightly.

There was a pause. Vee could hear the conversation echoing in her head and knew it was all wrong, a kazoo and a flute trying to pipe the same tune. She gave the box a little rattle, tried a smile and then remembered what they were supposed to be collecting for, and let her face drop. 'Widows,' she repeated. 'And orphans.'

The man felt around in his jacket pocket and pulled out two threepences, and then he coughed, and took a moment to catch his breath. 'Fifty years of chalk dust,' he said. 'One should never underestimate the far-reaching consequences of education. Your young fellow sounds as if he's doing rather well for himself, though.'

The door closed, and before Noel could reach for another bell, Vee grabbed his wrist.

'Not yet,' she hissed. 'We have to talk.'

She looked over her shoulder, but no one was watching. 'Over here,' she said, and led him to the cluster of salvage bins on the corner. Out of interest, she lifted the lid of one of them and a cloud of flies sizzled through the gap. She dropped it hastily.

'What's the matter?' asked Noel.

'We're telling people you're my boy and then you're using words like . . . like "original" and "hence". No one from St Albans ever says "hence". And you should say "my mum" not "my mother" and anyway you just don't sound right. You sound as if you come from somewhere posh and I sound—'

'Common,' said Noel.

Vee coloured. 'You don't say things like that about people,' she said. She fiddled with her hat. She thought she'd been look-ing smart and now she felt like a greasy rag. 'You don't know anything about me,' she said. 'I was at school till I was fifteen, I was clever. I wanted to be a teacher.'

Noel looked back at her. The expression on his wide, plain face wasn't cheeky or defiant, but baffled. It occurred to her that he hadn't used the word 'common' as an insult, merely a description. Which in some ways was *worse*.

'But I had to say something,' said Noel. 'You got it all wrong when he asked about my school timetable.'

'Yes, but that's another thing that people'd think is strange. Children oughtn't to talk back and say when their mums are wrong about things. I hope you don't speak like that when your . . . your . . .'

Her mind was a blank. Who was it that he lived with?

'Anyone would think *you* were the grown-up,' she amended.

Noel looked down at the pavement, so that she could see the wandering pink of his parting. His hair was full of summer dust.

It needed a wash and a trim, she realized; she'd almost forgotten that she was supposed to be looking after him.

'Do you?' she asked.

'What?'

'Talk like that at home?'

'Yes,' he said, fiercely. There was nothing he hadn't been able to say to Mattie. He turned and walked away along the street, through a blizzard of returning flies, and Vee hurried after him.

'Don't you see, we can't both do the talking,' she said. 'We don't match and people will think it's strange and if they think it's strange then they might start asking around and before long we'll be up to our neck in it, won't we? Or I will, anyhow. It might only be a bit of fun for you, but for me it'd be trouble. Worse than trouble.'

'But what if someone asks me a question?'

'Just nod or shake your head.'

'And what if they ask me a question which requires some kind of *answer*?'

There was contempt in his voice; she could almost have struck him again, if it hadn't been a public place.

'Look,' she said, thrusting her face into his, 'we can't be *noticed*. You said that – hiding in daylight.'

'Plain sight.'

'Yes, well then, you're a clever boy, aren't you? It's obvious, I was all wrong about you at the start. But you've got to practise what you preach.'

He carried on walking, but more slowly.

'What do you mean, you were wrong about me?'

'Well, I . . .' Vee huffed a bit, searching for an answer. '. . . I didn't think you were all there,' she said, finally.

He turned and stared at her. 'You thought I was *feeble-minded*?'

'You had a bit of a blank look, that's all. And you didn't say much, did you? And you packed a fur coat. In June.'

'Not for wearing,' he said. 'It's a memento.'

'And the rock?'

'A memento mori.'

'And there you go!' she said triumphantly. 'That's why you can't do the talking. Every time you open your mouth, out comes Latin.'

Along the road, a front door smacked shut. The pregnant woman, a shopping bag over one arm, clipped briskly towards them.

'Oops-a-daisy,' said Vee, loudly, crouching down. 'Let's do this up, otherwise you'll come a cropper, won't you, my little lad?' She undid his sandal strap and then fastened it again on exactly the same hole.

The woman walked past, scarcely glancing at them.

Vee straightened up. 'Hiding in plain sight,' she said.

'Yes, if I were *three*,' said Noel. 'Ten-year-olds don't get their shoes fastened by their mothers.'

'Some might.'

'Only if they're—'

'What?'

Noel paused. 'Feeble-minded,' he said. 'Ask me a question,' he added.

'What?'

'Ask me a question. Anything. Ask me how old I am. Go on.'

Vee shook her head, helplessly. 'Why?'

'Just ask me.'

'All right. How old are you?'

Instead of answering, Noel stared past her along the road, his face empty.

'Oh, I follow you,' said Vee. 'And why aren't you at school?' There was no change in his expression, and it struck her that he looked not so much soft in the head, as shocked sideways, as if someone had fetched him a whack with a sandbag.

She put a hand on his shoulder. It was like squeezing a

bicycle brake, all wire and tension. 'This is my lad,' she said, experimentally. 'He's not said a word since we lost his dad. He comes with me everywhere.'

She rattled the box.

'All right,' said Noel. 'Now I'll pretend to ask you something. So, what happened to his father?'

Vee opened her mouth. She had a dozen answers straight off; she could have been a story-writer, she thought, if she'd had the chance and the education, it came so easily to her. *He was on the last boat back from Dunkirk, and then we heard from his sergeant that he'd dived into the water to rescue a pal. He was the last one out of their billet, they left him with a Gatling. He was last seen on the road to the French coast, trying to help a little boy and his granny . . .* She could see herself talking, enjoying the tale; she could see herself spinning a long yarn, one that would trail behind them as they went from doorstep to doorstep – and snag, and knot, and loop dangerously around their ankles.

'So what happened to his father?' repeated Noel.

Vee sighed.

'I don't like to talk about it,' she said. 'Not in front of the boy.'

'And why isn't he at school?'

Vee let go of his shoulder, and took his hand instead. 'He stays home with me. The doctor said it was best for a while.'

'All right,' said Noel. He detached his hand from hers. 'Let's give it another go.'

1st September 1940
Dear Mr Churchill
I expect you've been very busy so won't write a long letter, just a few thoughts I've been saving up.

We have moved to new accommodation so please note different postal address.

1. There is still a lot of crime about. There was another smash-and-grab raid at the jeweller's in Victoria Street last week the second in two months, and also a burglar broke into the house of a friend in my congregation on Tuesday and stole a carriage clock and six bananas (her son is in the merchant navy). There are not enough police about. The one who came round after the burglary didn't even look for clues, and my friend said he was out of breath just bicycling from the station. Also, the flat we are in now only came empty because the woman who lived here before was claiming the allowance for five evacuees who'd all gone back to London and she did a flit before they could arrest her, so there's another example. No one said what happened to all the extra rations she claimed either, there was nothing in the cupboards when we moved in. We need more Police on the Streets, not sitting eating plates of tinned peaches and custard sauce from a brand-new jar in the back basement of St Albans Police Station, which is something a friend of mine saw through the window one evening.

2. *We keep getting sirens but they're all false alarms here. The man in the shop underneath our flat lets us use his basement shelter but it's too much for me to get all the way down there and then back up when it's just a practice. What such as me need is something in our very own living room like an iron box or a cage big enough for 2 or 3 people to sit in, here's a little sketch:*

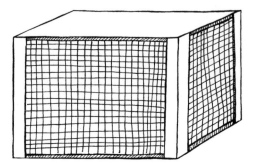

3. *I don't know if you know this, but when Alvar Liddell on the wireless says Nazi on the news broadcast he says it in a different way to the way you say Nazi, you say it Narzee and he says it Nartsi. People have noticed this, and when I met my cousin Harold at the Abbey Tea Rooms last week he told me that he's even heard jokes about it. I thought you ought to know. Alvar sounds a foreign name to me.*

4. *I have been listening to 'Beat the Band' on the wireless and when I wrote the answers down last week I noticed something very strange. The first letters of each of the songs if you wrote them in a row spelled OFF TMW. Now there were no raids on the British coast reported on Thursday (the next day), so you can see how I'm putting two and two together (OFF TOMORROW). A spy in the BBC could be signalling, I think checks should be made. I am going to keep a list for you.*

Well I think that's all for now. I saw your picture in the paper last week and I hope you don't mind me saying that I wonder if you're getting enough fresh air.
Yours faithfully,
Flora Sedge

6

Before leaving Croxton's Scrap Metal for the last time, Vee had gutted a couple of sprats and dropped the flaccid insides down the back of the gas-fire.

The new flat, for which she'd paid three weeks' rent in advance (*three weeks!*) was above a bookshop. It had a proper bathroom, and its own front door. The council offices were five minutes away; Vee dropped round there one morning to pay off her rates arrears and it occurred to her, as she walked home, that for the first time in her adult life she didn't owe any money to anyone. It was odd – unbalancing – not to have that particular worry; it was as if she'd been walking round for the last twenty years with a sandbag over one shoulder.

By the end of the summer, she and Noel had rules and a routine. They took a mid-morning train outward (not too crowded, not too empty) and returned mid-afternoon. Four hours' collecting was enough; the box was usually heavy by then. They changed their destination daily, taking buses from the stations, testing and comparing areas. St John's Wood was too rich, Kilburn too Irish, Camden had too many policemen. They stuck to the north-western suburbs, to houses crammed with the respectable poor.

Noel varied the beneficiary of the collecting box, keeping careful notes of the daily totals. By mid-August, RAF Widows and Orphans were clearly winning over those from Dunkirk.

In Kingsbury, one afternoon, they saw a dogfight, chalk lines scribbled across a wide blue board, one mark scraping diagonally downward, ending in a puff of black on the horizon. Half the street came out to watch, and there was a cheer as the Heinkel went down. People came up to Vee afterwards and stuffed money into the box. She thanked them and smiled sadly, keeping her eyes on the ground; she was learning.

On the way back, before getting the train, they'd treat themselves to a cup of tea and a bun, and Vee would talk, releasing half a day of pent-up chatter. It took Noel a while to realize that it wasn't a monologue, it was one side of a conversation, peppered with questions and hopeful gaps. When he first began to fill in the spaces, she looked startled, an odd light in her eye, like a dog brought up on bread scraps who'd been given a lump of liver for the first time.

'I need to look for some Sanatogen for Mum.'

They were seated in Fay's Tea Room, Fortune Green. It was a Friday, the last day of the school holidays, and they'd done very well; one man had given two and six. On Monday, they'd be back on afternoons only, the bounty halved.

'Why?' asked Noel.

'What do you mean, why?'

'What does your mother need Sanatogen for? What is it, exactly?'

'It's a tonic wine. Perks you up. It's hard to find in the shops now, though.'

'Couldn't you just get ordinary wine? Or beer?'

'Mum doesn't drink.'

There was a pause while they thought about this. 'There's wine and wine,' said Vee, defensively. 'My mother drinks it for health, not for . . . for . . .'

'Getting blotto?'

Vee let out a snort, and tried to cover it by taking a

mouthful of tea; she'd had a sudden, startling image of her mother drunk. 'You can't say things like that,' she said.

'Oiled?' suggested Noel. 'Pickled. Soused. Three sheets to the wind.'

'How do you know all those?'

'Jingled, smashed, tanked to the wide? I was paid to learn them.'

'*Paid?*'

'As an aid to the expansion of both memory and vocabulary.' *Roget's Thesaurus*. Mattie had chosen a word, and then rewarded Noel a penny a synonym.

Vee shook her head. She was beginning to relish Noel's oddness; it was like talking to someone who'd been raised on the moon.

'"Fuddled", they say round us,' she offered. 'Do I get tuppence?'

She felt gay and invigorated, her handbag full of money. On the way home, after they left St Albans station, she crossed the road to the Red Cross Comforts shop. 'Won't be a moment,' she said to Noel, and opened the door.

She nearly closed it again when she saw Mrs de Souza, the shoe-shop owner's wife, a red volunteer band around her arm. She was wearing a crisp little apron and resting her ringed hands on the counter, so that everyone could see she had a diamond the size of a pea on one finger. She said nothing to Vee, only looked down her nose, but there was a woman sitting beside her, crocheting, who had a friendly sort of face, and Vee gathered herself together.

'I've not come to buy,' she said, 'just to make a donation.'

She unclipped her handbag and though she'd meant to give a shilling, she found herself taking out a whole half-crown instead. 'Shall I put it in there?' she asked, making sure that both women could see the coin before it dropped into the box beside the till.

'Well, that's *very* generous of you, I must say,' said Crochet, 'isn't it, Mrs de Souza?' and the frozen-faced cow had to nod, though it looked as if someone had put a hand to the back of her head and given it a push.

Vee glided out of the shop as though on a gilded barge. She couldn't remember when she'd ever felt as good, not ever.

On the Monday afternoon, they went to Hornsey. Noel got off the bus they'd taken from Kentish Town and snuffed the air. There was a breeze blowing from the south-east, and it brought with it a peculiar smell: burnt sugar, vinegar, cooking gas.

'It couldn't be those bombs, could it?' asked Vee, doubtfully. Over the weekend, the East End of London had caught it badly – it had been on the morning news, and then again on the train, everyone talking excitedly. They said the whole sky had been black with German planes, and the water in the docks had boiled. Eight thousand dead, according to a thin-lipped man with an umbrella. 'A number of casualties', according to the wireless. Vee had been nervous on the journey there, half-expecting to see London flattened, but it looked no different from usual: rows of bins, sandbags, balloons like a giants' birthday party above the rooftops.

Noel was studying the gazetteer. 'Let's try the streets behind the reservoir,' he said.

'Is it RAF today?'

'Pilots' Benevolent Fund.' Noel took the collecting box out of his gas-mask case and dropped in the usual pennies. 'Let's go, shall we? We can cut across here.'

They climbed a set of steps and found themselves beside a bleak, oblong pond, level with the rooftops. A woman was throwing crusts to a solitary swan.

Cast thy bread upon the waters, thought Vee. 'Someone's got food to waste,' she said.

The swan-feeder shook her paper bag over the water, and

then carefully folded it, and started to walk along the path towards them. She cut rather an odd figure, tall, her clothes mismatched: a skirt down to the ground, a tweed jacket, a beret.

'Good morning,' she said, smiling.

She might have been good-looking once, thought Vee – she had the kind of high-cheekboned face that keeps its shape even in age, but her complexion was the colour of cheap mince, her teeth all whistling gaps.

'Mrs Aileen Gifford,' said the lady, extending a hand. 'Lovely to see you again. We met at Frank's christening.'

Vee shook it, nonplussed.

'And is this your son?'

Noel looked blankly past her, in his usual clever imitation of a half-wit.

'Delightful,' said Mrs Gifford, resting a hand briefly on Noel's head. 'I have always liked boys. I shall certainly contribute to your cause.' She plunged a hand into her jacket pocket, and took it out again. Her fist was closed around a mass of coins; one by one she fed them into the collecting box. 'Delightful,' she said again, and drifted off.

'Twelve shillings and fourpence,' said Noel, quietly.

'*Twelve . . . !*' Vee stared after the woman. 'Cracked.'

'You don't know,' said Noel, fiercely. 'She might not be, she might be ill, you can't just say things like that about people.'

He walked off, in the opposite direction to Mrs Gifford, and after a moment of surprise Vee hurried after him.

It was an average sort of take. Not counting the early windfall, they made a guinea and ninepence in two hours, calling at every other house, along one side only of selected streets, ringing no more than two bells per house; it was better to keep moving. There were no awkward questions, nothing that Vee couldn't cope with. 'You from round here?' one woman asked.

'Just the other side of Chalk Farm,' said Vee, vaguely. 'Thank you kindly for your contribution.'

In any case, today when people answered their doors, their eyes slid past Noel and Vee and towards the sky.

'They'll be after Buckingham Palace next,' said a man with scars on his knuckles. 'Lord Haw-Haw was saying,' and he gave them threepence, and a barley sugar for Noel.

'Shall we finish this street and call it a day?' asked Vee. She was beginning to feel nervy, as if the fear in the air were like cold germs and she was coming down with a dose.

'We've got another quarter of an hour,' said Noel, the sweet clicking between his teeth, 'at least.'

'Yes, but . . .'

He was already at the next house, pressing the top bell. Vee followed him reluctantly.

'Just one more, then,' she said.

They heard someone singing, a wordless melody coming slowly down the stairs, and then the door opened.

'Lovely to see you again,' said Mrs Aileen Gifford, extending a hand. 'We met at Jenny Allstrop's wedding.'

She was now wearing a tea-gown with, on one shoulder, a corsage of limp felt roses and on the other, a silver medal on a striped ribbon.

'We're collecting for the Pilots' Benevolent Fund,' said Vee, 'but you already gave us—'

'Do come in, I'd be delighted to help such a very worthy cause.'

Mrs Gifford drifted away along the hall.

'*Should we?*' mouthed Vee to Noel, but he was already following the woman.

There were three doors off the hall, and as they passed the third, it opened and a man in a warden's boiler suit came out, carrying his helmet. He glanced up the stairs after Mrs Gifford, and then gave Vee and Noel a grin. He had a pitted face, and eyes as mild and brown as a heifer's.

'There goes the living story-book,' he said, 'new tale every minute, none of them true. It's years of –' he mimed lifting a bottle to his mouth '– sent her right round the bend. Came from gentry, too.' He winked at Vee, and she smiled primly and put a hand on Noel's shoulder. The man lingered.

'Invited you in, has she?'

'That's right. She wants to give us a contribution.'

'I wouldn't go if I was you.'

'Why ever not?'

'Not a good example for the lad, is it?'

Vee could see Mrs Gifford's ankles, unstockinged and scaly, disappearing round the corner.

'Thank you, but I'm sure we'll be all right.'

She could feel him still watching as they climbed the stairs.

'I was just about to run a duster around when I had a visitor from Venezuela,' Vee followed the voice up another half-flight.

'It was the sister of my piano tutor, she couldn't stay long, she left her coat and one or two other items that I haven't had time to tidy away. And here we are,' said Mrs Gifford, opening a door. 'Do come in.'

Vee hesitated, but Noel stepped forward with apparent eagerness. The room was in shadow, the blackouts fully drawn and only a dim central bulb supplying any light. 'Lemon wafer?' asked Mrs Gifford, bending over and moving something that clinked emptily. 'Or perhaps a macaroon? I'm sure I have some left over from the garden party.'

'I won't, thanks ever so,' said Vee. She couldn't work out what she was looking at. There didn't, at first sight, appear to be any furniture; rather, the room was filled by a low-level mountain range, a series of gentle foothills surrounding a flat-topped central peak. It was the penetrating smell of mothballs that made her realize they were actually mounds of clothing arranged around a bed.

'Do take a seat,' said Mrs Gifford, waving a gracious hand as if indicating a choice of chaises longues.

'I won't, thanks ever so,' said Vee again, just as Noel said, 'Thank you.' He plumped himself down on a pyramid of coats and gave Vee what appeared, in the gloom, to be a reproving look.

She gave the box a rattle, and spoke rather too loudly. 'We're only here to do some collecting. We can't stay.'

'And I'll have a macaroon,' said Noel. 'That would be very nice.'

'*We should go*,' she hissed at him.

He ignored her.

There weren't any macaroons, of course. Mrs Gifford, talking gracious nonsense, burrowed around in the room as urinous smells billowed up beneath the camphor, and Noel sat as rigidly as if he were attending a tea party at Kensington Palace.

'We'll be missing our train,' said Vee, trying again. She gave the box another rattle.

'*Train train go away*,' recited Mrs Gifford with a light laugh, crouching beside the window. 'And here it is!' There was a click and then a prolonged rustling sound, as if she were rifling through autumn leaves. She straightened up with a crumpled piece of paper in her hand, which she passed to Noel. 'How you've grown – as tall as a Scots pine! It must be all the swimming. I expect you'll need to stock up on tuck when you get back after Michaelmas, won't you?'

'I expect so,' he said, huskily.

'All boys like cake, don't they? And I've been saving this one for a very special occasion.' She slid a hand under the bed-clothes and brought out an object swaddled in grey flannel. As she began unwinding, it became clear that the wrapping was actually a suit of long winter underwear, liberally stained. 'And *voila!*' she said, brandishing the very small Dundee cake at its centre. 'A slice for all?'

Vee found herself walking backwards whilst gabbling apologies.

'Shall we see one another at Hamish's gathering?' asked Mrs Gifford. 'I understand it'll be splendid. That's if we don't have another thunderstorm, there was a terrific one just last night.'

'Yes, that'll be lovely,' said Vee, 'pleasure to meet you.' She pulled at Noel's arm and he followed reluctantly.

'Bye!' called Vee, clattering down the stairs. On the first landing, she waited for Noel to catch up. He came slowly, smoothing out the creases in the piece of paper he'd been given by Mrs Gifford, and when he reached Vee, he held it up, level with her eyes.

It was a twenty-pound note.

She might have gone on gawping at it for several minutes, her eyes waltzing across the inked curlicues, if, from the hall below, she hadn't heard a key turn in the lock.

'Handbag, *handbag*,' she hissed, urgently, opening it, and Noel refolded the note across a set of old creases, and tucked it next to her compact.

The front door closed, and then there was silence. Someone was standing in the hall.

Vee put her finger to her lips and Noel nodded.

They waited. After what felt like half a year, there was the sudden stamp of boots up the stairs, and round the corner came the warden.

Vee smiled guiltily. 'Hello again.'

'Still here?' he asked. 'I thought I heard something.'

'We're just going.'

'Mrs Gifford cough up, did she?'

'Sixpence,' said Vee, her mouth dry. He wasn't a policeman, but he had a uniform. And a watchfulness that belied the grin. 'We have to get going,' she said. 'My son wants his tea.'

'Who are you collecting for, anyhow?'

'Dunkirk Widows and—' She felt, rather than saw, Noel flinch. 'I mean . . .'

The warden tilted his head to read the inscription on the box. 'Pilots' Benevolent, it says on there.'

'We collect for all sorts.'

'Kind of you.' He held Vee's gaze. Beautiful eyes, she caught herself thinking; pity about his skin – he must have been one giant pimple as a youth.

'We like to do our bit,' she said, trying to look modest and go backwards down the stairs at the same time. 'I expect you're busy yourself.'

'Not as busy as Jerry. You from round here?'

'Chalk Farm.'

'Which road?'

'Donald Street. Come on laddie, pilchards on toast for you when we get home.'

She grasped Noel's shoulder and steered him down to the hall, and when she risked a look back, the warden was still at the bend of the stairs, but he was looking upwards towards Mrs Gifford's room.

Once outside, every bit of her seemed to tremble, panic and excitement combined.

'You heard that rustling noise when she was getting the banknote,' she said to Noel. 'There's more where that came from; she's stuffed with money, *stuffed*. And she's taken to you. If we go back there we—' She heard a footstep and whipped round, expecting to see the warden hurtling after them, or a copper with a whistle, but it was only a postman, crossing the road.

She lowered her voice, but she couldn't stop talking, the words were flying out. 'We'd only have to go once a fortnight, I expect she'd be glad to see you. It's a kindness, really, it's not as if she's spending it on anything, we'd not be depriving her, though we'd have to stay clear of that fellow, he knows some-thing's up. Wonder if he works shifts? We could find out, the warden's post must be round here somewhere, shouldn't be hard to track it down. Chop chop,' she said to Noel, giving him a little push; he was moving like someone wading through water. They turned the corner to the bus stop, and there, twenty yards beyond it, was a concrete pill box with a red 'D' painted by the door, and outside it a lady warden in overalls, smoking a cigarette and gazing skywards. Ask and thou shalt be given, thought Vee. She parked Noel by a garden gate – didn't want to be recalled, later, as the woman with the kid who was asking questions – and walked over to the smoker.

'Ever so sorry to bother you,' she said. 'I just wanted to check who the warden is for Chetwynd Road.'

'It's Mac.'

'Mac?'

'Ray McIver. He does four till midnight – wait around for ten minutes and he'll be here. Or can I help?' She was blonde with sausage curls and a good figure, but one of her eyes was lower than the other so the curls and the figure wouldn't ever be more than icing on a rock-cake.

'I was only wondering.' Vee was already moving away, avoiding questions. 'Thanks for your help.'

The bus nosed round the corner.

'Stay away from him,' said the warden, indistinctly.

'What?'

'Bit of advice for you. Stay away from Ray McIver.' The woman pinched out her fag, and ducked into the pillbox, leaving Vee with her mouth open. Was this – surely not – was this *jealousy*? Was Sausage Curls viewing her as a rival? She stuck out her hand for the bus and watched her reflection slide into view. You couldn't see much between the strips of tape on the window, but at least her eyes were on the level and her wave was natural. She tried a smile.

'You getting on?' asked the conductor. 'This isn't a boodwah.'

It wasn't until she and Noel were standing on the train, squashed against a compartment door, surrounded by soldiers, that a key difficulty occurred to her. She'd never had a twenty-pound note in her life. What on earth could she do with such a thing? Who might change it for her without asking questions?

'Fag for the lady?' enquired a corporal.

'Don't mind if I do.' She smiled at him as he lit it, and then realized that his other hand was sliding across her rear end. She jerked backwards and crushed his knuckles between her right buttock and the door frame. 'Oops,' she said, 'ever so sorry,' and he wrenched his hand away and muttered 'Stringy old bitch', which sliced her to the marrow.

She turned her head away and glanced down at Noel. He had his face pressed to the glass and his shoulders were twitching. For a horrid moment she thought he was laughing at her, and then she heard a watery breath.

'What's wrong?' she asked. 'Have you got a pain?'

He didn't answer, just went on crying quietly.

'Cheer up,' she said. 'We'll be home soon.'

Their new flat was much nearer the station than the old – just over the footbridge and down a lane that ran past the Masons' Hall. Noel cried the whole way home, and their downstairs neighbour Mr Clare, who was arranging paperbacks on a shelf outside his bookshop, asked 'Whatever'th the matter with Thunny Jim?'

'Tonsils,' said Vee, opening the next door and pushing Noel in ahead of her. She closed it, shutting them both in the little turnaround at the base of the stairs.

'Now what's this?' she asked. 'You can't go around bawling. Whatever got you started?'

His face had lost its usual blankness; he looked like a toddler, features flailing.

'Go on,' she ordered.

His words, when they came, were so breathy and broken that she had to bend to catch them.

'I miss Mattie,' he said.

'Who's Mattie?'

'My godmother that I lived with.'

'Is that the one in Hampstead, you said her name that first night? The lady doctor?'

'She wasn't a doctor, she had a PhD. Her thesis was on Thomas Fuller and the origins of wit.' Speaking seemed to decrease the flow of tears. He lowered himself on to the bottom stair and rested his head on his knees.

'So who were the people I sent the postcard to?'

'Just some people. Mattie's cousins. I had to go and live with them when she died.'

'And they never replied,' she said, wonderingly; it was the first time she'd even thought of it. 'And what made you think of your godmother all of a sudden?'

Noel squashed his face against his legs. 'Before Mattie died she got ill,' he said, his voice muffled. 'She got senile dementia.'

'What's that?'

There was a pause. He licked the salt off his knees. 'It's when old people go mad.'

Madness. Needles and straitjackets. The booby-hatch. Screaming in corridors. She knew what that was like.

'And you were living with her when she started to go . . . you know . . . ?'

'Yes.'

She thought of Noel sitting amidst the chaos of Mrs Gifford's room. She remembered his eagerness to enter the house, his composure in the face of the squalor within, and something inside her seemed to twist, and then loosen.

'Well,' she said, 'you poor lad.'

For a while, neither of them spoke. From upstairs came a man's voice, warmly patronizing, talking about indigestion.

'It's the radio doctor,' said Vee. 'Must be nearly half past five. I'll have to set out supper. You hungry?'

'No.'

'Go on. You can have my egg.'

After a moment, he nodded.

'Good boy,' she said, 'up you go, then.'

7

The Bull was packed, even though there was a sign at the bar that read 'No Beer, No Spirits'.

'Not seen you in here for a while,' said Win Jackson, as Donald sat down with a ginger ale. 'Someone says to me you'd been done over but I didn't believe them. I says, "I don't believe you," and this chap says, "Honest as I speak, someone's done Donald Sedge over," and I says, "I don't believe you." Was you, though?'

'Dispute,' said Donald. 'Over a lady. You should have seen the other bloke.' He took a sip. The snug was a riot of Venetian mirror-glass and he could see his own face six times over, from every angle. The bruising had gone, but his nose had only recently re-emerged from its cushion of swelling and it was not the nose that he had known before; it wasn't deformed or grotesque, but there was an angle to the bridge that was unfamiliar. Donald turned his head from side to side, trying to gauge the effect upon his profile, and then he lit a cigarette and watched himself inhale. He tried to blow the smoke out through his nostrils, but they were still partially blocked, and only a thin jet came squirting out of the left one, like steam from a kettle.

'I never met a tart who was worth a fight,' said Win, reflectively. 'She from round here?'

Donald shook his head.

'Thought as much. When you said that, I thought, "She can't be from round here, because the tarts round here, they're not worth a fight." Got a fag? Ta.'

'Where's everyone else?' asked Donald, looking around for the other regulars. He didn't want to get stuck on his own with the biggest bore in Hertfordshire. 'Win' was a nickname, short for 'Winchester Repeater'; the man would send you crackers in fifteen minutes.

'There are tarts you'd fight for, and tarts you wouldn't,' said Win, 'and the ones round here, you *wouldn't*.'

'I said, where's everyone else? Where's Cyril Brixley?'

'Cyril's joined the navy. I said to him, "You can't swim," and he said, "They'll give me a lifebelt." Can't hardly believe that, can you? Joined the navy and he can't even swim. Not a stroke.'

'Frank Collingbourne? Arthur Gee? Harry Stanley?'

'Frank's gone to Egypt with the Welch Fusiliers. He said, "Don't tell anyone, it's a secret, but they're sending us to Egypt." I said, "If it's a secret, why are you telling me?" which had him stumped. Arthur's navy as well, though he *can* swim, and Harry's joined the RAF because he says tarts go for the uniform. I said to him, "What have you joined the RAF for?" and he said—'

'What about you?'

'—he said, "Because I've heard tarts go for the uniform,"' finished Win, determinedly. 'I'm reserved, aren't I?'

'I thought you worked at the barber's.'

'Joined the specials in March, and they're taking me on permanent. The station sergeant called me into his office and said, "How would you like to join the force permanent?" and I said, "I only joined the specials in March," but he said it's all the fifth columnists, the country's chocka with spies, they need more police on the lookout and I'm just the sort they want. I arrested two enemy aliens last month.'

'What happened?' asked Donald, curious in spite of himself.

'I was proceeding westward from the Market Cross when I heard two women talking in a foreign tongue behind Waterend Barn about ten forty-five at night – you know, the place where they have the weekend dances?' Donald nodded, and Win carried on reading from his imaginary police notebook. 'I stopped them and inspected their identity cards. On discovering they were registered enemy aliens, I pointed out to them that it was an offence for them to be absent from their registered addresses after ten thirty p.m. A week later, they appeared before the Bench charged with an offence under the Aliens' Movement (Restriction) Order 1940. Each was fined five pounds. Matter of fact,' added Win, leaning forward and speaking conspiratorially, though it was hard to hear him through the din, 'they were here in the Bull this evening, on the other side of the lounge bar. One of them's a bit of all right. Blonde.'

'So they're not spies?'

'*They're* not.'

'Who is, then?'

'Oh no, you won't get me like that,' said Win, as if evading an elaborate and cunning ambush. 'The girls said the same thing to me that night, they said, "We're not spies," and I said, "I'm not saying you're spies, I'm saying you're absent from your registered address after ten thirty p.m. at night, which is an offence under the—"'

Having reloaded, he rattled on. Over by the bar, somebody dropped a glass and there was a cheer and a surge of khaki.

'All over my fooking boots, you fooking fooker!' bellowed a northern voice.

Donald glanced around, clocking the faces. It was ridiculous, he knew, but he kept expecting to bump into that bastard Fielding, now in uniform and thirsting for further vengeance. The worry of it had kept him at home, long after he could have resumed his career; he'd had a few offers, sent on from the old address. There was one that had come only today in a cream envelope, lined with maroon tissue, the paper watermarked, the handwriting beautiful, dark violet ink, a flowing purple filigree across the page. *I am writing to enquire about your availability on the morning of Thursday, 29th October in Kensington, London, for a task for which I believe you are heartily qualified.*

There'd been no mention of money in the letter, but the writer had used the phrase 'mutually agreeable arrangement', which Donald sensed might be an opportunity to raise his rate again. The 1904s were being called up now, which meant that the letter-writer would probably be well into his thirties, someone with a substantial career and cash to spare. 'JD' he'd signed it. It would be a gentlemanly sort of name. Jasper. Jolyon. Bespoke suits. Gold cufflinks. A house with a basement and a bell-pull and a hall floor like a marble draughts board. *Mr Sedge Esquire? Do come in.* Tea in cups that matched, served on a table whose legs were all the same length.

He had almost written to accept, but couldn't dispel a nudging nervousness at the prospect of travelling into London. Aside from the bombs, he didn't know his way around. He'd never even been on the underground and Londoners were sharp, on the lookout for country types; he wanted to appear worldly and smooth and was afraid he'd arrive on the doorstep of JD's house two hours late and robbed blind.

He'd never been taught anything *useful*, he thought, bitterly. School had wasted him, had never considered that a man might want a wider life. Sums on slates and rows of pot-hooks, a fortnight off for the harvest every year, and here he was at nineteen, afraid to visit his own capital city. One day he'd take taxis everywhere, or have a Bentley with a chauffeur in a pearl-grey uniform and white gloves . . .

'Pardon,' said Win, over a noise like a burst tyre, and Donald found himself back in the world of farts and cider, the taste of gingerless ginger ale sickly on his tongue.

'Here, I haven't told you about the burglar what keeps stealing fruit off people,' said Win. 'The sarge called me in to his office and he said, "You won't guess what this chap keeps nicking," and I said, "I'm no good at guessing, Sarge, you'll have to tell me," and he said, "Fruit," and I said, "You're having me on," and he said, "I'm dead serious, he steals fruit."' He drained his glass. 'Another one?'

Donald shook his head. 'No, I'm off.' He left half the drink and pushed his way to the door.

It was moonless, as dark as if someone had thrown a black cloth over the town. Donald waited for a few seconds, and saw a white line emerge gradually from beneath his feet and slide into the night: the painted stripe that marked the edge of the pavement. He switched on his torch, aimed the faint splash of light a yard or two ahead and started to walk slowly, one arm extended to fend off lamp-posts. The town lost all familiarity in the blackout; distances stretched, a hundred yards seemed half a mile, turnings disappeared or multiplied.

He crossed the road by the Co-op, and nearly got his nose sliced off by an invisible bicycle flying along in the centre of the road, and then he stumbled over a sandbag on the opposite pavement, flung out an arm and hit something that screamed.

'Sorry.'

'You haff a torch?' A hand clutched his arm, and the light jerked up to reveal red lips and a long white face, blonde hair curling to the shoulders, a humming-bird brooch on the coat lapel. 'Can we borrow you? We haff flad badderies.'

'Where are you heading to?'

'Not far. What is your name?'

'Donald.'

'*Duck!*' she shrieked, her voice splintering off into giggles.

'My name is Birgit and I must warn you I haff to hurry home because I am an *alien*.'

She leaned in to whisper the last word, and her brooch speared him in the neck with its beak.

'I was just talking to someone about you,' he said, swaying back.

She looked delighted. 'Is it true?'

'A local policeman.'

'Oh yes, he was very, very cruel.' Despite this, she sounded buoyant. 'So many people are suspicious and yet every day I'm in the factory, working and working for the war effort. I haff a great big machine and I swivel, punch, lift, swivel, punch. I am getting very *strong* – like you,' she added, and gave Donald's bicep a squeeze. 'Where do you live?'

'The end of this road.'

'And we are at the hostel by Brickett Wood Common. It's very kind of you to walk with us, Mr Duck, with your great big torch!'

'Brickett Wood? That's back the other way.'

'Is it?'

'You've gone a quarter-mile in the wrong direction.'

'I *tolt* you,' muttered a voice from behind. Donald looked round but could see nothing but a shape in the darkness, a pale blob beneath a knitted tam.

'I am such a silly *goose*!' said Birgit, brightly. 'Right and left and left and right are not my friends and they neffer will be my friends! In fact, they are my enemies! War on left and right and right and left!' Her voice was very loud. 'And now we will haff to hurry. Come on, Mr Duck!'

'*Warum musst du immer so schreien?*' asked the voice from behind.

'No,' said Birgit, 'I am not always shouting, Hilde, I am speaking clearly because I am a foreigner and I want the English to be able to understand my accent, and not to hear me muddering in German like you do all the time, like a *troll*. You can understand me, can't you?' she asked, tightening her grip on Donald's arm.

'Yes. You're German then?'

'No!' The peal of laughter nearly took his ear off. 'I *hate* Germans.'

'Austrian,' said the small voice from behind.

'But I love the English, and I love the English country and all the lovely birds and flowers, and the beer and cake and the lovely tea.' Every noun was accompanied by a bounce on the toes and a tug on Donald's arm; it was like taking a terrier for a walk. 'If I was English I would fight and fight to keep all the beer and cake and lovely tea.'

'*Österreichischer Kuchen ist viel besser,*' said the small, dark voice.

'No they are not, Hilde.'

'Yes they are. Austrian cakes are far bedder than English cakes, they are famous over the world.'

'You must try to ignore her, Mr Duck, because she is not a very happy or grateful person, and it is my bad luck to be stuck together with her, just because we are aliens. And I try hard to be happy and be a good pal and join in with all the fun!'

'Sachertorte is not like a jam sponge that anyone can make. People would come all the way from another country to eat Sachertorte.'

'So are you not in the army, Mr Duck?'

'My name's Donald Sedge.'

'Yes, but Duck is my little joke!' He flinched away before Birgit could laugh again.

'I'm in a reserved occupation,' he said, and the phrase felt perfect in his mouth.

'What is that?'

'I can't talk about it. It's hush-hush.'

'Oh, but of course I understand. Loose lips sink ships! Be like Dad keep Mum!'

'Shud *up*, Birgit,' said the voice from behind.

'Don't tell me to shud up, please.'

The other girl replied in German, and a hissed argument ensued, Donald's arm jerking back and forth with every exchange.

'Left down here and then on the right,' said Birgit, mid-harangue. 'The big house with the tree.'

'*Small* house,' said Hilde, disparagingly.

'Don't listen please, Donald. It is very comfortable and pleasant.'

'The curtains are made of *sacking*.'

'We are very grateful to the people of England.'

'By my house in Wiener Neustadt the kitchen maid had bedder curtains.'

'I shall sing a song so you can't hear her voice. Do you know "Can I Forget You"?'

'This one?' asked Donald, raising the torch and catching the bottom half of a gatepost, with an old sign reading *The Beeches* and a newer one advertising it as a hostel for women workers. It occurred to him that he'd heard of it; the place was known locally as 'The Bitches'.

Birgit disengaged her arm. 'Thank you so much,' she said, warmly. 'It was very, very kind of you to take us all the way home. Wasn't it, Hilde?'

There was a mutter in reply, drowned by a series of girlish screams from the other side of the road, and the noise of a man pretending to be a lion. Birgit did another of her gay laughs.

'And now that will be Avis and Pam back from their dance. Avis! Pam! Are you back from your dance? Have you brought a wild beast with you?'

'Hello, Birgit,' replied one of the girls, without enthusiasm. 'Haven't got a couple of fags, have you? Avis and I are all out – the boys kept pinching ours.'

'Of course.'

'Handing out fags?' asked the lion, jovially. 'Got one for me? Tell you what, I'll take one for now and one for later. You don't mind, do you?'

'No, no.'

'And maybe one for the morning – you can spare it, can't you, for a soldier boy?'

'Oh yes,' said Birgit, brightly. 'I haff plenty.'

'Getting a secret stash dropped in by the Luftwaffe, are you?'

'Oh yes, we aliens are kept very well supplied.'

'In that case, I'll take a couple more.'

Birgit let out another scream of laughter, and Donald heard a sharp sigh from the darkness next to him.

On impulse, he raised the torch. Birgit's companion had turned and was walking away, one hand trailing along the panels of the garden fence.

'Are you all right?'

She turned. She was short and pale, her dark hair scraped back and tucked into her hat. She looked as if she were about to pass out from disgust.

'I chust cannot listen to this,' she said. 'With Birgit everything is funny. The food, the chob, the rudeness of people to us – all is ha ha ha ha *ha*.'

There was an answering burst of laughter from behind them, Birgit's shriek a beat or two behind the others.

'Day after day I have to listen,' said Hilde. 'They even put me on the next machine so I would have a *frent*. Luckily I cannot hear her because of the noise.'

'I got told this one today,' said the soldier, over Birgit's yelps. 'Might be a touch ripe for the ladies, but here goes. This slip of a tit goes up to the bar and she says to the barman, "Pull us a pint, Charlie," and he says . . .'

Hilde stood unmoving while the filthy joke unwound, and

then, as the punchline slithered past, she raised her eyes and for the first time looked directly at Donald.

'I should not have to listen to this sort of talk,' she said. 'This is not what I am used to. At home we had a pastry cook. I studied the *harp*.'

Something happened inside Donald's chest: he felt a gasping heave, like the shudder of a beached fish, and for a moment he thought he must be dying, but his heart pounded onward and Hilde continued to speak, her voice low and emphatic.

'And they make us share a room. It is filthy. There is a woman who calls herself a cleaner, but you could grow *marshrooms* in the skirting boarts, she uses the same cloth which also is for the lavatory and I know this to be true because one day I watched her, even though she tried to hide from me. At home the maid would clean the skirting boarts twice a week with lemon chuice and every year they were painted again so they were always fresh. When we arrived at The Beeches I complained about the skirting boarts and the warden was so rude I thought I would have to leave, but of course, there is nowhere to go. We are not welcome anywhere.'

She was looking past Donald's shoulder, her hands, in crocheted gloves, clasped together as if praying. 'Sometimes there is so much rudeness that I have to close my eyes and think I am sitting in our summerhouse at Wiener Neustadt, with my skedging book. Skedging.'

There was a flare of light, and Donald turned to see one of the other girls leaning forward over a match, a cigarette between orange lips.

'Ta everso,' she said, flapping her eyelids at the soldier.

He looked back at Hilde. It was like switching his gaze from one of his mother's hat decorations to a real flower. His heart flailed again.

'What did you sketch?' he asked, and the voice didn't sound like his own.

'Various things. Horses. Clouds. '

'And what do you enjoy doing now? In your time off, I mean?'

'There is nothing that I enchoy doing. My life is horrible.'

'The pictures?'

'I went once. There was a stain on the seat and the man beside me was old and disgusting.'

'Did you sit upstairs or downstairs?'

'Downstairs.'

'You get a better class of person upstairs. There are half-crown seats in the circle.'

'Half-*crown*?'

'My treat. When could you go?'

'Go where?'

'To the pictures with me. Wednesday evening?'

She looked at him with irritation, as if he'd suggested she work an extra shift at the factory.

'Oh, *Hilde*,' said Birgit, roguishly from the darkness. 'Are you coming in or do you wish to keep *talking*?' She managed to souse the last two syllables with a bucketful of filth.

'I wish to keep talking,' said Hilde, restoring the word to instant cleanliness.

With much sniggering, the other girls opened the gate and went up the path. The front door snapped shut.

'So what do you want to talk about?' asked Donald.

'I don't. I chust want not to talk to Birgit. If I wait a short time she will be asleep when I get to our room.'

For a full minute there was utter silence. Donald had lowered the torch, and all he could see of Hilde was her feet. They were clad in dainty black Oxfords with tassels on the laces; he had sold many similar pairs in his time at de Souza's ('A classic choice, madam. And may I interest you in a pair of shoe trees?').

She had tiny feet – he'd estimate a size 3, double C fitting – and he imagined kneeling before her, while she rested her small heel in the palm of his hand. The thought caused another unexpected throb, lower down this time.

In the darkness, he heard Hilde take something from her handbag.

'Need a light?' he asked, quickly feeling for his matches.

'I am eating a biscuit I have safed from luncheon.'

He heard the soft crunch of it between her teeth, and tried to think of something smoothly fascinating to say. And failed.

'You like biscuits, do you?' he asked.

'Yes.'

'Any sort in particular?'

'Vanillekipferl.'

'Would those be Austrian biscuits?'

'Yes.' She coughed on a crumb and he hovered his hand above her back, but didn't dare touch, didn't trust himself (for the first time in his life) not to carry on touching.

There was another minute of silence.

'I will go now,' said Hilde. 'Good night.'

'Come to the pictures on Wednesday.'

'I am sure Birgit will come to the pictures with you.'

'I don't want to go with Birgit.'

'Why not? She has blonde hair and a *figure*.'

'Because she's common. You're . . .' He paused, and then the perfect word came to him. 'Uncommon.'

There was a short, surprised pause.

'I know nothing about you,' said Hilde. 'I do not even know what you look like.'

Mutely, Donald held out the torch, and she took it and shone it back at him. He tried for a pensive expression, head tilted in thought.

'What is wrong with your neck?'

He straightened. She was thorough; the light traced a semicircle and lingered on his profile.

'Roman,' she said, and he thought he could detect a hint of approval in her voice. She placed the torch back in his palm.

'What else do you want to know?' asked Donald.

'Such things as your family. Your studies, your chob, why you would choose to live in this small place.'

He didn't hesitate; never had a fork in the road been more clearly marked. To one side lay the dingy truth.

'Donald Sedge de Hannay,' said Donald, moving effortlessly in the other direction. 'And I was born in London. I won a scholarship to study mathematics at Cambridge but before I could take any of my exams I got a letter. It asked me to come to an interview at an address in Whitehall . . .' He could see himself, knocking three times on an unmarked door, murmuring a password through the letter box. *Come in, Mr Sedge de Hannay, we've been expecting you.* The dry handshake, the shrewd assessment, the tricky questions. 'After being interviewed for sixteen hours I was taken straight to a training camp in the Highlands and taught how to shoot, ride and navigate blindfold without a map.'

He risked a glance at Hilde. She was looking faintly puzzled. 'So why are you choosing to live in this small place?' she asked, again.

'Secret government work. I might be moved at any time, but I can't tell you anything more under pain of death. By firing squad.'

'What is that?'

'They'd shoot me.'

'I see.' She seemed curiously unimpressed by this last piece of information. 'And what chob is your father?'

'A banker.'

And his mother wore large hats and satin gloves, buttoned up to the elbow; he had three older sisters, all married, and when he went up to London in the Austin Tourer, he stayed at his club and dined late. He could describe the carpet in his room, the bed linen, the bloodstone tie-pin he wore with the green silk tie – it was the life he should have been leading . . .

Hilde was speaking. 'I beg your pardon,' he said, hastily.

She gave a short sigh and repeated the question.

'I was asking, what is showing at the pictures?'

8

The lines around her eyes were like peg-marks on a dried sheet. Vee patted some more powder over them, and applied a second coat of lipstick before smiling at herself in the compact mirror. 'Hello, Harry,' she mouthed. 'Long time no see. Can I have a word?'

And then, before her nerve could fail her, she left the arcade, where she had just spent nearly an hour queuing for some hake (and if the fat woman directly in front of her hadn't turned out to be running a civil servants' billet – *nine portions*, she'd taken – Vee might have actually got some) and crossed the road to Fleckney's Garage.

It was busy, as usual. It had always been a going concern, a smart purpose-built premises, brick and tile, even a panel of stained-glass in the side window, showing a green sports car racing along a purple road. Harry had been lucky. Though of course he'd had to marry the boss's daughter to get it, so you had to weigh the benefits of money in the bank against the daily sight of Jenny Fleckney, who'd always looked like a municipal lamp-post and who hadn't grown any lovelier with age.

Vee edged past a spill of oil. 'Have you seen Mr Pedder?' she asked a boy in stained overalls.

'Pit,' he said, nodding towards the back of the garage. Hammering was coming from beneath a police van, and a familiar liquid whistle, like an evening blackbird. Vee bent her knees and tried to peer under it.

'Mr Pedder?' she called.

'Who's asking?'

'Vera Sedge.' There was a clatter, and a pause, and then Harry's face appeared between the front wheels, his expression horrified.

'Hello, Harry,' said Vee, 'long time no see. Can I have a word?'

He didn't move, but his eyes darted past her to see who might be watching.

'Won't take long,' said Vee.

'You can't come in here.'

'Why not? People do.'

'People with motors.'

'Well . . . I could be thinking of buying one.'

'Don't be soft, they're all up on bricks for the duration. It's only official and business now.'

'That's what I'm here on. Business.'

She drew herself up, and gripped her handbag.

'Oh Christ,' he said. 'All right. Come to the office.'

He didn't offer her a seat, but she sat down anyway. Harry wiped his hands on a rag, and stood by the office door, gnaw-ing on a thumbnail. She hadn't expected him to be pleased to see her, but it wasn't nice to see the panic in his eyes. They were fine eyes, all the same: navy blue, with Donald's long lashes. His hairline had slipped a bit, but he was still handsome.

'You look all right,' she said to him, shyly.

'I thought you was in Harpenden.'

'We moved to St Albans last year. You must've seen me passing the garage enough times, I'm always about.'

He shook his head. 'Too busy to notice. What do you want, Vee?'

There wasn't a speck of sentiment in his voice, not a particle of pleasure. She tried to keep her tone light.

'Just a bit of a favour.'

'I can't give you no money,' he said, quickly.

'I wasn't going to ask for any.'

'Jenny does the books, see. She's in charge of all that, now her dad's dead. She's got a head for figures. I'm the mechanical side, and she's accounts, she's red-hot on all that, checks the ledgers four times a week, you can't get nothing past her.'

'I said I wasn't going to ask for any.'

'Well, what do you want then?'

'You could be a bit polite,' she said, stung. 'I've never made trouble for you. I could've, but I didn't.'

'How could you have?'

'You know how, you know *exactly*. When I caught for Donald your mother gave me money to get rid of him.'

'To look after him.'

'Don't make me laugh. She gave me the address of that doctor in Glebe Street.'

'You chose to go, she didn't take you there.'

'But I changed my mind, didn't I?'

'And kept the money.'

'The doctor had already taken it, I *told* you.' She'd run down the stairs, leaving her knickers and cash behind, and when she'd gone back five minutes later, he'd refused to answer the door. God knows her life had been crammed with humiliation, but the memory of begging through a letter box for twenty pounds and a pair of peach crêpe camis came pretty near the top of the list.

'I could have made trouble and I didn't,' she repeated, wearily.

'None of it would have stuck,' said Harry. 'He doesn't even look like me.'

'He does now.' And it was true, though it wasn't until this second that she'd thought of it. The change to the shape of Donald's nose was slight, but it had altered his face, pulled the flesh tighter across his cheekbones so you could see the structure beneath. 'He looks a damn sight more like you than your daughters do. Same height, for a start.'

He opened the office door and jerked his thumb. 'Out.'

She shook her head, beginning to enjoy the encounter. It was like the rare occasions on which she'd downed a whisky: a few seconds of wincing and then fireworks all the way. 'I want a favour, Harry. I need to change a banknote.'

'What sized banknote?'

'Twenty.'

'*Twenty?* Where did you get that?'

'Someone gave it to me.'

'Did they heck.'

'As the Lord God is my witness,' she said, solemnly. 'An old lady of my acquaintance.'

'If it's all above board, then why are you coming to me? Ask a bank.'

There was a pause.

'I'll take nineteen pound ten for it,' she said.

Harry smiled and pushed the door fully open. 'Out you go.'

'Nineteen and six?'

'No.'

She continued sitting, though without a plan in mind. All she knew was that Harry was nervous, and she wasn't; not any longer. His gaze flicked towards the office clock. 'You've got to go now, Vee,' he said.

'Why? You expecting Jenny?'

She knew from his face that she'd guessed correctly. He moved his shoulders as if shifting a harness.

'Please, Vee,' he said.

'Oh, so now you're being pleasant?'

'Have a heart, I'm a family man.'

'I've got a family too,' said Vee, shrilly, 'in case you've forgotten. Four mouths to feed.'

'*Four?*'

'One's an evacuee. A half-wit cripple,' she added, virtuously. 'And Donald has to be careful with his health, and my mother's been an invalid since the day I told her I was expecting.'

'All right, all right.' He shut the door hastily. 'I'll change the bloody thing.' There was a strongbox in the corner and he took a bunch of keys out of his pocket and began to sort through them. 'Give me the banknote, then,' he said, over his shoulder, crouching down.

Vee took the creased rectangle out of her handbag. 'I want it all in change,' she said, hearing the rustle of notes.

'Twenty quid in *change*? You'd need a bloody wheelbarrow.'

'Nothing larger than a pound note, then.'

He inspected the twenty carefully, while she folded the notes and counted the coins into her handbag.

'Thank you, Harry,' she said, politely.

He wasn't looking at her. He locked the box, and peered round the door again. 'I'll take you through the back,' he said, 'just in case. And don't let me see you here again.'

He scuttled ahead, but she took her time, arms wrapped around the leaden handbag. Behind the garage was a walled yard, with a long, open-sided shed on the left and a padlocked gate at the far end. Harry had almost reached the latter when he turned on his heel and raced back past her. 'Left the bloody keys in the bloody office. Stay here,' he ordered.

Vee waited. A pair of swallows twisted past her and up into the eaves of the shed. 'Handsome is as handsome does,' she said, out loud. For a few moments in the garage, waiting for Harry to catch sight of her, she'd felt extraordinarily young, a sixteen-year-old wearing a bottle-green cloche and riding a borrowed bicycle over the ruts to Colney Heath. The act of actually speaking to him seemed to have had the opposite effect: she'd been flung forward, right over the handlebars and into middle age. Her back hurt.

She heard a tiny splash, and then another. It took her a second or two to spot the islands of bird droppings that had fallen from the swallows' perch into the puddle beneath. And then she moved forward and peered more closely, not quite able to understand what she was seeing. The bird droppings were drinking up colour, changing from black-and-white to a brilliant crimson, and the puddle itself was dark red, fed by a red rivulet that ran from beneath the chassis of a wheelless van, parked within the shed.

She checked that no one was in sight, and then she stepped into the shadows and walked around the van. Behind it was a row of dustbins, one of them on its side, and it was from the latter that the dark liquid was still trickling. Beside it lay a large funnel. The air was heavy with fumes. She lifted the lid of the next dustbin along and it was heaped with something spongy and red – and she almost shrieked before she realized that she was looking at loaves of bread, steeped in red dye. The third bin was filled to the brim with petrol, and she knew, then, what Fleckney's garage was up to – filtering dyed government petrol to sell to civilians. She put back the lids and hurried out to the yard again.

Harry wasn't in sight, but half a second later an apprentice came out, holding the keys self-importantly, and Vee thanked him as he opened the gate. 'What's Mr Pedder like as a boss?' she asked, innocently.

'All right,' said the boy.

'And her? Mrs Pedder?'

He didn't reply but his expression was eloquent. Vee cradled her handbag and found herself almost smiling. She had hoped for a pinch of old passion and instead she'd come away with a hefty slice of knowledge; it wasn't such a bad bargain. She'd certainly have no trouble changing another note from Mrs Gifford.

9

Dear Uncle Geoffrey and Auntie Margery,
I'm sorry that I haven't written a proper letter to you since I've been
in St Albans. I hope that you are well. I am living at a different
address now, above a bookshop (see top of page) but still staying with
the same, very kind, family, who have been very generous in buying
me delicious things to eat and new clothes, etc. How I would love to
be able to repay their generosity.

Noel paused, pen in hand, and looked up at Vee.

'Carry on,' she said. She was at the mangle, water cascading out of a pair of Donald's trousers and into a zinc tub.

'I can't think of anything to write.'

'Of course you can.'

'They don't care how I am anyway.'

Vee stopped hauling at the handle, and pushed a knuckle into the small of her back.

'Use your noggin,' she said, irritably. 'If they send a letter to Croxton's and it's returned with "Not known at this address" on it, the next thing we know they'll be sending a policeman down from London to find out where you've got to.'

'Up from London.'

'Don't give me cheek, just write the letter. Say what the weather's like.'

Noel cast his mind back to the handwriting exercise Mr Waring had set them the previous day.

The weather at present is mellow, fruitful and misty, and a great
many of the mossed cottage trees are bent with apples. We're hoping
that the hazel shells will soon be plumping with a sweet kernel.
Yours sincerely
Noel

'Done,' he said, folding the sheet of paper carelessly and crushing it into the envelope.

'You can post it on your way to school, and make sure you do. No more lies.' After he'd told her about Mattie, she'd prised him open like an oyster, scooped out all the grey slime and most of the grit. 'And take Mum's with you as well,' she added.

Noel thumbed through the pile of envelopes on the sideboard.

'Who's died?' he asked, pausing at a black-edged envelope.

'Cousin Harold's wife, back in August. No loss.'

'And why is your mother writing to Mr Herbert Morrison?'

'She says he's stolen an idea she had.'

'What idea? And why is she writing to Mr Arthur Askey?'

'Don't you need to get to school?'

'I was only wondering. Curiosity's not a criminal offence.'

'Killed the cat, didn't it?'

'Without curiosity we would still be troglodytes.'

'Latin again.'

'Cave dwellers.'

'We might have been better off. No rates. Oh *damnation*.' There was a sharp crack as a shirt-button went through the rollers. 'Get off to school. I'll see you at the station at one.'

He clattered down the stairs and slammed the front door. Smiling faintly, Vee scanned the floor for shards of button. It wasn't until she'd collected all the pieces that she realized that Donald had come into the kitchen, and was standing silently, blotting his chin with a scrap of newspaper.

'Cut yourself, love? I'll look for razor blades again – Woolworth's said they might have a batch in this month.'

He didn't reply, just stood staring out of the window. He'd not been himself for a fortnight now – up before ten every morning, and hardly dabbing at his food. Vee edged closer.

'How about a piece of toast? I've some dripping left from yesterday. Or there's a slice of mince pie from last night.'

'Just tea.'

'Or I could open a tin of pilchards. You're fond of pilchards. I've been saving them for you.'

Donald shook his head. 'Like I said, just tea.'

She poured him a cup and watched anxiously as he drank it, scanning him for pallor, shakes, a rash, but he didn't look ill, exactly. More as if he were wrestling in his thoughts with something huge; Jacob and the angel, she thought, beside the ford Jabbok. She touched the hollow of his shoulder. 'Is there anything I ought to know about? Anything I can help you with?'

It seemed to take a moment before he heard her, and then he looked round, nodding. 'Clean shirt for this afternoon,' he said. 'And my brogues need a rub.'

At the pictures, Donald had once seen a trailer about a man from Venus with an invisible death ray; when it was turned on, people half a mile away would start fainting and clutching at their throats. He was reminded of it by the steady accumulation of bodily symptoms as he walked towards Brickett Wood: a tightening of his chest by the time he reached the common, contraction of the stomach before he could even see the red gables of The Beeches and a strange bleaching of his entire vision occasioned by the sight of the front gate. He had to stand for a minute, taking deep breaths, before he felt able to continue up the path.

'Is Miss Neumann in?' he asked, and the maid disappeared without answering, leaving the door ajar.

Donald waited. The smell of luncheon meat with a syrupy undertone of tinned peaches seeped from the hall. Hilde had said the food was terrible and she was half-starved but that she would rather actually die than eat meat you could cut with a teaspoon. There was a tin of ham in Donald's right-hand jacket pocket.

'She says she won't be down for a quarter hour,' said the maid, returning. 'Shall you wait in the parlour?'

It was a comfortless room, furnished with two hard chairs, a locked glass-fronted bookcase and *The Light of the World* hanging on the wall. Donald stepped over to look at the picture; there'd been a copy in his schoolroom, and he'd never felt any particular emotion when viewing it, but now it was all too easy to see himself in the sombre greenish figure, knocking hopelessly at an ivy-clad door.

Over the past thirteen days, he'd taken Hilde to the pictures three times and to the Abbey Tea Rooms twice, and she'd not smiled once, though he'd noticed that the first taste of an eclair had lifted her mood a little. On their last meeting he'd presented her with a marcasite brooch in the shape of a bow, which she'd scrutinized gravely, and at the hostel gate that evening she'd let him kiss her, a brief dry brush of lips which had left him filleted.

In the parlour, he sat down, closed his eyes and saw Hilde; it was as if the inside of his head was a room, plastered with her photograph. In it, she was wearing her grey mac and her knitted tam. She had never actually taken either of them off during their meetings, and he tried to wrench his mind away from the scarcely bearable fantasy that she was wearing nothing at all beneath her coat. Certainly, her legs were always stockingless, the skin of her calves as pale as watered milk. He thought again of her feet, her tiny feet. She had mentioned, last time, that she had no nail-scissors, and he had spent an entire day trying to buy some in St Albans, and had been forced, in the end, to purloin his grandmother's pair with the mother-of-pearl handles. He slipped a hand into his breast pocket to check they were still there and his fingers met the other little gift he had for her.

There was a step outside the door and his eyes snapped open.

'I am very, very tired,' said Hilde. 'Birgit talked in her sleep for the whole night and I have had *one* hour in total.'

He saw, with a shock, that she was wearing something different: a maroon beret that didn't hide as much of her hair as the tam, so that he could confirm what he had guessed: that it was not only dark but very curly.

'I've brought you these,' he said, producing the nail-scissors.

'Thank you.'

'And this,' he added, bringing out the ham; he would save the final gift until later. Hilde studied the picture on the tin.

'Not enough fad,' she said. 'By my house the ham had fad *this* wide.' She held her finger and thumb an inch apart. 'But I will take it upstairs and hide it while Birgit is out.' She disappeared again, leaving just a hint of mothballs. From somewhere within the house came the crash of pans, and the snipped tones of a wireless announcer.

'I am too tired to go all the way into the town,' announced Hilde, returning.

'We could get the bus.'

'*Bus*,' she said with contempt. 'In Wiener Neustadt we had a Tatra 57. It was cream and dark red.'

'You can't get the petrol here.'

'I would think that people who work for the government would get petrol.'

'Yes, but I can't arouse suspicion. I have to get around like everyone else, keep a low profile. They warned me about that early on, it was part of the training.'

'I see.'

'So, is there anything else you fancy?'

'Fancy?' She frowned, missing his meaning. 'Nothing is fancy here, there is nothing that is nice to see, or buy or touch. The blanket on my bed upstairs I would not give to a *horse*. In Wiener Neustadt we had a silk cover on the ottoman as smooth as the ice. You would sid on it and slide.'

He had an image of her white body slipping across an ottoman and for a moment was unable to speak.

'I meant, is there anything else you'd like to do?' he asked, hoarsely. 'What about a walk in the wood? It's dry out.'

The path was a ribbon of fallen leaves.

'You're starting nights, aren't you?' Donald asked, after a hundred yards of silence.

'Yes.'

'How long for?'

'A month.' She stopped walking. 'There is mud under the leaves. I only have one pair of good shoes.'

'We could sit down.' There was a convenient fallen bough; he took off his jacket and draped it over the lichened bark. Hilde sat hunched, her arms wrapped around her shoulders.

'Are you cold?'

'No.'

He felt in his pocket. 'I've got another present for you,' he said. He drew it out, a slim packet that he'd swathed in a clean handkerchief and tied with string. She unknotted the latter carefully, winding it round her hand before unwrapping the square of cotton. There was a short, surprised pause, and her face seemed to brighten; she looked suddenly very young.

'For skedging?'

'Yes.'

Delicately, she opened the box and withdrew one of the sticks, holding it cautiously between her fingertips.

'I do not know the English word.'

'Charcoal.'

'But it weighs *nothing*,' she exclaimed. There was a pale patch on the branch beside her, where the bark had been stripped away by a squirrel or a bored child, and she bent and wrote the letter 'A'.

'Will you draw something for me, Hilde?'

'I have no paper.'

'I can get you some.'

'It has to be correct paper. For skedging. Any paper will not do.' She glanced at her smudged fingers and frowned as if she hadn't expected to see them marked.

'Is charcoal different in Austria, then?' he asked, and she threw him a furious look.

'No. Just the same. *Exactly.*' Quickly, she put the stick away. Her face was no longer bright, but sealed shut, like a slammed door. She stood up and started walking fast, back towards the hostel, and Donald hurried after her.

'What's the matter, Hilde?'

'I'm tired. I am tired all the time.'

'I wish you didn't have to work.'

'I wish it too.'

'I wish you'd let me look after you.' He caught her by one shoulder and she swatted at his hand as if it were a horse-fly, and carried on walking.

'I'll get you the special sketching paper,' he called after her. She didn't turn.

'I'll get you a motor car.'

She stumbled and he hurried to catch up with her.

'I will,' he said. 'I'll get you anything you want. Anything. Make a list. Long as you like.'

This time when he touched her shoulder, she stopped and

leaned against him and the soft weight of her body seemed to turn him inside out.

'My home,' she said. 'I want my own home.'

Later, walking back into town, he tried to remember how much was in the shoebox he kept under the bed, and in the Gladstone bag on top of the wardrobe. One thing was certain: he was going to need more.

10

Before leaving the flat, Vee sprinkled a little rose water on to her handkerchief. She and Noel had made three further visits to Hornsey Rise over as many weeks and Mrs Gifford had happily donated sixty-three pounds seven shillings and a bone button, but on the second occasion she had unearthed an album of photographs from some crusted corner and had spent a good forty minutes going through it – a barmy flow of half-completed anecdotes: *this is Bunny you met her in Dorset such a lovely girl with hair down to her unmentionables she survived the* Lusitania *by climbing up on a table and this is Celia at the march can you see how tall she is she could throw a stone clear over the statue of this is Alethea, we'll be seeing her later she's popping over from Little Venice if she's back from Ralfie Henderson's house party, well of course you were there, weren't you, did you try the punch, I believe it contained absinthe* . . . In the dim light, one grey smudge had looked much the same as the next and Vee had staggered out into the twilight with spots before her eyes and the smell of unwashed knickers clinging to the folds of her coat. 'Next time she gets out the album, tell her we've got to go because we're meeting Bunny at Ralfie's in ten minutes,' she'd said to Noel, but he hadn't found it funny; he was still rather po-faced about the old besom.

The banknotes were in a secret hiding place in Vee's room; one more visit to Hornsey and she'd take them to the garage.

She was looking forward to seeing the shock on Harry Pedder's face. The small change she'd already spent on a black-and-white scarf in La Mode and a pair of grey leather gloves from the stall at the good end of the market. The gloves were as pale as ash and as soft as a baby's bottom; she hadn't worn them yet – just kept them in her bag and touched them every now and again. She'd bought a book of detective stories for Noel too, from the second-hand shop under the flat, and he'd read them in an evening, deaf to conversation, not even looking up when she'd dropped a tray. 'I might try reading one myself,' she'd said, though she didn't quite mean it, couldn't imagine having the time to sit and flip through pages. In any case, spending the money had been as good as a holiday. If she'd had to choose between a week at the seaside and the opening snap of a purse full of coins, she knew which she'd settle for . . .

'Here, sonny,' said a man who'd squeezed on to the train at West Hampstead. 'Do you want this? I found it on the platform. I know what you kids are like about shrapnel.' Noel took the heavy brass disc, one side shiny, the other dull and stinking of explosive.

'It's the base of an AA shell,' said the man, encouragingly, as if he'd handed Noel a kitten and was urging him to tickle it under the chin. 'Bit of a find, that.'

'Ooh, what do you say to the gentleman?' asked Vee, giving him a nudge.

'Thank you.'

'*Thank* you,' repeated Vee, trying to camouflage Noel's lack of enthusiasm. Her gaze, though, had already strayed back to the window. In the week since they'd last travelled into London, the Luftwaffe had kicked lumps out of the north-west suburbs. Odd gaps had appeared in the streets at right angles to the line, glimpses of indoor plumbing, sprigged wallpaper, a picture askew on the wall of a floorless room; but it was the terraces that ran alongside the railway that had really caught it – whole rows tipped over, as if Gulliver had stood at one end and given a push, leaving a slush of bricks topped with slate. Poor people's houses, she thought, jerry-built and Jerry-wrecked.

The compartment door slid open. 'Just to tell you,' said a level voice behind the usual crush of khaki, 'the wobbler's sounded at Hampstead, so once we get there we'll be stopping at the station until further notice. Blinds down, please, and we advise passengers to lie on the floor for their own safety.'

There was a derisive laugh. 'I've seen blokes spit on this floor,' called someone. 'You going to pay for the sanatorium when I get TB?'

'Damn sight cheaper than paying for your head to be sewn back on.'

There was another laugh, less hearty than the first.

Vee helped to pull the blind down, and the train crept forward in darkness. They could hear the swoop of the siren now.

'Probably another false alarm,' said a woman. 'We had Lord knows how many yesterday.'

And then, from beneath the siren, a low, irritable buzz, like a fly trapped under a blanket.

Vee put out a hand for Noel, and encountered one of his ears.

'You all right?' she asked, giving it a pat.

'Yes.' He didn't sound too certain.

The fly was joined by another fly; there was a series of distant dull bangs, like someone stamping on a cardboard box, and then, tremendously loud, the stutter of guns.

'That'll teach 'em,' said someone, venomously.

At the station, the train emptied and Vee and Noel spent an hour in a dank basement shelter beneath the waiting rooms before the all-clear sounded. The air outside smelled sweet and autumnal. 'You'd think we were smack in the woods,' said Vee, looking round. Hampstead Heath station was in a cut, and there was nothing to see but a scrubby embankment, with a palisade of red-brick mansions at the top.

'Come on, then,' she said, gesturing towards the train, but Noel stood as if planted in cement, his head turned towards the station exit.

'*Dulce Domum*,' he said.

'Are you *ever* going to speak in English?'

'Home Sweet Home. In *The Wind in the Willows*, they walk past Mole's house, and he smells it and he can't bear not to go back and take a look at it.' He knew the illustration so well, Mole's snout raised yearningly, Ratty scurrying on oblivious.

'What?' Exasperated, Vee looked at the station clock. 'It's already four,' she said. 'That warden'll be going on shift.'

'Oh, please.'

Vee had never heard him use that word before; he had never asked for anything, only demanded, or waited silently and infuriatingly until she at last gave in.

'So your godmother's house is near here?'

'A ten-minute walk. Please, Mss Sedge.' Another first, though there was something about the way he said her name that sounded odd.

She gestured him towards the exit and then had to hurry to catch up. They crossed a road and were straight away among tall trees, on a sandy path. Up ahead, she could hear a chorus of ducks.

'Did you . . .' she turned his words over in her mind, '. . . did you call me *Miss* Sedge just now?'

'I might have done. Accidentally.'

'It's *Mrs*.'

He shrugged. 'All right,' he said. 'Only it honestly doesn't matter to me. My parents weren't married either. Mattie says that legitimacy is overvalued as a gauge of—'

She dragged him round to face her, and bent down so that she was on a level with his ears. 'It's *Mrs*,' she hissed. 'I'm a *widow.* I married a man called Samuel *Sedge* and he *passed on* fourteen years ago, so don't give me one of your lectures. You don't know everything. You might be clever and have been to a good school but you don't know everything. You don't.' Her throat was closing like a fist, and she turned away and gave her own cheek a vicious pinch. It had worked in the past; it didn't quite work now.

Behind her, a small, almost unrecognizable voice said, 'Sorry.'

She nodded, tightly.

They carried on walking, and the curve of the path brought them out by a broad pond.

'Wish we had some bread,' said Noel, subdued.

'Bread?'

'For the ducks. I didn't intend to make you upset. It was only that it seemed odd, your mother being Mrs Sedge and you being Mrs Sedge as well, and I put two and two together.'

'Well, you need to work at your sums,' she said, sharply. 'He was a second cousin. Older than me.'

'Your cheek's bleeding.'

She gave it a swipe.

Five years of bloody hell. She hadn't expected much out of the marriage. He'd been maimed during the Great War and was living off a tiny pension and odd jobs, but she didn't have much choice (seven months pregnant with Donald) and God knows he'd needed a wife; he'd been eating bread and scrape for every meal and the inside of his cottage looked like a shed, one chair, no curtains, clean but lifeless. She hadn't expected much out of it, but she'd got less, seeing as how Wipers hadn't only taken his left arm above the elbow, but part of his mind as well. He never slept, she never saw him sleep, not once. As time went on, he'd stopped speaking and then had taken to his bed. He'd ended up in Doulton Grange Asylum and had died at forty-two, face down in a pond in the hospital grounds, and seeing as the water was only two inches deep it had been ruled a suicide secondary to chronic melancholia, which meant that she didn't even get a widow's pension. All a disaster.

'It's still bleeding,' said Noel, and he held out a handkerchief.

'Thank you.' She pressed it to her eyes and then her cheek.

They were crossing a square of heathland now, having taken some complicated path through an elder thicket, and there still wasn't a sign of a house.

'You wouldn't know you were in London,' she said. 'Much further, is it?'

'No.' She followed him round a stand of birch trees and through a hole in a hedge and saw a sunken lane sneaking off to the right.

Noel scrambled down to it and started to run, past the green-painted gate of Mrs Holroyd, the clematis arch of the Wimbournes, the rustic pergola of Major Lumb. Vee caught up with him at Mattie's front gate and together they looked at the four-square villa, up to its windowsills in grass, but otherwise unchanged.

'It's a palace,' said Vee. 'Look at the size of it . . .'

There was no need to ask whether anyone was living there; ivy was actually growing across the door frame.

'Do you want to try and get in?' she asked.

Noel thought of the mess within and shook his head. 'I just wanted to make sure it was still here.' All the time they'd been in the underground shelter, he'd been imagining a smoking crater, singed pages floating above the ruins. 'We can go now,' he said.

Vee lingered, gazing up at the frontage. 'I'm surprised it's not been rented on. Nice place like this.' She looked round and saw that Noel was already heading off, picking his way between the ruts. She hurried after him. The lane sloped upward; a single lorry was parked at the top, the cab empty.

'Well, heavens above,' said Vee, breathless. 'What is this, the Cheddar Gorge?'

In front of them was a giant excavation, ninety yards across, littered with empty sacks.

Noel took a deep breath. 'This is where I found Mattie,' he said, speaking rapidly and without inflection. 'She left the house when it was dark, and I couldn't find her until I went out again the next morning. She was right near the bottom of the pit and she was half-buried in sand, otherwise she would have frozen to death. Her feet were navy blue, and the hospital said they were frostbitten, the skin came up in blisters that looked exactly like purple grapes and they were going to have to amputate her legs at the knee only she died the night before the operation. I thought she was dead when I found her because her face was grey but then she groaned, and I covered her up with the beaver coat and then I found I couldn't climb up the same way that I came down, I kept causing avalanches.'

'How did you get up?' asked Vee.

'I went to the far side, and there was a tree root sticking out, like a rope. When I got to the top . . .' He frowned, thinking about it; there'd been an icy mist, knee-height, and a buttery sun, bright but heatless.

'What?' asked Vee.

'. . . I saw an enormous dead log, with a pattern on it, a black-and-white pattern. And then I saw it wasn't a pattern, it was a flock of magpies, and there were ten of them. I kept thinking it must mean something significant.'

'One for sorrow, two for joy,' began Vee, 'three for a girl, four for a—'

'But that rhyme only goes up to seven,' said Noel. 'Five for silver, six for gold, seven for a secret never to be told.'

Vee shook her head. 'Goes further where I grew up. Eight you live, nine you die, ten you—'

She hesitated.

'What?' asked Noel. 'What?'

'It's not very nice.'

'Tell me.'

'Ten you eat a bogey pie.'

Noel gave a laugh like a hiccup. 'Anyway, I ran all the way back round and I banged on Major Lumb's door, and he phoned an ambulance and they came and got Mattie. So that's what happened, I've told you all of it now, every bit. We can walk to Mrs Gifford's from here, it'll be far quicker than going back down and taking the bus.'

The only people they saw as they crossed the Heath were the female crew of an AA gun. They were sitting in their trench, a row of cheerful disembodied heads in tin hats. They waved as Noel and Vee walked by, and lobbed a screwed-up paper bag of cough candies over the perimeter fence.

'I was thinking,' said Noel, cheek bulging, 'that we should start collecting for bombed-out families.'

It was as they left the Heath, emerging abruptly from a willow-shaded alley into a street of shops, that they felt the change; a tension, a shrill of chatter, women talking in clusters. There was a reddish fog above the rooftops to the east and the air smelled of vinegar and fireworks. An ambulance was labouring up the hill towards them, while another hurtled in the opposite direction, bell ringing.

They crossed the road and turned into a side street. Halfway along it, Noel's shoe caught a fragment of glass and sent it spinning into the road. There was more glass further on; a woman in curlers was sweeping fiercely. At the corner, a yellow feather floated by, and then a purple one.

'Over there,' said Noel, pointing to a window opposite. The words 'SHIRLEY ANNE – MILLINER' were visible above an empty window. Heliotrope ribbon hung in loops from the sill.

'I don't like this much,' said Vee. 'Should we go back?'

Noel shook his head and turned the corner. The next street was full of people, a shifting civilian crowd, odd figures in uniform, a woman in a tin hat. A few yards down, an ambulance was parked diagonally across the road, and beside it a fire engine with its wheels on the pavement. Next to the vehicles, a house was missing. It had been removed neatly as if with a cake-slice, the party wall intact: paisley paper downstairs, roses for the bedroom. On the low dome of rubble, a man was lying full length, a tack hammer in his hand.

'*Quiet!*' shouted the warden.

On the other side of the rubble, like a framed picture, was the back garden, cabbages growing and a row of washing on the line, every item maroon with brick dust. There was dust in the air as well, an abrasive mist that caught the throat.

'That's the lady warden we met,' said Vee.

'*Quiet!*' shouted Sausage Curls again. 'We do not need *sightseers*, we need *quiet*.'

'I bet she's the sort who always enjoyed shouting. The war's just given her the chance to get paid for it.'

'Come on,' said Noel. 'Mrs Gifford's street's next right.' Except he was afraid that it would be gone, just as he'd thought that Mattie's house had gone. His heart seemed to stumble as they turned the corner, and then it steadied again. Nothing had changed, except that a few yards along, a section of the road had been roughly fenced off by lengths of scaffolding propped on upturned crates. Beyond the makeshift barrier there was a hole, the size and shape of a coffin.

'What happened there?' asked Vee, peering over as they passed. They rang the top bell at number 14 and waited. After a minute or two, Noel backed up a few paces and looked up at the second-floor window.

'The curtains are open,' he said. 'They've never been open before.'

Vee frowned. 'Maybe she's out feeding the swans.' She pressed the bell again, and then stepped aside as the door opened. A pram nosed its way out, followed by a fat, pale young woman in a blue knitted hat, her face furrowed in concentration as if wheeling a pram through a doorway was a skill on a par with juggling bananas.

'Do you know if the top floor front's in?' asked Vee.

'Sorry?' The young woman looked round, and then carefully applied the brake before tucking a blanket a little more firmly around the occupant. 'Who are you asking about?'

'The lady on the top floor, Mrs Gifford.'

'She's been taken away.'

'What?'

'After we got back she went all loopy.'

'Got back from where?'

'Well, I don't know where *she* went, but I went to my auntie on Booth Street.' The woman rechecked the blanket, her head momentarily disappearing inside the hood of the pram. 'Do you think it's a bit cold for her?' she asked, reappearing. 'We've been under the stairs since lunchtime and they need fresh air, don't they? Only she's delicate.'

'Oh.' Vee peered in, compliment ready ('She's going to be a real old-fashioned beauty') and found herself looking instead at a boot-faced toddler sitting up with a bottle in her fist, like a tramp in a church doorway. There was a pause. 'You've got her well-wrapped,' she said. 'You were saying about the lady on the top floor . . . ?'

'There was a time-bomb a week last Thursday' – the woman nodded towards the hole in the road – 'and the warden evacuated the whole street and we weren't allowed home till the army came and took it away on the Saturday. And when we got back in Mrs Gifford started screaming and slamming doors because she said someone had been in her room and all her pins had gone, and they had to take her away. In an ambulance.' She took a handkerchief from her pocket and reached into the pram. 'Perhaps they'll put someone nice in there now. The landlord said when the room was cleared he had to wear his gas mask.'

'Cleared . . .' repeated Vee, faintly.

'Nothing but old clothes and the salvage people wouldn't touch them, said they were all germs, so the whole lot had to be shovelled up and incinerated. They came with a truck.'

Vee heard a bleating noise, and for a moment thought it was herself, but the woman bent solicitously towards the pram again.

'Pins,' said Vee. 'What did she mean by pins?'

'Where is Mrs Gifford?' asked Noel, loudly. He had been lurking with the usual dull expression, but Vee was failing to ask the most important question, and the woman with the baby was taking off the brake and preparing to leave. She slid him a startled look, as if a lamp-post had just spoken.

'How should I know?' she asked. 'A loony bin, I suppose, and not before time.' She wheeled the pram away.

'Your baby's got a face like an arse!' called Noel. Vee grabbed his arm and dragged him in the opposite direction, his legs galloping involuntarily along the pavement. She didn't release him until they had rounded the corner, and when she did so she gave his elbow a little shake.

'You shouldn't say things like that.'

'Stupid woman.'

'Even stupid people think their babies are beautiful.'

'More fool her.'

They started walking again, slowly.

'Well, that's that,' said Vee. 'I thought it was too good to last.' She slipped a hand into her bag and touched the grey leather gloves. 'Back to the usual next week then? RAF widows? Noel?'

His feet slapped along the pavement.

'Noel?'

He said nothing more, though Vee tried a variety of tactics, from offering a mint to pointing out objects of interest ('Look at that fire engine!'). She was used to his conversation now, the

long words, the oddity and arrogance; half the time she didn't
know whether to clout him or applaud. It wasn't nice, getting
the silent pudding back again.

'That's the fourth rat I've seen this morning,' she remarked,
as they turned the corner into Kentish Town High Road. There
was no response from Noel, and when she glanced at him
he was no longer there. She wheeled round. A pack of sailors
was clogging up the pavement, and she shoved her way
through, getting her backside squeezed in the process, and at
once saw Noel with his face pressed to a pawn-shop window.

'What are you doing?' she asked.

He pushed his finger against the window, and she saw a
jumble of objects on a shelf: a pewter jug, a dish of jewellery,
a brass telescope, a medal draped over a wrought-iron
book-end.

'It's a hunger-strike medal. She had one like that,' said Noel.

'Who?'

'Mrs Gifford. She was wearing it the first time we saw her,
when she asked us into the house. Her medal had a stain on the
ribbon like that.'

The stripes were of purple, white and green; the stain looked
like red wine. Above the ribbon was a bar with 'For Valour'
written on it, and beneath it a tarnished silver disc.

'And look,' said Noel, 'in the saucer, the gold safety pin with
the bit of flint. They got that for throwing stones at Parliament.
And there's a Holloway brooch as well, can you see the
portcullis and the arrow? Mattie had one of those too.'

'Why? What for?'

'Going to gaol,' said Noel, impatiently.

'Gaol?'

'Mattie was a *suffragette*. And see that bar next to the brooch?'

'With the numbers on?'

'Those'll be dates of imprisonment.' He tapped his fingertips
on the glass, at first distractedly and then with an insistent beat.

157

'Her *pins*,' he said. 'Mrs Gifford said that someone had taken her pins.'

'Hoy!' It was a shout from the shop door, a short man with a moustache. 'Get off that bloody window.'

Vee flashed him a smile and caught Noel's hand. 'What are you getting at?' she hissed, as the man disappeared again.

'Someone stole her pins from her room and pawned them.'

'And if they did?'

'Well, that's *wrong*. It's a *crime*.'

She waited for him to realize what he was saying, but he was too busy being indignant.

'We have to get them back for her,' he said.

'What?'

'They're special, they're . . .' he screwed up his face in an effort to make her understand, and he heard Mattie's voice in his head, more clearly now than at any time since she'd died: Mattie at full blast, Mattie impassioned, oratorical. 'They're *earned*,' he said. '"Suffrage" and "suffering" are historically linked and the reason that you have a vote now is because women like Mrs Gifford were prepared to break the law and take the consequences, not once, but over and over. They suffered so that *you* might have a say.'

His face had gone quite pink; Vee bit back a smile.

'I've never voted in my life,' she said.

'Well, you should. People have died for your vote.'

'I didn't ask them to.'

'They took on the struggle so that you wouldn't have to.'

'Oh, don't make me laugh, what did people like your god-mother know about *struggle*? Struggle as a hobby, maybe – struggle as something she did when she wasn't sitting reading a *book*.'

Noel looked at her with hatred, and then bobbed down, cross-legged on the pavement.

'What are you doing?'

'I'm not moving until we get them back.'

'What?'

'I want to get them back and find out where she's gone and go and give them to her.' He was shouting, the 'g's like a shower of stones.

'Get up.'

'No.'

'Up now or I'll slap your legs.'

'No.'

Vee looked around, desperately. People were staring. 'He's not right,' she mouthed at an old man who'd paused, walking-stick in hand. 'Shell shock. Poor little thing.' She crouched down beside Noel.

'Get *up*,' she whispered, gripping his shoulder between her nails. He didn't flinch. After a moment she stood again, and felt the sour familiar surge of heartburn.

Little sod, she thought. She shouldered her bag and went into the shop.

The man with the moustache was sitting on a stool behind the counter, a newspaper open in front of him over which he was cutting his nails.

'Sorry about earlier,' said Vee. 'My little lad got very excited. He thought he saw some bits that belonged to his nan in the window there.'

The scissors paused, and the man lifted his heavy gaze towards her.

'What you implying?'

'Nothing. They reminded him, that's all. I'm not saying they were hers.'

'All above board here,' he said.

'I'm sure. I was just wondering how much they'd be.'

There was a sharp click, and a hangnail winged across the shop.

'Not everything in the window's for sale.'

'No?'

'Some are still on ticket.' He put the scissors down and closed the paper with a sigh, saving his clippings for later. 'What were you looking at?'

She followed him over to the window. 'There's some brooches and pins in the saucer. Suffragette souvenirs, I think they are.'

He shook his head. 'Not for sale. They only came in this week.'

'Oh.'

She caught sight of Noel, on his feet now and staring fixedly at her through the glass; it was like being watched by a plain-clothes copper. 'And this?' she asked, unhooking the medal.

'Same lot. Come back in a month. If he hasn't collected, I'll consider an offer.'

'Are they, er . . .' She lost the thread of what she was saying; there was writing on the disc at the bottom of the medal.

Aileen Gifford
Fed by Force 1/3/12

She blinked at the caption, read it again. It hadn't occurred to her that Noel might actually be right, that these bits had truly belonged to Mrs Gifford. *Fed by Force.* She closed her hand over the medal.

'How much?'

'That's silver, that is. You'd be looking at five bob.'

'I'll give you six. To have it now, I mean.'

'Can't do that.'

'Six and six.'

He shook his head. 'Can't.'

'Why ever not?'

'Wouldn't be right.' He held out his hand for the medal and, feeling baffled, she dropped it into his palm. Moral scruples in a pawn-shop owner! It was like a bailiff mouthing psalms as he carried off your furniture.

Then she had a thought: it wasn't morals, it was mammon.

'Regular customer, is it?' she asked. 'Someone who brings you lots of stuff?'

'I couldn't say.'

'These bits belong to a Mrs Gifford, she had them nicked from her room when she got bombed out.'

'I wouldn't know.'

She had another thought, snapping neatly on to the first.

'Get a lot in here the day after a raid, do you? All sorts of things left lying about, I'd imagine.' And who'd be able to resist the odd lucky find: a purse blown into a garden, or a wristwatch lying in the rubble? But the right sort of person could make their own luck – make a business of it, especially if their job was to be on the spot, unquestioned, *official*.

'This regular customer of yours,' she said – and she knew the answer before she spoke – 'he wouldn't be a warden, would he? With bad skin? McIver?'

The man's face closed, but not before she'd seen fear on it.

'I can't help you,' he said. 'Got to do my shutters.'

And she found herself skittering out of the shop ahead of him, as if swept with a broom, the door jangling shut behind her. By the time she turned, a bolt had been drawn across.

'Did you get them?' asked Noel.

'No.'

'Why not?'

'Because they're not for sale.' She jerked her head and did some frantic acting, and he stared at her open-mouthed.

'What?' he asked.

'Not *here*. Wait till we're somewhere private.' She set off briskly for the station and he trailed after her, bleating questions while she hissed at him to shut up. The platform was full, the train fuller, a carriageload of ATS, big, plain, noisy girls, bulging out of their khaki. That's where all the rations go, thought Vee. And they were so *happy*, with their bellowed conversations about men and dances, all nicknames and secret jokes and snorting abbreviations. Vee tried to imagine herself at eighteen, whisked off to learn how to mend trucks, everything found and not a whit of responsibility, a clean start, a new life on a platter. Heaven. She smiled at the fatty next to her, and was offered a fag.

'*Now* can you tell me?' asked Noel, when they got off at St Albans.

'Remember that warden we met at Mrs Gifford's? It was him that pinched them, he must take something to the pawnbroker every time there's a raid. Half the stuff in there's crooked, I wouldn't wonder – they'd keep the small bits in the window and sell the rest on, split the profit. And you know what?' Realization dawned as she spoke. 'I bet he took all Mrs Gifford's money as well. Just walked in there when she was gone and searched around, found the pins and the banknotes. He'd know nobody would believe her if she reported it, poor old soul.'

'Who should we tell?' asked Noel.

'What?'

'Should we tell the police here, or should we go back to Kentish Town?'

'The police?' She turned and looked at him, to see if he was joking, except he never told jokes.

'Are you cracked? How can we go to the police? What could we say we were doing there? How would we even know she had money unless we were getting some of it ourselves?'

She could see him thinking, sifting through ideas. 'We could . . . we could tell them that . . .'

'We're telling them nothing,' said Vee. 'Nothing.'

'So you'd let him get away with that sort of behaviour?'

He sounded like a county court judge; Vee had an urge to

laugh. 'What about us? What do you think we're getting away with?' she asked.

'It's not the same. People give us money, we don't take it. What we're doing isn't nearly so bad.'

'That's not how policemen think.'

'Well, they should.'

'Well, they don't.'

He stuck out his lower lip, childishly, and Vee felt suddenly cold. He was ten. He was *ten*, and he still thought the whole thing was a game; he was cross with Ray McIver for cheating and now he wanted to tell teacher. What a fool she'd been; she could scream at the risk she'd been taking.

'Noel.' Her voice was a fraction of her normal volume, and he looked at her with suspicion.

'What?'

'Do you know what would happen if we got caught?'

He made no effort to answer her.

'I'd go to gaol, and you'd go to a reform school.'

There was a pause. Noel looked past her, at the Boy Scouts dragging a salvage cart along the road.

'But he shouldn't get away with it,' he said, again.

So that's that, thought Vee. She smiled and nodded, and said, 'Let's get home, shall we?' but inside she was banging the lid down on the whole business. They'd been lucky for too long; from now on she'd have to go collecting on her own. And then she saw herself sitting silently on the train, trailing solo along blasted streets, peering at the street map which Noel always read with such ease, and the thought was dismal and she knew that she wouldn't stick it. Perhaps the time had come to get back in touch with Vic Allerby, to sew a few hatbands, lie low for a while. Another idea would come along.

They were very nearly home by the time Noel spoke again, and Vee had already moved so far and so fast away from the collecting lark that she had to struggle to follow his argument.

'What if we went back to that warden and said we knew he'd done it? And told him we'd call the police if he didn't return everything to Mrs Gifford.'

'No.'

'Why ever not?'

Vee paused, remembering the fear on the pawnbroker's face, and the words that the woman warden, Sausage Curls, had used. *Stay away from him.* What if it hadn't been jealousy at all, but a genuine warning?

'Because,' she said sharply, 'that'd be asking for trouble.'

11

That night, St Albans caught its first bomb; at chapel on Sunday morning, the congregation was still vibrating with the thrill of it.

'I *knew*,' said Mrs Williams, surrounded (for the first time in her life) by interested listeners. 'I heard the whistle as it dropped and I said to Idris, "It's got our name on it!" and he said, "Well let's hope it's spelled wrong," and I said, "Shall we get under the stairs?" and he said, "Too late for that, girl!" and then he threw himself on top of me.'

First time for everything, thought Vee. The bomb had landed on the shed and Mr and Mrs Williams had survived uninjured, though a chicken had been blown straight through the kitchen window.

'And which of us,' asked the Reverend Pilcher from the pulpit, 'as Satan was conducting his business overhead, did not ask the Lord, "Pray take this cup from me"?'

Vee nearly raised a hand. She had spent most of the raid in the basement of the bookshop beneath the flat, Mr Clare, the owner, having knocked on their door at nine, just after the siren sounded. Donald had been at the cinema, so Vee had left a note for him, roused her mother and Noel, and gone downstairs for what had turned out to be a two-hour social event.

'I have a thurprithe guaranteed to make the time thpeed by,' said Mr Clare, holding up a booklet entitled *Blackout Fun!* and smiling to reveal teeth like old toenails, grey ridges flaring into yellow. 'They've been thelling like hot thauthageth. What shall we thtart with?' A fine mist of spit obscured every word.

They had begun with Bus Stop, a word game which Noel had won, followed by Silly Rhymes and My Son John Went to Market, both of which he had also won, his mouth bunched tightly to guard against looking too pleased, and then Vee had offered to nip upstairs and make a pot of tea, since Mr Clare had been free with his smiles and she was in need of fresh air and a clean view.

It was a full moon and the road was a stripe of chalk, the houses newly whitewashed. For a moment all was quiet, and then from the north she heard a deep repetitive mutter, like a throat being cleared. The mutter was joined by another, growing steadily louder until, with a roar like a mill-race, two planes crossed overhead, clipping the outline of the moon so that for a second they were perfect silhouettes. Off to London, thought Vee. She waited for the mutter to disappear again before letting herself into the flat. Under the noise of her feet climbing the stairs, she heard other, smaller noises: the hurried rustle of paper and the snap of a lock, and when she opened the kitchen door, Donald was standing by the table, a closed Gladstone bag in front of him.

'You're not off somewhere are you?' she asked.

There was an odd flush to his cheek. 'Sorting a few things. Didn't expect you.'

'What things?' she asked, but he didn't answer, just lifted the bag from the table – one-handed; there was no weight to it – and carried it back to his room.

She heard the creak of the bed-springs as he lay down.

'All clear's not sounded yet, love,' she called through the door on her way back out with the tea, but there was no reply from Donald, only a thin scream from the sky and a thump that rattled the crockery, and that was the Williamses' bomb –

dumped by Jerry on the way home, like a fag-end thrown out of a lorry window.

In the chapel porch the next day, the story was on its umpteenth retelling. 'Not a pane of glass left in the house,' said Maud Williams, 'not a plate left on the dresser.'

Vee's mother scratched something on to her slate and held it up for Mrs Williams to see.

'No,' said Mrs Williams. 'We couldn't cook it, Mrs Sedge, it was flat, like a cut-out of a chicken.'

Through the thinning crowd, Vee saw the minister's wife collecting hymn books and remembered yesterday's resolution. Now that it came to it, she felt less keen on lying low if it meant rearranging Mrs Pilcher's shed again. She lingered too long and the woman caught her eye.

'Were you wanting to speak to me, Mrs Sedge?'

'I was just wondering whether you still needed any help in the house?'

'Oh . . .' Mrs Pilcher's expression teetered between huffiness and hope. 'I seem to remember you told me you were much too busy. You kept having to take your evacuee to the hospital to get his leg checked.'

'Yes, but he's such a lot better now. Stronger. The doctors said it was all the good food and sunshine he's been getting.' Both women looked across at Noel. He was leaning against a pew, reading a book while absently sucking the end of his tie. His face was the usual shade of whey.

'Such a plain child,' said Mrs Pilcher, and Vee felt an unexpected pang of indignation.

'He's clever,' she said.

'Really?' Mrs Pilcher's tone was doubtful. 'Well anyhow, Mrs Sedge, I shall certainly consider your offer. In the meantime, could you help me put these in the cupboard?'

The brittle silence lasted all of thirty seconds, before Mrs Pilcher caved in and asked her back four afternoons a week.

★

She'd thought that Noel would sulk when he heard the news, but his reaction was shocked – wide-eyed, as if she'd spat on the pavement.

'But we can't just *stop*,' he kept saying, his voice shrill. 'We have to go back and sort things out.' In the end she got cross, and told him to stop pestering her.

When Mr Waring announced the outing there was a groan.

'Fresh healthy air,' said Mr Waring.

'It's foggy, sir.'

'A light mist.'

'Sir, I can't get these boots muddy or my foster mother says she'll hit me with a big stick with a nail in, sir.'

'Coats on,' said Mr Waring. 'Form into twos. Every pair take a sack from the corner.'

'Why, sir?'

'I shall tell you when we arrive at our destination.'

'I'm not joking about the stick, sir.'

'We are not walking across a ploughed field, Pursey. Your boots should remain pristine.'

'I don't know what that means, sir. Is it good or bad?'

'Can anyone define "pristine" for me?'

'Unsullied.'

'Thank you, Bostock.'

It wasn't a dense yellow, like a London fog, but white and diaphanous. From his solitary place at the tail of the crocodile, Noel could still catch the odd glimpse of Mr Waring at the head, as they crossed the road from the school and made their way uphill towards the cathedral.

'My auntie told me she's expecting,' said the girl in front of him to her partner. 'She says it's a boy because she's sticking out so much at the front.'

There was an explosion of giggles.

'Assemble over here,' called Mr Waring. The air was filled with cawing, and Noel could dimly see the dark blotches of a rookery overhead. 'Your task is to collect conkers.'

'We going to have a tournament, sir?'

'They are for the war effort. According to the instructions from the Ministry of Supply, the conkers must be husked before being placed in the sacks. We shall spend half an hour here, and your sacks will be weighed when we return to school, with the heaviest receiving a prize.'

'What sort of prize, sir? A book?'

'A Mars bar.'

The crocodile split and scattered, in a frenzy of hunting. After a minute or so, Noel bent down and picked up a single green cobble.

'Not interested in the prize, Bostock?' asked Mr Waring, from behind him.

'Not really, sir.' Noel broke the husk apart, revealing two glossy half-moons. 'My godmother told me that they did this in the Great War as well. They said they needed them to make cordite, but they were never used and there were piles and piles of rotting conkers outside railway stations.'

One of the Ferris twins dashed past, hesitated, and then nipped back.

'D'you want those?' she asked Noel.

'Yes,' he said. She pulled a face and dissolved into the mist again. From nearby came the sound of a scuffle.

'I imagine,' said Mr Waring, 'that the current request is as much about benefitting morale as munitions.' The invisible fight grew louder, and the teacher raised his voice. 'Conkers obtained by *force*, Madeley, will be discounted. Do you hear me?'

'Yes, sir.'

Mr Waring thrust his hands into his pockets, and looked over his shoulder at the cathedral. A row of buttresses receded into whiteness, the clefts between them like sea caves.

'Have you been into the Abbey, Bostock?'

'No, sir. I'm an atheist.'

'And I a Catholic. My father's house has many mansions. Come and have a look.'

They entered through the wide west door. Inside, someone was playing odd notes on the organ. There was a smell of Jeyes fluid, with just a hint of incense.

'Largely Norman,' said Mr Waring. Noel heard the scuff of his own footsteps disappear into the vastness of the nave. He thought of dinosaur bones, of the lofty vaults of the Natural History Museum, of Mattie's stick clipping along the aisle of the Palm House at Kew. He'd forgotten there could be so much space within a set of walls.

'I think we should make a pilgrimage to the shrine, don't you?' asked Mr Waring. 'Do you know the tale of the three miracles of St Alban's martyrdom?'

Noel shook his head. The pilgrim's path flowed like a stream up the north aisle, the flagstones darkened and polished by a thousand years of footfalls – cloth slippers, leather boots, hobnails, rubber soles. 'St Alban,' began Mr Waring, his voice assuming the heightened emphasis of the classroom, 'was a citizen of the Roman town of Verulamium around the end of the third century. He sheltered an itinerant priest, was converted by him, and then when the Romans arrived on the doorstep he exchanged clothes and went to be executed in his stead. First of all, he was led out of the city and over a river which ran dry in order for him to cross. He then complained of thirst, and a spring bubbled out of the ground in front of him, and finally' – they skirted a wooden screen, studded with carvings – 'when Alban was beheaded in front of a large crowd, the executioner's eyes dropped out.'

'His eyes?' repeated Noel, startled. 'Why his eyes? Why didn't his axe-arm drop off – wouldn't that have been more appropriate?'

Mr Waring pursed his lips, pondering the question. The shrine lay just ahead of them, tall and narrow, a stone liner anchored in the sea of faith.

'Perhaps it was because he'd been witness to an injustice.'

'Or perhaps,' suggested Noel, 'it meant that the last thing he ever saw would stay in his mind for ever and ever.' An eternity gazing at a jetting neck stump; it was both horrible and superb.

'Of course, appropriate punishment is very much an Old Testament phenomenon,' said Mr Waring, still in teaching mode, 'an eye for an eye, a tooth for a tooth. The New Testament takes quite a different viewpoint – "Vengeance is mine, sayeth the Lord. *I* shall repay."'

'But what if you don't believe in God?' said Noel, and his voice was suddenly urgent. 'Who'll repay then?'

Mr Waring glanced down at him.

'Do I take it that you have a specific repayment in mind?'

'Yes.'

'Can you tell me more?'

Noel hesitated, choosing his words. 'There's been an injustice. Someone took some things from someone else and the person who took the things ought to get punished and the person who lost the things ought to get them back again, but the only other grown-up who knows what happened won't actually do anything about it.'

'Why not?'

'Because she – because this other grown-up is afraid of getting into trouble for doing something else. Something that isn't nearly as bad as the other thing.'

'A venial as opposed to a mortal sin?'

'Yes. If "venial" means "not nearly as bad".'

'"Pardonable" would be the definition. Have the victims of this different sort of badness offered their pardon?'

Noel paused. 'The victims don't actually know that they're victims,' he said.

'They don't?'

'No.'

'Well now . . .' Mr Waring clasped his hands together and clicked the knuckles like press-studs. 'That would be what we'd call a moral dilemma. Is a crime any less wicked because its victims are unaware of its perpetration?'

'Yes,' said Noel, with certainty. No one who had contributed to Vee and Noel's charity-box had ever been carted off to an asylum, screaming that they'd been robbed. 'So now something really bad — a mortal sin — isn't being rectified. And it ought to be. It *ought* to be.'

'I see.' Mr Waring's expression was troubled. 'Were I having this conversation with one of your classmates then I would assume that an overactive imagination was at play. But that's not the case here, is it?'

Noel shook his head.

'I thought not. Bostock, it's not the job of a ten-year-old to—'

'Mr Waring!' Valerie Gibbs, a girl with a perfectly spherical face and an air of prissy certainty, came hurrying around the carved screen. 'There's a great big fight out the front of the church, and people have started throwing conkers, and Audrey Ferris has been hit in the eye, and I think she might have been blinded. That's why I ran in church, I wouldn't normally, of course, because I know it's wrong . . .'

Mr Waring followed her out. Noel lingered. Just beside St Alban's tomb was an iron frame, studded with candle-holders, only one of which held a candle. A notice beside it informed the public of the necessity of saving wax for the purposes of the string industry. *Please light the candle solely for the duration of your prayer, and then extinguish.* Noel lit it and stared at the wavering blue flame. Not a prayer, obviously, but a vow; there was no one within earshot and he spoke loudly.

'Vengeance is mine, sayeth Noel Bostock. *I* will repay.'

He fished a threepenny bit from his pocket, stuck it in the poor-box, and left the candle burning.

When he got back to the flat after morning school, Vee was out at Mrs Pilcher's and Donald was sitting at the kitchen table eating cold boiled potatoes with a wedge of ham, and looking at Noel's *London Gazetteer.* Beside it was a blank pad of writing paper.

'Do a letter for me,' said Donald, without preamble or a question mark.

'What sort of letter?'

'Best handwriting.' With the tip of his knife, he pushed the pad towards Noel. 'Dear Mr JD.'

'I don't have a pen.'

'On the sideboard.'

Noel uncapped it and removed a hair from the nib.

'Is it a business letter?' he asked.

'Why?'

'Because business letters are written in a different style to personal letters. They're more formal.'

'Just write it. Dear Mr JD.'

'I should put the signatory's address first, and then the recipient's and then today's date.'

Donald looked at him expressionlessly. 'Dear Mr JD . . .'

Noel started writing.

'. . . I will meet at the address you gave at the time you gave to discuss terms before completing the job you said. Yours faithfully Donald Sedge.'

'That's more of a note than a letter.'

'Got any friends at school?'

'No.'

'Can't think why. Do the envelope. It's er . . .' Donald consulted something in his pocket; a page crackled. 'Flat 4, Pembroke Mansions, 195 Exhibition Road, Kensington, London.'

'That's the same road the Natural History Museum's on,' said Noel.

'Is it?'

'South Kensington tube.'

'You know it?'

'I should say I do. I've been there hundreds of times.'

Donald hesitated, and looked again at the open page of the *Gazetteer*, the roads like a tangle of snipped threads. 'Fancy a day out?' he asked Noel.

'When?'

'Thursday morning.'

'I've got school.'

'Skip it.'

'All right.'

Noel lifted the tea towel that covered his own plate. A pile of cold boiled potatoes was arranged next to a smear of grease in the shape of a small slice of ham. He looked at Donald suspiciously.

'Post this after, will you,' said the other, blandly, smoothing on the licked stamp with his thumb. 'And gran's got some too, haven't you, Gran?'

There was no reply from the armchair, just a faint thread of music from the headphones – a dawdling violin – and the whisper of the pen as it glided across yet another page of yet another letter to Cousin Harold.

'Why can't *you* post it?' asked Noel, emboldened by the absence of ham.

'Got to rest after meals,' said Donald. 'Doctor's orders.'

He lit a cigarette and opened the *Daily Express* to an illustrated fashion spread.

CIVILIAN MEASURES

If you're not in uniform, the rule today is 'less of everything' – narrow collars and no turn-ups mean cloth saved and style gained!

When he'd got the money, and after he'd got Hilde's presents, he'd go to a tailor, get something made-to-measure. *Donald, you're so smart.*

'Where's the best place for tailors in London, then?'

Noel shrugged. 'I don't know. Savile Row?'

'Savile Row.' Syllables of luxury, lolling on the tongue. 'We'll go there after,' he said. 'Make a day of it.'

PART TWO

12

'You'll never guess who's died,' called Vee, joyfully, opening the front door. 'I'd just left Mrs Pilcher's and I was in the fish queue and Ada Press in front of me was talking to that red-headed woman from the Post Office, and I heard her say . . .'

She paused with her scarf half unwound, the smell of what the fishmonger had claimed was cod (but which clearly wasn't, unless cod happened to be spelled W.H.A.L.E) oozing from her basket.

Something was missing; there was a gap in the coat-hooks where her mother's navy gaberdine should be hanging.

'Mum?' As she spoke she was already searching the silent flat – Donald out somewhere, Noel at school.

'Mum?'

In the bedroom she shared with her mother, the wardrobe was open, the only clothes still hanging in it Vee's own. She stood staring, open-mouthed, and then swung round to look at the dressing table. A fine dusting of talcum powder outlined the missing hair-brush, the ivory comb. Propped against the mirror was an envelope bearing Vee's name.

She snatched it up, and then couldn't open it; her fingers felt huge and jointless, like washing tongs. In the end, she pulled up the flap with her teeth and shook out the single page.

Dear Vera

As I've always said, you never know just what's around the corner. I didn't want this to come as a shock to you, Vera, but then I thought that it's better to be truthful than beat around the bush. Mr Chamberlain was beating around the bush for at least a year and look where that got him, if he had gone after Hitler sharpish then perhaps none of this would have happened, as I pointed out in my last letter to him. I have always felt it's my duty to offer help and advice to those in need, but it's not often taken, or sometimes it's taken and then I am given no credit. For instance I've read that iron indoor shelters like the one I suggested are going to be all the rage, but it is Mr Morrison in the government who is taking the credit and no doubt the profit.

Harold says I should have kept a copy of my letter, setting out my idea for an iron indoor shelter, but it's too late now. Anyway, Vee, I shan't beat around the bush. You know that I have been corresponding with Harold in his troubles for many years. Since his wife passed on he has been very lonely and his daughter is now married and in the family way and never visiting, just because Harold won't speak to her husband (Scottish). In his time of loneliness my friendship has been a great solace to him and last month he asked for my hand in marriage to which I have agreed

Vee sat heavily on the bed and the springs twanged bathetically.

and we will marry this morning in Harpenden Town Hall. Harold and I didn't want any fuss and the registrar said that if I could mouth the words so he could see them it would all be legal, together with my signature.

Harold says he will look after me through Thick and Thin because as you know, Vera, since that terrible day when I had my brain seizure I can scarcely lift a hand around the house and I am only being honest when I tell you that Harold thinks lately I have not been looked after as well as I should have been. I know you are busy,

*Vera, and it has been a great sadness to me that I haven't been able
to help you as I'd like, but meal after meal has been left cold for me
instead of fresh cooked, while you've been out and about taking the
evacuee to his hospital visits and so on. When I've needed a pot of tea
or something picking up you have not been there to help and last
week when I ran out of ink it was three days before you remembered
to get me some and in the end I had to go all the way downstairs
and borrow a bottle from Mr Clare in the bookshop.*

*Harold says I will never want for anything once I am married, and
of course I hope you will visit us when you can spare the time, Vera.
Harold has an electrical washing machine.*

I remain your affectionate mother

Flora Brunton (note married name)

*ps Did you know that Donald has been walking out with a
German?*

pps I have taken my ration book

Vee lay back on the double bed. The ceiling had a pattern of
cracks that looked vaguely like a swastika.

'My mother has eloped,' she said.

Harold was tall and stooping, a shopfitter with arthritic knees
and the ability to take a ten-second anecdote and stretch it out
for a full hour. His wife – his *first* wife – had rolled her eyes
whenever he spoke. His stories had no shape to them, no
climax, no way of distinguishing whether the end was nigh, or
whether there was still another twenty-five minutes to sit
through – it was like eating your way through slice after slice of
a plain loaf, without even a dab of jam to relieve the tedium.
And that was what her mother had chosen: after twenty years
of loving servitude, Vee had been thrown over for a washing
machine and a bore.

For a moment she thought she was going to cry, but her eyes
seemed to have lost the know-how.

Twenty years. Her mother had been skimming the fat off a

pan of stock when Vee had told her she was expecting; she'd dropped the spoon in shock, reached for a cloth, slipped on the grease and fallen forward, rapping her head on the tabletop with a noise like a cleaver hitting a chop. And when she'd opened her eyes the next day in the cottage hospital, she'd not been able to say a word, and ever since then Vee had been breathing guilt, drinking it, wearing it next to her skin like a suit of long underwear. She'd tried to atone, God knows. She'd tried to fill her mother's life with little luxuries, had never asked for help, had never burdened her with her own troubles. She'd treated her mother like a spun-glass ornament that might shatter if carelessly handled, except that now it seemed that it wasn't an ornament she'd been tiptoeing round all these years, but a bloody great unexploded bomb – a couple of cold lunches, a missed cup of tea and *boom* . . .

Vee closed her eyes and actually dozed for a moment or two, and then woke with a start and forced herself to her feet. Only sluts and invalids slept during the day. She straightened the eiderdown and plumped her mother's pillows, covered with eau-de-nil sateen instead of cotton, because the texture of the latter irritated her delicate skin. The plumping went on for rather a long time, and then Vee took the pillows and threw them across the room at the framed photograph of her mother on the beach at Broadstairs, scoring a bull's-eye with the second. 'Apologies if the service here wasn't up to scratch,' she said, out loud, her voice a coarse shout. 'See if Harold gives you bloody sateen. See if Harold tries never to turn over in bed, in case the noise of the springs wakes you. See if Harold goes into nine different shops to try and get ink for you. *Nine!*'

Someone was ringing a handbell on the street outside and she went over to the window and saw two Boy Scouts, one fat, one thin, pulling a handcart piled with old clothes. She snatched up the pillows and the photograph and looked around for what else she could grab.

The Scouts had almost reached the High Street before she caught up with them. 'Salvage,' she said, between gasps, offloading the pillows, the chalk, the galoshes, the umbrella, the half-eaten packet of Parma Violets.

The boys exchanged glances. 'We're just collecting rags today, missus,' said the fat one.

'Won't kill you, taking a bit extra.'

'But—'

'Put them in the bin if you don't want them.' She threw in the photograph with such force that the glass cracked, and then she went back to the flat, closed the curtains, kicked off her shoes and climbed under the eiderdown. She was asleep in seconds.

This time, waking up was like climbing out of a pit; she kept slipping back down, her eyes gummed with clay. In the end, it was the smell of fish that pulled her into the afternoon light. The whole flat smelled like Whitstable quayside.

She retrieved the basket and slid the stinking grey overpriced slab into a pan of water. Then she leaned against the kitchen table and tried to clear her head. 'My mother has eloped,' she said again, and it sounded no saner than the first time. She'd have to tell Donald, of course, and she tried to imagine how he might respond to the news, but she couldn't; he was as sealed as a nut, a riddle inside a mystery, and instead she thought about what Noel would say. He'd be home soon and then she'd have an evening of it ('Strictly speaking, an elopement is a marriage without parental consent, which in this case would be impossible, so you really ought to find another term for it . . .'). She looked at the clock and felt the room jolt. It was half past six; Noel should have been back hours ago. Any other child you'd say that they were out playing with friends, but Noel didn't have any friends and in any case she'd never seen him do anything as childish as *play*.

In detention, she thought, for correcting the teacher too many times.

She made tea and listened to the wireless, but couldn't settle. It was years since she'd been in a house on her own; she didn't know what to do with herself. The announcer's voice reminded her of Noel, scrolling out the long words.

At seven o'clock, she jammed on a hat and went to find him.

'Bostock?' said Mr Waring, standing at the door of his lodgings with a book in his hand, a finger marking his place. 'He wasn't at school today.'

'Are you sure?'

'I take a register. Had he been present I would certainly have noticed.' His voice was mild but precise, every sentence perfectly formed, ten out of ten for grammar.

'Well, where was he then if he wasn't at school?'

'Mrs—'

'Sedge.'

'Mrs Sedge, could I ask your connection to my pupil?' He looked, as well as sounded, like a teacher – rumpled flannels and a tweed jacket, an air of looking down at her, even though he was the same height. His grey moustache had a sepia fringe from pipe-smoke.

'He's my evacuee,' said Vee.

'And did you see him actually leave for school?'

'No, I went to work early.'

'Well, perhaps he decided to . . .' There was a pause. Mr Waring glanced at the page number and took his finger out of the book. 'I was going to say "play truant", but that doesn't seem very likely, does it?'

'No.'

'Have you tried the library?'

'It closed at six.'

She realized she was fingering the large bone button at

the neck of her coat, as if it were a St Christopher medal.

'The trouble is that I don't know where to look for him,' she said. 'There isn't anywhere else. Unless he's friends with some child I don't know anything about. Is he?'

'No.'

'No, I didn't think so.'

She looked up and down the twilit street, gnawing her lip. 'There isn't anywhere else,' she repeated.

'I'm sure that no harm will have come to him. We are, after all, in a safe zone.'

It took a moment for her to register the waggish tone of voice; teachers and unfunny jokes, she thought – they were inextricably linked, like damp and bronchitis. 'I'll try home again,' she said, turning away. 'Maybe he's back by now.'

She'd only gone a yard or two when he called her name.

'I've just remembered something,' he said. 'I had rather an odd conversation with the boy last week. He was preoccupied with the idea of vengeance.'

'Vengeance? For what?'

'An unspecified theft. He was concerned that no one was seeking justice for the victim. He implied that the only other witness was also engaged in crime.'

Vee flinched, as if flicked with a whip. 'He makes up stories,' she said, mechanically. 'Reads too many books.'

'So you'd suggest this was merely childish fantasy?'

'Yes.'

She was twisting the coat button again and it was suddenly in her hand, the thread broken. She looked at it, stupidly.

'He's an unusual child,' said Mr Waring. 'Do you know very much about his family?'

'He doesn't have one.'

'So you truly are in loco parentis.'

More Latin. She guessed the meaning and nodded.

'Then your obvious concern does you credit.'

'Cast thy bread upon the waters,' said Vee. 'He's been a help to me.'

Mr Waring smiled, sweetly and unexpectedly, with the look of someone who'd just spotted an old friend. 'Give,' he said, 'and it shall be given unto you; good measure, pressed down and shaken together, and running over.'

'Luke 6,' supplied Vee. 'I'd better go,' she added. 'It's getting dark.'

'Should you, perhaps, call in at the police station? If you're worried.'

Briefly she met his gaze, but it was too clever; she was worried he'd pick the truth out of her like a splinter, and she hurried away, nodding as she went.

13

It had been a mistake to bring the suitcase. It was half-empty and the ammonite kept rolling from one end to the other, shifting the handle in Noel's grip at every step. It was like walking a badly trained dog.

Since leaving for the station, he'd been waiting for Donald to ask him why he'd brought a large item of luggage on a day trip to London, and had even prepared an answer ('I'm going to see if I can bring back some shrapnel to sell at school') but the question hadn't been asked, and now they were nearly at their destination.

'It's those houses there,' said Noel, gesturing to the north side of Exhibition Road. 'So can I go now?'

'Hmm?' Donald, mentally lunching at the Ritz with Hilde (consommé followed by salmon, Hilde in a white fur stole, *Oh, Donald, I am so heppy*), glanced down at Noel, with the expression of someone noticing a piece of lint on their trouser leg.

'Can I go now?' repeated Noel.

'Go where?'

'To look around for shrapnel, so I can sell it at school. That's why I've brought the suitcase, you see.'

'No, stay right here. I'll be out in half a tick and then I'll have to get to somewhere else, a drill hall or something like it. You'll have to find the way.'

'Why?'

But Donald was already crossing the road, straightening his jacket as he went, smoothing his hair, taking a letter out of his breast pocket. He had spent half the journey sighing and examining his profile in the train window, and the other half cleaning the dirt from under his fingernails with a matchstick. 'What wine d'you have with salmon?' he'd asked, just outside Watford, and Noel had instantly given Mattie's answer: 'A good wine. All other considerations are mere pretension.' And for the first time since Mattie had died, the thought of her had actually been *nice*, a simple pleasure – like having the back of his neck stroked – rather than a bone-deep ache.

He set the suitcase down. He'd planned to drop into the Natural History Museum (just to see the diplodocus) before sneaking away through the usual crowds and abandoning Fat Donald, but the road, usually nose-to-tail with taxis and charabancs, was empty, the museums shuttered and sandbagged. The stone walls of the V & A looked as if they'd been attacked by a giant with a pea-shooter.

As Donald mounted the steps of number 40 and pulled the bell-wire, Noel sat gingerly on one end of his suitcase and started to work out how many words he could make from the letters of *diplodocus*:

Did
Dip
Disc
Plod

The door was opened by a seedy-looking man in his fifties, his skin lemon-tinged, his eyes peering wetly between crumpled lids.

'Yes?' He was wearing a tweed jacket, gone at the elbows, and a maroon paisley scarf, spotted with grease. There was a bicycle with a basket in the hall behind him, and a cold smell of mildew.

Donald glanced again at the number on the door to check he'd got the right house. 'My name's Sedge, I believe I'm expected.'

'Yes, yes. Close the door.' As he spoke, a tiny sausage dog skidded out of a side room into the hall and threw itself at Donald's ankles, barking.

'Don't, Rexy,' said the man, stooping to pick it up, 'naughty laddie.'

'I'm supposed to be meeting a Mr JD,' said Donald.

'In the drawing room,' said the man, setting off back along the hall, the dog peering vindictively over his shoulder. 'Follow us.'

Donald looked once more at the letter in his hand; the man's voice matched the expensive paper, but if there had once been money in this house, it had long gone. He hesitated, trying to work out how little he'd accept; eighty, he thought – if they offered him less than eighty, he'd leave. He had standards to maintain.

The barking had started again and Donald followed it into the room.

It took him a moment to understand what he was seeing. The man who'd answered the door was sitting hunched in a wing chair, knees primly together, the dachshund on his lap. A second man, with a pale, smooth face and a fawn hat, stood beside him, like a guard. A third was silhouetted in front of the window.

'This him?' asked the one with the hat, and Donald felt fear spike him like a fork to the heart – they were coppers, *coppers*, and he spun round and ran for the entrance, footsteps close behind him, his own hand lunging for the latch. He pulled at it, caught just a breath of outside air, a glimpse of a small figure standing on the pavement and then he was suddenly shoved forward so that his head smacked into the door, slamming it shut.

His right arm was grabbed and dragged behind him, twisting the shoulder muscles like a wrung sheet.

'Don't scream,' said a voice close to his ear. ''Cos if you think that hurts, then you haven't felt *nothing* yet.'

The world slid in and out of focus and Donald tried to catch his thoughts but they were like minnows, dodging out of his grasp. There was only one that strayed within reach; he snatched it and held on.

'I'm not who you think I am.'

His shoulder heaved in its socket and he found himself being turned and steered back towards the drawing room.

The dog was still barking.

'Can I take Rexy out to the garden now?' asked Paisley Scarf. 'Poor little chap's crossing his legs.'

The yelping disappeared out of the door and down a set of stairs.

'You'll regret this,' said Donald. 'I'm not the person you want.'

'Aren't you now?' asked the figure by the window. His voice was an odd snuffle, air spilling through the words.

'I was visiting a friend, I got the wrong address.'

'Did you?'

'My name's de Hannay, I work for the government.'

'Bollocks you do. I *know* you.'

The figure stepped forward, out of the glare from the window.

'Oh Christ,' said Donald. Not a policeman but Fielding, the bookie's runner from Leicester – Fielding, changed and ruined. The sharp-featured face had been blunted, the nose-tip a puckered groove, the upper lip bunched and darned, a soft gap where the row of top teeth should have been.

'You did this,' said Fielding.

'I didn't.'

'Two weeks into basic training and some yellow bastard tries to shoot off his own fucking fingers and misses and gets me right in the fucking face. But *you* did it, you mug. You passed the fucking medical and look what you done to me.'

'My name's de Hannay, I'm looking for Mr JD.'

'There's no JD, you arsewipe. The poofter what lives here is a punter who owes us half his bloody house and wrote the letter I told him to write and he won't say nothing when we start on you, he'll mind his own fucking business and play deaf. And blind. And dig the bloody hole afterwards.'

There was another heave on Donald's arm, and the pain was no longer just in his shoulder but everywhere, circling his body like an iron coil.

'I work for the government,' said Donald, and he sounded like someone else, his voice strangulated but steadfast.

'Shut *up*.'

'Hush-hush job. I was watched coming in here. They'll be looking for me if I'm not out in five min—'

The doorbell rang.

'I told you, I told you they were watching,' and through the swimming red haze he could see Fielding's eyes flicker and there was a tiny loosening of the grip on his arm.

'He's talking bollocks,' said Fielding. He edged over to the window and peered round the curtains. 'It's a kid,' he said, disgustedly.

The doorbell rang again, followed by a tattoo on the knocker.

'Go and tell him to fuck off,' said Fielding to the other man, reaching into his pocket as he spoke and taking out a short blunt object that, with a click, became a long, sharp one. 'You can leave Fatty Arbuckle here.'

Donald swayed as he was released, his arm dangling like a weighted sack.

'The boy's just a decoy,' he said.

'What?'

'They don't send agents to a front door. They'll be waiting round—'

'Shut *up*, will you?'

But there was a slender note of doubt in Fielding's voice. He sidled over to the curtain again and – with no plan, no direction, nothing but the memory of Robert Donat jumping from a moving train and the thought of Hilde's feet nestled in their size 3 Oxfords – Donald turned and stumbled from the room, cannoning into Paisley Scarf as he rounded the corner. A small object fell, bounced and barked; Donald staggered on. Ahead of him was a set of stairs leading downward, behind was a confusion of noise: a yelp and a curse, the thud of body on floorboard as Fielding tripped and fell, a tearing scream, a hysterical yodel from the dog.

'I'm *stabbed*,' shouted Paisley Scarf, 'oh good *God!*' and Donald was down the steps and through a damp blue scullery and a door that opened on to a nest of brambles that dragged at his trouser legs, so that he had to lift his feet as if walking through waves. There was a garden gate at the end and then he was in a cobbled lane with a row of garages opposite and the certainty that a knife was half a garden behind him and there was one garage door that was open, only one. A white-haired man stood dumbly, cloth in hand, as Donald pushed past him and dived through the open door of the black car that stood on bricks, its paintwork shining like the toe of a squaddie's boot. He lay across the seats, his face pressed into the leather, his mind a roaring blank.

There was a short silence, a crisp footfall and then the garage door slammed shut. A bolt slid home and in the darkness someone cleared his throat.

Noel had just let go of the knocker when the door was answered by a man with a fawn hat and a pale, grave face.

'What is it, sonny?'

'I'm collecting for books for servicemen overseas,' said Noel, calculating that anyone living so close to the museums might think that public education was important.

'You *bastard*!' shouted someone inside the house. Footsteps vibrated.

Wordlessly, the pale man slammed the door, but not before Noel had glimpsed some kind of fight taking place in the hall behind him, an arm arcing blood across the wall, a singing snarl like the whine of a petrol saw.

He crouched and peered through the letter box, looking for Donald. He saw the man in the hat take a flying leap over a tumble of bodies and run for the back of the house and then a dark shape leapt into view, inches from Noel's face. Teeth snapped at his fingers.

He let the flap drop and quickly walked away. His palm was sweaty on the suitcase handle, and his mouth as dry as if he'd been chewing blotting paper. He thought of a wooden puzzle he'd been given for his first Christmas at Mattie's – a street of houses, the façades removable so that you could see cooks in kitchens, children in nurseries, a lady brushing her hair, a gentleman reading a newspaper. It revealed a world of calm and quiet activity, whereas the truth was that you never knew, when you lifted the flap, who you'd find hitting whom, who'd be crying in the corner, who'd be steeling themselves to jump from a window. There were bombs outside, but inside was worse.

'I don't care in the slightest who you are or what happens to you,' said the voice in the darkness of the garage, 'but I should like Violetta to remain unharmed.'

There was a clatter of footsteps in the mews, a couple of unintelligible shouts, and then one garage door after another was savagely kicked.

'Sedge! *Sedge!* I know you're in one of these.'

The hollow crash of foot on wood came nearer, was suddenly, thunderously upon them, and then past again, as the bolt held.

Beneath the lavender smell of leather polish was the reek of Donald's own sweat. He felt peeled by fear, as if there was only the core of him left, a loose swatch of nerves draped across the seats.

'She's a Type 44 Bugatti, you know. The finest tourer ever built.'

Yards away, a garage door burst open. Something metallic fell over. The shouts were briefly muffled.

'I bought her from an Italian who had been using her to ferry his mother's dogs between her flat and Hyde Park – I used to see him every day, driving along the Cromwell Road, and it was like watching . . . calligraphy. You wouldn't believe the lines of her, the curves. She flows. She's like a ribbon in the wind.'

'SEDGE!'

'I should have moved her somewhere outside London, I suppose, but I wanted to keep her where I could see her every day. I've reinforced the garage roof, though that wouldn't do much good if we were to catch a thousand pounder . . .'

More kicks, and then a baffled roar of rage and a series of loud cracks – cobbles maybe, slung with random fury. Glass smashed; a stone juddered across a corrugated roof.

'Don't think you're safe,' shouted Fielding, his voice all mush and snuffle. 'Never think you're safe, because you're not safe, you're a DEAD MAN, Sedge.'

A final rock was lobbed along the road, a gate squealed and slammed.

There was silence for a long while and then the soft squeak of cloth on paintwork.

'I ought to tell you that she was named after a real Violetta. Someone I once left behind, assuming she'd still be there when I came back. Stupid of me, of course.'

A little solidity had returned to Donald's body, and he struggled to sit up. He sat, swaying, in darkness, hardly able to believe that he was still alive.

'Violetta,' said the man again, softly.

And Donald knew that urge, that need to hear a name, to feel the lovely shape of it in one's mouth.

'Hilde,' he said. 'Hilde.'

14

Noel had written his plans lightly in pencil on the end-papers of *The Roman Hat Mystery*. He re-read them on the tube from Kensington and was satisfied by their rhythm and logic, their orderly progression through the imperatives:

Day 1
> *Arrive at Kentish Town library.*
> i) *Return The Roman Hat Mystery (after memorizing and then rubbing out plans).*
> ii) *Research and make list of asylums in North London.*
> iii) *Find telephone box, call asylums and locate Mrs Gifford.*
> iv) *Retrieve Mrs Gifford's items under cover of darkness.*
> *Go home*

Day 2
> i) *Deliver anonymous letter denouncing Ray McIver to Kentish Town police station.*
> ii) *Return items to Mrs Gifford.*
> *Return to St Albans*

At Kentish Town station, the platform stank, a compound of sweat and urine left over from the night-time shelterers. Rows of bunk beds had been pushed back against the wall and as Noel made for the exit he passed a warden attempting to wake a late sleeper whose liquid snore bubbled onward, regardless of shakes and bellows.

Above ground, there was already a queue for the coming evening, pale shabby families with blankets and bundled babies, parcels of food and coughing grandmothers.

'You was supposed to *share* them blimming chips with Eileen,' a woman was complaining, over the sound of weeping. 'She won't get nothing now unless them ladies come round with biscuits.'

'Frankie!' someone else was shouting. 'Where's Frankie? Anyone seen Frankie?'

No one gave Noel a second glance as he steered his suitcase around a knot of toddlers and into the sunlit High Street. It was balmy for October, the sky cloudless and a pale slice of moon already visible.

He had nearly reached the library when he felt the hand close over his shoulder.

The rattle of the knocker came long after midnight. Vee had been sitting halfway down the stairs, fully clothed, ears straining the darkness; she sprang to open the door and Donald pushed through like a bullock forcing a gate, shouldering her aside, his breathing harsh and rapid.

'Whatever's the matter?'

He was already taking the stairs, two at a time. Vee hesitated, and then she stepped outside and looked up and down the empty street. Nothing moved in the moonlight; the only sound was the tinny shriek of Mr Clare's gramophone, seeping round the bookshop shutters.

Her son was in the kitchen, sitting hunched in darkness, head on hands.

'What's the matter, Donny?' she asked again, switching on the light. 'You're not ill, are you?'

'Turn it off.'

'Why?'

'OFF.'

He had never raised his voice to her before. Her hand trembled as she reached for the switch.

'They mustn't know I'm here,' he said.

'Who mustn't?'

'I'm in danger.'

'What do you mean?'

'You've got to take a letter round to someone.'

'Who? Why?'

He was already on his feet, raking through the dresser drawer.

'Where's Gran's writing paper?'

'Gran . . .' She had to swallow before she could speak, all the troubles of the day lodged in her throat. 'She might have taken it with her. She's not here, Donny, she's left. She's gone off and married Cousin Harold. She did a flit when I was out shopping, must have been planning it for . . . for . . .' Her voice tailed off; her son wasn't listening. He had grabbed a torch and a stub of pencil and was busy writing on the back of a bill, his half-lit face all pallor and shadow, like a guiser's mask.

'Are the police after you, Donny?' Black market, she thought, hams and whisky, his skills as a salesman once again in use.

'Not the police. Worse. I'll have to leave.'

'Leave? What do you mean?'

He didn't answer, just carried on with the note, and she caught herself thinking how nice his handwriting was; as neat as any teacher's.

'Where will you go?'

'Ireland maybe.'

'Ireland? *Ireland?*'

She groped for a chair and sat heavily.

It was as if her life was being deliberately unpicked, the seams parting, the whole thing dropping shapelessly to the floor.

'What will you do there, all on your own?'

'I shan't be on my own.' He folded the note and slid it into an old envelope, crossing out the address and substituting a single word. 'She's on shift at six, so you have to get there before she leaves The Beeches. The factory bus goes a half hour earlier.'

He held out the envelope and after a second or two Vee took it and stared at the name. 'Hilda?'

'Hilde.'

'She the German? Mum wrote that you were—'

'She's not German, she's Austrian. It's the hostel up at Brickett Wood Common and you need to give it right into her hand, not to anyone else, only to her.'

'How will I know which one she is?'

'She's smaller than you – dainty, with dark hair, she wears a knitted hat. Don't tell her you're my mother.'

'Why not?'

He leaned back in the chair, and it creaked in protest.

'Just don't. Can you get me something to eat? I've had nothing all day, not a scrap.'

'But what if she asks who I am?'

'Say I'm your lodger.'

The torch on the table flickered twice and went out. There was a pause and then Vee heard herself speak.

'Lodgers pay rent,' she said. The gasp that followed was her own; she clapped her hand to her mouth, and her mind slid sideways to her other lodger. 'Where's Noel?' she asked, between her fingers. 'Have you seen him?'

And when her son didn't answer, she fumbled her way across the room and snapped on the light.

'The curtains are up, there's not so much as a chink outside,' she said, over his protest. 'I asked if you'd seen Noel.'

Donald frowned vaguely. 'Is he not back?'

'Back from where?'

'Kensington.'

'*Kensington?*'

'I had an appointment this morning and he knew the place.'

'You took him to London?'

Donald nodded.

'You took him to London and you didn't bring him *back*?'

'I told you, I'm in trouble. I'm on the run. He knows his way around, that's why I took him.'

'So where is he then?'

'How should I know?'

'Because you *should*, you *should* know. Because he's ten, he's only *ten years old* and he's on his own and he could be anywhere and there's been bombers going over all night, I must have counted thirty, and you're sitting there saying, "How should I know?" as if it wasn't any of your fault he was there in the first place when you were the one who took him and you won't even . . .' She ran out of breath, her voice a bare squeak, and her son said nothing, just turned the letter round and round, his face set in its usual impassive lines.

Vee stood and looked at him, this large man in her kitchen who had never learned – never been *taught* – the meaning of obligation, and with a slow surge of despair that was almost like nausea she realized that the calamities of the day, every last one of them, had simply been lying in wait for her; not the actions of cruel fate but a series of tripwires lovingly laid by herself. She'd asked for nothing from her mother and her son and she'd expected nothing from them, either, and now she'd received nothing, not even thanks. She was face down in the mud, and on her own.

'I'll have to go and get him,' she said, matter-of-factly. 'I'll deliver your letter, since it means that much to you, and then I'll go and fetch Noel back. Do you need help with packing?'

He lifted his head.

'Holdall?'

'Under my bed. The zip's broken.'

'Shirts?'

'In your drawer. Six of them, all starched and ironed.' She left the room to get her coat, but her mouth kept moving. 'I hope your Hilda can iron. I hope your Hilda can cook and sew and wash and queue for half the day and then search every flipping shop in St Albans for razor blades when she's got fifty dozen other things to do . . .'

'He had a suitcase.'

'What?'

'Noel. He had a suitcase with him.'

'Oh.' She came back into the kitchen. 'So he meant to stay.'

The house on the Heath, she thought, leaping ahead – that's where Noel would be, he'd sneak in there somehow – and she knew in the same instant that she'd never be able to remember how to get back there; it had been tucked away like a crumb in a rug and she had no idea of the address. She stood and thought, and then crossed swiftly to the dresser and grabbed a card that had arrived from Noel's uncle and aunt just a week before. Five minutes more and she was ready, three banknotes from her secret store folded carefully in her purse, her torch and a spare battery in her pocket, her blue plush hat on and her sturdiest shoes, seeing as she was about to walk all the way to bloody Brickett Wood and bloody back again.

'I'll take that,' she said, twitching the envelope from Donald's fingers and dropping it into her bag. She turned to go, and then found herself swinging round again, like an unlatched gate.

'You'll be gone when I come back?' she asked.

'I should think so.'

His head was bent and he was cleaning under one of his nails with a matchstick; Vee gazed at the nape of his neck. It hadn't changed a bit in nineteen years. Not a bit. The skin there was still pale and tender, traced by a line of little soft baby hairs and she could remember exactly what they felt like, the fairy tickle of them on her fingertips, the weight of his warm head cupped in her hand. She drew in breath. 'You'll take care, won't—'

'You ought to hurry,' said Donald. 'And don't forget to give it straight to her, not anyone else.'

She stamped down the stairs like a four-year-old, and a steaming rage propelled her most of the way to Brickett Wood along lanes blue-striped by moonlight. It wasn't until she was back on a metalled road, houses looming on either side, that she realized she'd been talking out loud to herself the whole way – shouting, probably, judging by the raw tightness in her throat. Her body seemed to thrum like an engine.

She didn't know which of the houses was The Beeches, but it didn't take long to find one with a charabanc waiting outside, the driver asleep behind the wheel, and only a few minutes later the front door opened and a procession of girls began to drift down the path, yawning, pushing hair into turbans, coughing through the first cigarette of the day. Their pale faces were featureless in the darkness, their speech a sleepy jumble of complaints.

'. . . not what I call a chop. Chip, not a chop . . .'

'. . . feet are killing me . . .'

'. . . fourteen and six they were charging, and I said to the woman—'

'. . . so absolutely *hilarious*!!' The last words were said in heavily accented rising shriek and Vee jerked her gaze towards the speaker, and saw that she was too tall and blonde to be Donald's girl.

'Was not funny at all,' muttered another voice, also foreign.

'He was very *very* funny but you have no sense of humour. He pretended to be a man with chust one leg and then we danced the Paul Chones. *Backwards!*'

The volume of the last word seemed to send a shudder along the line.

'Birgit, I've had three hours' sleep and if you don't shut your gob I'm going to shut it for you,' called someone from the back.

The blonde laughed merrily. 'But in these nasty times it's nicer to be cholly than be sad, isn't it?'

'It'd be even nicer if you'd just shut up and—'

'I've got a letter for Hilde,' said Vee, interrupting before someone (possibly herself) gave the blonde a well-deserved slap. There was a gasp and a sudden movement in the line and a small figure stepped forward, hand outstretched.

'My ledder,' she said, peremptorily.

'All right, all right,' said Vee, rattled. 'I just need to make sure I've got the right person. You're Hilde . . .' She didn't know the surname, she realized. 'Hilde who's Austrian.'

'Yes, *yes*, give it to me now, please.' The girl was still holding out her hand, and now she waggled the fingers impatiently. She was an unimpressive-looking little thing, a small mouth in a small face, hair tucked into an ugly knitted hat.

Reluctantly, Vee took the letter from her bag and the girl snatched it from her and aimed a torch at the envelope. There was a split-second pause and then a cry of obvious disappointment.

'This is not a *ledder*!'

'Of course it's a letter.'

'It's not a ledder with *stamps*, from another *country*.'

'Sorry, I'm sure.'

Hilde stared at the envelope as if willing it to sprout postmarks.

'It's from Donald Sedge,' said Vee. 'My . . . lodger.'

There was a pause, and then a muffled reply. 'I will read it later.' The torch went out and Vee heard the crackle of paper being carelessly stuffed into a pocket.

'But it's urgent. I've just walked two miles to deliver that.'

'I did not ask you to, did I?' Her tone was hateful, but Vee could have sworn the girl was close to tears. There was a toot from the bus, and they both jumped as if jabbed with a spike. Hilde turned and hurried after the others.

'Well good *luck* with that one, son,' said Vee, bitterly. Love was blind, everyone knew that, but in this case it was also deaf as a post. She watched the bus move off, its shuttered light a yellow smudge in the darkness, and then she crossed the road and began the long walk to the station.

15

'Would you like a biscuit?' asked Margery Overs. She spoke with a sort of gulping girlishness that contrasted oddly with her appearance.

'I won't thanks,' said Vee. 'I've not long had my tea.' She smiled, and shifted slightly in her chair to hide the noise of her stomach. The truth was that she hadn't eaten since the morning – one fly-blown currant bun at a café in Kentish Town – but since entering the Overs' basement flat in Mafeking Road she had told such a string of lies that it seemed only natural to tag on another.

Margery set the plate down and, for the umpteenth time, glanced over at the window, not that you could see anything through the shutters.

'Mr Overs will be home any minute now,' she said. 'He'll just be dropping into the grocer's after work. He has to do all the shopping for me, I'm afraid.'

She was a pale, heavy woman and her skin had a glassy tinge that put Vee in mind of uncooked hake.

'Have you been ill?' she asked politely.

'Um . . .' the woman glanced around the room, as if the answer might be pinned to the wall somewhere, '. . . oh dear. It's so hard to explain. I can't go out you see, Miss Gifford, it's a nervous complaint. I haven't been out for a number of years.'

There was a long pause during which Vee became acutely

aware of the low ceiling, the perfect, polished tidiness of the flat. She tried to imagine Noel living here but she couldn't picture it, couldn't see how he'd fit.

'You won't mind if I give Mr Overs his evening meal when he arrives, will you, Miss Gifford?'

'No, of course not.'

'Because he'll have just the half hour before he has to be out again on his warden's shift. He does four evenings a week, till midnight, and yesterday he was on his feet for the whole shift, not a cup of tea passed his lips and it was five hours before the all-clear sounded. There's a nice bit of brisket in the oven for him.'

'Oh, that'll be a treat.'

'Yes, Mr Overs has always liked brisket. And it's not too dear either.'

'No, it's quite reasonable. When you can get it, of course.'

There was a further pause, during which Vee heard the creak of the clock, readying itself to chime the hour. Six tiny bell-tones followed; she rallied herself for yet another attempt.

'Mafeking Road's not all that far from Hampstead Heath, is it? Wasn't that where Noel lived before he came to live with you?'

And there it was again: an actual flinch, as if Noel's name was a flung pebble, with the power to sting.

'No, not all that far,' said Margery, faintly, and then a key sounded in the lock and she almost sprang to her feet, teetering across the room like a spinning top.

'You'll never guess,' she said, as the door opened. 'The St Albans billeting officer's here. A Miss Gifford.'

'No trouble with young Noel, I hope?' Geoffrey was all teeth; when he smiled it was like someone opening a piano lid.

'Oh no,' said Vee, standing to shake his hand. 'He's very well. It's a routine visit. I'm seeing all the families of the evacuated children and asking routine questions. Which we need for our routine paperwork.' She winced inwardly; how did council officials actually talk? She'd met enough of them over the years, but she'd always been too busy panicking to take note.

'Miss Gifford first called here this morning, but I said to her that since our connection is through your side of the family, Geoffrey, I'd prefer it if you were able to talk to her.'

'I hope that didn't inconvenience you too much, Miss Gifford?'

'No, not at all, I had a whole list of people to call on,' replied Vee, who had spent most of the day dozing on a bench next to a bus stop.

'I'll just fetch your supper.'

'Thank you, my dear. Do take a seat, Miss Gifford.'

Vee bobbed down on an armchair as Geoffrey removed his coat and smoothed the remains of his hair. He was almost as short as his wife, and had a round, pink face bisected by a pair of wire-rimmed spectacles.

'I seem to remember that you're a relation of Noel's godmother,' said Vee, seizing her chance. 'His godmother that lived near here.'

'That's quite correct, Miss Gifford. She resided in the vicinity of Hampstead Heath.'

Ah yes, *that* was how council officials talked.

'I remember now. Noel told me that it was a sizeable residence in . . . er . . . ooh, now what was the name of the—'

'Supper!'

Vee leaned back with a hiss of frustration, which she tried to cover with a cough.

'Do please forgive me for eating in front of you, Miss Gifford, but my wife has probably alerted you to the fact that I'll have to leave again shortly.'

'No, you go ahead, I know how hard you wardens work. Don't mind me.'

Margery sat down beside her husband and watched with

evident pleasure as he ate. 'Delicious, dear,' said Geoffrey, between mouthfuls, 'absolutely delicious.'

They were a dull enough pair, thought Vee; based on Noel's remarks, she'd expected a couple of monsters, not Darby and Joan. And their flat was really quite pretty, as opposed to the sterile dungeon that he'd hinted at. Margery, it appeared, spent much of her day embroidering chair-covers while Geoffrey was presumably responsible for framing the prints that lined the walls: sunlit meadows and woodland scenes – the outdoors for a woman who never went outdoors – and a few photographs: Margery as a young woman, pretty in an anxious sort of way; Margery and Geoffrey's wedding day, Geoffrey already balding, Margery gazing at him as if she'd just said 'I do' to Rudolf Valentino; a baby whose wan blob of a face was framed by a cross-stitched bonnet; an elderly woman and a child sitting on a garden bench.

'Oh,' said Vee, rising. 'Is that . . .?'

'That was my cousin Mattie, yes. And young Noel, of course.'

Noel was a little blurred, all knees and elbows, the woman utterly solid, like a granite outcrop; Rock of Ages, thought Vee. The pair were looking at each other; a firm look, like a handshake.

'I meant of course to come and see Noel in St Albans,' said Geoffrey, 'but his foster mother wrote to say that she thought an early visit might unsettle him. We send regular letters.'

Vee nodded sympathetically. 'I'd say that was good advice from Mrs Sedge. You'll be glad to hear that she's one of our very best and most experienced foster mothers.'

'Is that so?'

'Oh yes. Honestly I wish half the ladies were as conscientious and caring as she is, she really is a marvel. In fact, I was only saying to my assistant last week that it's a pity that we can't pay people like Mrs Sedge a bit more than the other foster mothers, seeing as she's worth at least two of them and my assistant said to . . . to my *other* assistant that we really should get Mrs Sedge on a committee to talk about how on earth she manages it all.' She let Mrs Sedge linger briefly in the limelight – such a warm feeling – before moving on. 'And in any case I saw Noel only last week and he's looking top-notch, lovely rosy cheeks and no trouble with his limp and he especially sent you lots of love.'

Geoffrey paused, mid-chew, to exchange a startled look with his wife, and Vee realized that she'd gone too far. She made a play of searching through her bag, and drew out a tiny black notebook that had belonged to her mother, the matching pencil attached via a cord half an inch too short for comfortable writing.

'Just a few questions,' she said, quickly. 'Now, Noel is your . . . your nephew?'

Geoffrey swallowed his mouthful, with difficulty. 'Noel is actually no blood relation to me at all, Miss Gifford. His godmother, however, was my second cousin, and Noel's guardian.'

'So he's an orphan?'

'We believe so,' said Geoffrey, primly, the set of his mouth precluding further questions along that line.

'And he lived with his godmother in her house in . . . ?'

'The Vale of Health.'

'And is that the name of a road or a . . . ?'

'It's a dead-end lane that cuts into the south side of the Heath.'

Bingo. Vee began to close the notebook, and then realized that she ought to ask a few more questions, just for the sake of authenticity.

'And it's all official, now, that you're Noel's guardians?'

Geoffrey shook his head. 'The wheels of the law are never swift, Miss Gifford, and the solicitor in question has moved out of London for the duration. Eager as we are to assume the responsibility' – his wife closed her eyes – 'we shall have to wait until a meeting has been arranged. And even then I believe the necessary paperwork may take some time.'

'I see. And is there anything you think it might be helpful for Mrs Sedge to know about the boy? Like . . . er . . .' Vee cast around for something, anything, '. . . his favourite colour? Hobbies?'

Geoffrey's habitual smile became a little fixed. 'We never found Noel to be very enthusiastic about hobbies.'

'No?'

'Spying on people,' said Margery, in a muffled voice.

'Last Christmas we bought him a John Bull printing set, hoping it might spark his interest. But he didn't take to it.'

'He ruined it.'

'Margery—'

'He *ruined* it, Geoffrey. You were dog tired, it was your only evening off and you went all the way to Barnet to buy it from a man in the office.'

'Margery—'

'It was good as new, not a single letter missing, and you won't believe it, Miss Gifford, but we found it the next day lying outside the front door, in the pouring rain. *And* the scarf I'd knitted him with his initials embroidered at one end, and I'd made a Christmas cake as well, with real icing, and he just crumbled it up on his plate, and no one could say that we didn't try, Miss Gifford, but he's not an easy child and in six months we didn't get so much as a thank you from him, barely a word at all, just hatefulness, just . . . just . . . just . . .'

There was a pause. Margery blew her nose, long and hard.

'I seem to remember that he likes green,' she said, through the handkerchief.

Vee wrote FAVOURITE COLOUR GREEN in her notebook, taking her time over the letters. When she looked up again, Geoffrey was holding his wife's hand, gently stroking it with his thumb.

'Some pudding?' Margery asked him, tenderly.

'Well, I . . .' Geoffrey's sentence ended in a sigh. The first long note of the siren was lifting into the night.

His wife let out a mew of protest. 'It's *early*,' she said, 'and there's still ten minutes before you're expected at the post. You could have a slice of plum tart before you go.'

'No, no, dear, I'm afraid I'd better be off. Excuse me, Miss Gifford, while I get changed.' He rose, wearily, and left the room.

He was back a minute or two later, tin-hatted and wearing a boiler suit designed for a man six inches taller, the legs twin concertinas.

'I hope you have all the answers you need, Miss Gifford,' he said, as his wife helped him on with his coat. 'And of course we're extremely glad that Noel is so well looked after.'

He kissed Margery on the cheek and she clung to him, fussing over his buttons, her face blank with worry.

'You will be careful,' she said, 'won't you?'

'Mrs Overs will be sheltering in the cupboard under the stairs here for the duration of the raid,' said Geoffrey. 'You'd be more than welcome to join her, Miss Gifford. It will quite easily accommodate another footstool.'

Five hours knee-to-knee with Margery Overs. '*No!*' said Vee, forcefully, before she could think of an excuse. There was a slightly awkward silence. 'Because I have to get back to St Albans,' she added. 'To look after my mother. And son. So I'd better set off for the station straight away. Thanks ever so for your help.' She was moving towards the door as she spoke, hauling on her coat, ignoring Geoffrey's protests – 'I have to advise you in my capacity as a warden . . .'

The wobbler was still screaming as she reached the pavement and she paused to take the torch from her bag before setting off up the hill towards Hampstead; it was cloudier than last night, the moon a grey smear, the stars invisible. Somewhere to the north, a searchlight swung through the darkness.

She found herself gulping great mouthfuls of air, as if she'd been underwater; she knew, now, why Noel hadn't been able to stand it there. It wasn't the size of the place, or the tidiness – it was the *devotion*. A man should cleave unto his wife and be as one flesh, as it said in Genesis 2, but what it didn't say was that a love like that could be stifling to those around it, a velvet cloth that blocked out the rest of the world.

She felt cold, and deadly tired. 'I have to get back to look after my mother and son,' she'd said, but neither of them needed her any longer: Donald would be halfway to Ireland by now, that pinch-faced little harridan on his arm, while in Harpenden her mother was no doubt wedged on the sofa next to her new husband, listening to the electrical swish and thud of Cousin Harold's socks being thrashed into cleanliness. Her whole family, split and vanished.

She followed the dribble of torchlight along the pavement, and had barely gone a hundred yards (so far as she could judge) when the siren stopped. The ghost of it rang in her ears for a few seconds before new sounds took its place: voices from a shuttered pub, a man coughing on the pavement opposite, her own footsteps, one louder than the other as a boot-nail worked its way through one of her soles.

She came to a road, hesitated before crossing, came to another and knew that she was already lost. A few yards ahead, a fag end wheeled through the darkness and bounced in a shower of sparks.

'Excuse me, can you tell me the way to Hampstead Heath?'

A girl giggled and then murmured something.

'Lovely,' said a male voice, muffled and salacious. 'You're so *lovely* . . .'

Vee turned and started to retrace her steps; if she could find the pub again then she could get directions. She recrossed two roads and suddenly there was a tree ahead of her that hadn't been there before, and grit underfoot, and she stumbled over a split sandbag and dropped her torch. It went out as it hit the pavement, and as she knelt to retrieve it, she heard a new noise: the pulsing drone of bomber engines, low and directionless. Above the rooftops, a trio of searchlights joined the first.

She found the torch but the end had sprung off and the battery was gone, and after a hopeless search, sifting with trembling hands through sand that smelled of dog's business, she crouched on the pavement and listened to the distant dull crumps and thought of Noel, on his own and facing a second night of this. She reached for the words that might protect them both.

'Thou shalt not be afraid for the terror by night' – her mouth was so dry that the syllables clicked together like beads – 'nor for the pestilence that walketh in darkness. For he shall give his angels charge over thee, to keep thee in all thy ways.'

In swift answer, a light blinked in the sky overhead, followed by a sudden splash of rose across the clouds; a second later and the roar of gunfire reached her, loud enough to drown out the engines, each shell repeating the blink, splash, bang of the first, and Vee remembered those cheerful girls on the Heath, manning the big guns, and the thought was enough to get her to her feet, though her knees felt like sponges. She began to grope her way forward, running her fingers along the high brick wall that edged the pavement.

16

'Room for a little one,' said the shelter warden. 'Where's your ma?'

'At work,' said Noel. 'She said I should come here by myself if the siren went.'

'Find yourself somewhere to sit, then.'

The air was warm and damp; he could smell chips and the harsh whiff of disinfectant. In the dim light, there were no obvious gaps in the rows of seated figures, and he stumbled forward along a corridor of knees. 'Watch yourself,' said someone, sharply, as he trod on a foot. He reached the far wall without finding a space, and hovered aimlessly until a large woman shifted a buttock and he was able to cram in beside her. She settled back down again and he found himself pinned upright, scarcely able to breathe, the large woman on one side and a man with a running head-cold on the other.

Outside the guns were still popping. In the house on the Heath, it had sounded as if they were in the next room, the walls shuddering with every shell, and Noel had sat in the dark and gripped his thighs in panic until, during a pause in the gunfire, he'd heard the scrabble of mice, skittering around his shoes, and that had been enough; he'd fled down the lane and on to South End Green, and had found a public shelter next to the police post.

''Scuse all,' said the man with the cold, sneezing again. 'Wish I'd stayed in bed.'

'Wish you had too,' said someone opposite. 'It's bloody raining in here. I need a bloody umbrella.'

'I can't help it.'

'You can help not having a bloody handkerchief.'

'I don't like swearing,' said the large woman. 'It's not necessary and if you ask me it's the sign of a small vocabulary.'

'So you want me to sit here and come up with another word for "bloody" while he's drenching me three times a minute?'

'Sanguineous,' said Noel.

There was a huge thud – felt rather than heard – and one of the shelter lights went out. A woman shouted '*Oooh!*', and there was a rustle of nervous laughter.

'Anyone fancy a song?' asked someone.

'No.'

'They always sing in the shelter behind the Pond Street flats.'

'Why don't you go there then?'

'Just trying to cheer things up.'

'I'll tell you what would cheer me up,' said a man with a high, nasal voice.

'What?'

'A beer. Fetch me a beer and I could sit here with a smile.'

'Whisky for me,' chipped in another voice.

'And me.'

'Make mine a double,' called someone from near the entrance. 'And a bottle of champagne while you're at it.'

'Bottle . . . of . . . champagne,' said the beer drinker, as if writing down the request. 'Any more orders?'

'Jug of eggnog.'

'Can you do food as well?'

'Our staff are at your disposal.'

'I'll have a chocolate cake, then.'

'I'll have the same.'

'Cream horn, please.'

'Crate of bananas.'

'Joint of beef with Yorkshire pudding and sponge custard for afters. Mind, it has to be treacle sponge.'

'Turkish delight.'

'Gross of torch batteries and a new kettle.'

'Box of cheese straws.'

'Hair grips.'

'Ham.'

'My Leonard back again. My Leonard . . .' This last was a sort of howl that sliced through the laughter. For a long while nobody spoke.

'Now then, Mother,' said a man's voice, helplessly.

The woman next to Noel swivelled and reached down, nearly pitching him off the seat. When she straightened, he heard the slither of a paper bag, and then the sound of slow eating. Saliva filled his mouth.

'Can I have something?' he asked.

'What?'

'Can I have something to eat?'

'Cheeky so-and-so, where's your manners?'

'Please may I?'

'All right then – hold out your hand and don't ask for no more because you won't get it.'

He felt something round and cold on his palm: a boiled potato. He ate it in three bites; it tasted of nothing, and clung to his teeth like flour paste.

At the other end of the shelter a baby started crying, a thin, dreary whine that went on and on and Noel felt like joining in, flinging his head back and wailing because nothing had gone right since he'd come back to London and if he were to update his careful list, it would be a mass of crossings-out.

★

He'd never reached Kentish Town library. The hand on his shoulder had belonged to a grey-faced truant officer who'd been patrolling the High Road like a shark. She'd sunk her teeth into Noel's hastily invented story, shredded it, and then dragged her prey all the way to the council offices in Mornington Crescent, where a temporary classroom had been set up in the lobby.

For the rest of the day, Noel had sat between a half-wit boy and a terrifying girl with a cold sore on her lip. After a lesson on factors, they'd been instructed to write an essay entitled 'Why I Need to Go to School in Wartime' and Noel had produced nine pages of impassioned counter-argument, interrupted at intervals by the girl throwing spit-moistened paper pellets at his head.

By the time he'd been released, the library had closed. Instead, he'd gone to a café, been thrown out after making a cup of tea last for two and a half hours, and had then sat beside a bus stop and re-read his book until the siren had sounded and the streets had cleared, after which he'd made his way to the pawn shop where he'd seen Mrs Gifford's medals.

This was the part of the plan that he'd relished in prospect, allowing himself little tastes of the scene, as if it were a sweet held under the tongue. He'd be standing in a doorway close by, just another shadow in the blackout, waiting for an explosion loud enough to drown out the sound of an ammonite being lobbed through a plate-glass window. He'd be wearing gloves – both to avoid fingerprints and to protect himself from broken glass – and a scarf pulled up over his nose and mouth as a disguise, and once he'd retrieved the stolen pins, he'd flit off into the night, taking the back streets towards the Heath; unnoticed, untraceable . . . Of course, he'd probably have to leave the ammonite behind, but it would be lost to a noble cause and in any case he rather liked the idea that the only clue to the

Mystery of the Missing Medals would turn out to be one hundred million years old.

The plan had collapsed immediately and for the most prosaic and predictable of reasons: the pawn-shop windows had wooden shutters, padlocked into place. Noel had stood there for nearly half an hour, hanging on to the padlock as if it were a strap on the tube, sure that a solution would come to him if he could only think hard enough. (What did burglars use? Skeleton keys? Jemmies?) The night was full of sound: guns, aircraft, bombs; he could have broken every window in the shop with impunity.

He gave the padlock an angry rattle and the shadow of his hand – huge, a giant's fist – leapt across the shutters; the world was suddenly bathed in amber light and he jerked round and saw the High Street, actually *saw* it, every shopfront, every lamp-post crisp and vivid, the shadows as neat as if outlined with a narrow nib.

'*Hoy!*'

And high above the shops, swaying downward, a cluster of brilliants, a spangled pendant, mesmerizing, beautiful . . .

'You. *You!*'

Noel detached his gaze, dragged it over to the figure running across the street towards him and tried to bolt, but a hand reached out and snagged his arm; he found himself running on tiptoe, his collar in a vicious grip.

'Standing drooling at a flare as if it was bonfire night, you bloody little idiot! Don't you know that Jerry use those so they can see what they're going to *bomb*?'

The light flung their shadows in front of them; Noel could see his own scurrying legs, the dome of the policeman's hat.

'Where d'you live?'

'Primrose Hill.'

'What are you doing all the way over here then?'

'Visiting my gran.'

'Don't believe a word of it. Get *indoors!*' This last to a couple standing cuddling in the street. Noel's breath was coming in squeaks now, his bad foot beginning to flap.

'Where are you taking me?'

'Where d'you think?'

'I haven't done anything wrong.'

'Is that so?'

'Honestly I haven't, but I can give you some information about a crime. A real crime. I've got a letter I can give you with all the names and details.'

'What? Come on, pick your feet up.'

'There's a warden who's stealing things from bombed-out people.'

'What, just the one?'

'He's *stealing* things and then selling them.'

'They're all stealing. Whole of bloody London's at it.'

'But' – he tried to crane round; the policeman mustn't have heard him correctly – 'the man I'm talking about is an *air-raid* warden. He's supposed to be looking after the public. And that pawnbroker where you found me just now – he's receiving stolen goods!'

There was a series of barks which Noel realized was a laugh. His collar was suddenly released and he was given a gentle shove along a sandbagged passageway.

'Get yourself into a shelter, Sherlock.'

It was the tube station; Noel turned but his captor had already gone.

'You all right, son?' asked a woman ticket collector. 'Had a bit of a fright, have you?'

'I told that policeman about a *crime*' – his voice was loud and indignant – 'and he didn't do anything. He didn't even ask me the name of the criminal.'

'What sort of crime?'

'Theft. From people who've been bombed out.'

She nodded glumly. 'There's a lot of it going on.'

'But that doesn't mean that it shouldn't be stopped.'

There was a crash outside that jarred the whole floor.

'You'd better get downstairs,' said the collector.

'So you're saying that because it's common it's *acceptable*?'

'I'm saying that unless you get underground you're liable to get blown up.'

'You mean that collective safety's more important than collective morality?'

'Go downstairs.'

'Which makes us actually no better than the enemy that we purport to despise.'

'Gus!' – she was calling over his shoulder – 'Gus! I need a hand. Can you make this blinking little walking dictionary get into shelter?'

Noel turned before Gus could arrive, and started down the stairs, and it was only when he'd reached the bottom that he realized he'd left his suitcase on the pavement beside the pawn-broker's. As well as the ammonite, it contained a change of socks, a spare jumper and two tins of sardines taken from Vee's store cupboard.

He spent the night on the stationary 'up' escalator, since the platform was already full. An elderly man gave him a meat-paste sandwich, and a folded newspaper on which to sit, but it wasn't until the small hours that he finally slept; he woke to find people stepping over him, whole families streaming upward towards breakfast, work, school.

Above ground, a gritty wind was blowing and the road was littered with broken roof slates. Noel retraced his steps of last night and was pleasantly surprised to see his suitcase still sitting beside the pawn shop. He opened it and found that both tins of sardines had been swiped. He closed it again, and looked in the pawn-shop window and saw that the shelf on which he'd seen

Mrs Gifford's pins had been cleared and was now occupied by a row of Toby jugs and a stuffed badger.

After that, since it was the only thing he could think of to do, he walked home to Mattie's house – a long walk, up the High Road and clear across the Heath, a thin cold rain starting as he slogged the final half-mile and turning to sleet as he climbed awkwardly over the low fence at the back.

The kitchen door-key was under a flower pot in the summerhouse, just as it had always been. At first he couldn't turn it in the lock and then he remembered the old trick of leaning on the jamb, and the key swivelled so suddenly that he skinned a knuckle.

'Hello?' he called, pushing open the door. He waited for a moment, to give time for Mattie to reply ('And hello to you, young man'), though he knew of course that she wouldn't; the house felt as empty as a robbed tomb. One of the kitchen black-outs had fallen down, and in the grey light he could see that the sink was clear and the cupboards all closed; someone had been in at some point and tidied up. Someone had switched off the electricity too, and the gas, though the water still ran – pale brown, iron-rich, straight from the spring that fed the ponds on the Heath. He scooped a handful and tasted pennies.

Someone had tidied the dining room as well, and the drawing room, clearing the floors and tables, returning books to bookshelves, closing albums, shutting pencils in drawers, straightening the items on the mantelpiece, clapping the chess pieces back in their box so that the rooms looked neat and ordinary, as if anyone at all might have lived there.

Upstairs, the beds had been stripped, and the contents of the wardrobes folded into boxes. There was nothing left on Mattie's bedside table: her binoculars (for spotting birds), her copy of Fuller's *Worthies of England*, the little glass pot in which she kept her hairpins – all had been put away. The only trace of the previous clutter was a series of sticky rings that marked where she had placed her nightly sherry. He touched one with a licked finger and rubbed it across his tongue: dust and Harvey's Bristol Cream.

He started to hunt, then, for other tangible traces of the old Mattie. He found one of her slippers under the bed, the back trodden flat, a squashed moth on the sole ('Cheaper than using mothballs and twice the fun'). He found her toothbrush still in its pot in the bathroom, the bristles splayed out by the vigour with which she'd brushed. Her comb was on the windowsill in the same room; Noel raked it across his scalp, looked at himself in the mirror and saw a long white hair looped amongst his own short brown ones.

He pieced together an old shopping list of hers that had been cut up and rolled for spills and stuffed in a vase beside the drawing-room fire (*apples, spuds, chelsea buns, joint of beef, shilling each way on Finuken, 4.20 Epsom*). He discovered her gardening coat hanging on the back of the scullery door, a lozenge-shaped tin of her favourite extra-strong mints in one pocket, a pair of secateurs in the other. He ate a mint and felt the familiar scorching wind roar through his sinuses.

Best of all was the two-year-old copy of *The Times* that he found in the glass-roofed lean-to at the rear of the house. He sat in the armchair, with the yew tree scraping the window, and read the scathing pencilled comments in the margins (*'Rot rot rot'*, *'the Abyssinia question NEVER SETTLED'*, *'Yet more humbug!!!'*). It was like having the old Mattie right beside him.

The feeling dwindled, flattened by hunger. Noel ate the rest of the mints and searched the larder, finding nothing but a tin of limp, blue-tinged cream crackers, and an almost empty bread crock. The oddly shaped cloth-wrapped bundle at the bottom of it turned out to contain his godmother's jewellery. He glanced at the knotted jumble of beads and brooches and then quickly replaced it and shoved the crock right to the back of the larder, but it was already too late: the discovery had let the other Mattie back into his head, the later one, with her terror of imaginary robbers, her random hiding places, her wild accusations. The house felt precarious again, no longer like his home.

He stared at the sodden garden through the kitchen window, and wondered why the word 'home' seemed to linger in his head, in large, neat capitals. 'THERE'S NO PLACE LIKE HOME', to be precise, picked out in maroon beads on a yellow pincushion; for a minute or more he couldn't fathom where he'd seen such a thing, though he could clearly remember pulling off the beads and dropping them one by one behind a sideboard. Then, like a coin into a gas-meter, the memory dropped into place: it had been in the flat above the scrap-metal yard, where he'd first lived with Vee. With Vera. With Mrs Sedge. He still didn't have a comfortable term for her; she wasn't a comfortable person.

For the first time, he wondered what she'd thought when he hadn't come home from school. Perhaps he should have left her a note; after all, she'd given him her egg ration, once.

He stood and watched the rain. The grey afternoon grew gradually darker, and when he could no longer see the back fence, he roused himself and hunted fruitlessly for candles and matches. Later, when the guns started, he left.

The baby in the shelter carried on grizzling for so long that the noise ceased to sound human and became just another part of the raid, intermingling with sneezes and bombs and the rasping snore of a drunk. Despite her warning, the woman next to Noel gave him a second potato, followed by a Bovril sandwich, after which he dozed briefly, opened his eyes and saw Ray McIver.

'What's wrong?' asked the woman.

'Nothing.' His whole body was trembling; he stood up to see better.

'If you want the WC, it's in the corner. Just follow your nose.'

He nodded, absently, his feet taking him in the other direction, towards the little desk where the shelter warden sat knitting. Ray McIver was standing beside her, unbuttoning his greatcoat; he had brought the night air into the shelter with him – Noel could smell cordite, could feel a cold current ruffle past.

'We could prob'ly take another ten or fifteen if the kiddies sit on their mums' laps,' said the shelter warden. 'What's the problem with Bell Street, then?'

'Fractured water main – they're up to their knees. Got a match?'

McIver bent to light his cigarette.

'Busy night out there?' asked the knitter.

'Seen worse. Nothing in our sector so far, it's all down by the river tonight. Did you hear about Eddy Burden?'

'No.'

'He was going past an alley in the middle of a raid and he saw a tart in a white dress leaning against the wall.'

'Tipsy?'

'That's what he thought. He got a bit nearer and saw it was a landmine, with the parachute all wrapped around.'

'*No!*'

'It's true. Plenty of strange things going on out there in the dark.' He leaned against the wall, in no apparent hurry to leave, smoke trickling from his mouth. He looked untroubled, his eyes sharp and his body loose. No one who mattered was ever going to hold him to account, thought Noel; London was too full of public danger for McIver's small, private cruelties to be chased. The only people who'd ever care were the ones he'd stolen from and the ones he'd steal from next.

Noel took a step nearer and McIver glanced over at him.

'I know you, don't I?' he asked, mildly.

Noel nodded. There was no plan in his head, but he knew

that he was getting ready to do something. His heart whirred like a clockwork toy.

'So when are we getting all these extra people?' asked the shelter warden.

McIver ignored her. 'You had a collection box,' he said. 'You and that skinny piece.'

Noel nodded again. He could feel McIver's gaze, like a finger pressing against his forehead.

'Yes, I remember,' said McIver. He flicked the ash off his fag and seemed to relax again. 'They'll be round any minute,' he said to the knitter.

Noel took another, deliberate, step forward.

'You still here?' asked McIver, casually.

'Yes,' said Noel. Out of the corner of his eye, he could see heads shifting; the nearest row had started to realize that something was happening. He turned and saw an old man, a gangling girl, a woman with a baby.

'Anything the matter, love?' asked the woman.

'That warden over there is a thief,' said Noel. Her eyes widened in shock; the row of heads swung round to look at McIver. 'That warden,' said Noel, more loudly, addressing the whole shelter, 'is called Ray McIver and he's a *thief*. He stole money and jewellery from an old lady's room when she was bombed out and he's done it before and if—'

McIver was trying to say something, his face all rage and disbelief, but Noel's voice was speeding up and climbing to a shout; people were standing to see what was going on, people were gaping.

'—and if you get back after a raid and you've had something stolen it's most likely *him* who did it, it's most likely Ray McIver, and he's an air-raid warden at Post D in Solomon Road and he's arottenstinkingdirtyTHIEF.' Like a full stop, the door smacked open and a stream of people entered the shelter, wet shoes puddling on the floor, blankets steaming, and Noel ducked down and wormed between the elbows, following the draught outwards.

The guns were pounding and the sky was latticed with searchlights. He felt reborn, rinsed clean. He started walking, not knowing or caring in the slightest where he was headed, navigating from one white-painted lamp-post to the next, certain that tonight he was invulnerable, shielded by rectitude. 'You can't get me!' he shouted, when an engine whined overhead.

He felt utterly magnificent.

When a flare dropped, and he found himself in lurid day-light, he kept walking, his shadow marching triumphantly ahead of him.

17

It was the ears; Vee would have known them anywhere. She'd been fumbling along the road, cursing every sandbag, when the world was suddenly flooded with ghastly light and she found herself gazing at a film show taking place on the gable end of a house ahead of her: two shadows crisply silhouetted on the brick screen, one small, with a domed head, and one larger, with a bouncing gait and ears that seemed familiar.

She spun round and saw two yellow figures advancing along a yellow street – the illusion reversed, so that it was the more distant of the two who was actually taller, a full-grown man in warden's uniform, while the maker of the other shadow was only small, a small boy—

'Noel!!!'

She ran towards him. She saw Noel's mouth drop open, she saw the warden check his stride, she saw the man's face – furious, thwarted – as he turned away, and then a line of tracer bullets rose gracefully above the rooftops and the flare was shattered with the noise of dropped crockery. The darkness was instant.

'Noel. *Noel!*'

'I'm here.'

He was just in front of her, and she reached out and grabbed him by an arm and a shoulder and then by a cheek and an ear, and pulled his face towards her coat.

'Ow,' said Noel, a button digging into his lip. 'What are you doing here?'

'What do you think I'm doing? Looking for you, you silly beggar, outside in the middle of a raid and that man following you.'

'What man?'

'McIver.'

'Where?'

Her eyes had adjusted now, and she could see his pale face, struggling to look round. Beyond him, the empty road spooled into the night.

'He's gone now,' she said.

Noel pulled free. 'I was all right. I'd done it. I told everyone in the whole shelter that he was a dirty, rotten thief – I got my revenge.'

'And he bloody nearly got his! He was following you in the dark, you little fool. What were you *thinking*? No, never mind—' He was starting on one of his explanations, and she wasn't in the mood for polysyllables. 'Thank God I found you. I'd been doing some praying so maybe it works sometimes. Now, which way should we go?'

Noel shrugged, sulkily, the glory of five minutes ago already muddied.

'I don't know where we are,' he muttered. 'I left my torch in the shelter.'

'And I broke mine. Fine pair, aren't we?'

For a moment both were silent; from somewhere to their left, quite far away, came the long, shrill whistle of a falling bomb, and the phlegmy rumble of its impact.

'Come on,' said Vee, taking Noel's arm and giving it a little tug. They started to walk, following the pale line of the kerb.

Seconds passed. From exactly the same direction as before came exactly the same sequence of sounds. But louder, this time; nearer.

They broke into a trot; Vee pressed a hand to her chest, the scald of heartburn beneath her fingers.

The third bomb in the stick came down not with a whistle but with a wicked swish; it was still streets away, but the explosion shook the road. Window glass showered the pavements.

'*Run!*' shouted Vee.

The engine of the bomber was audible now, stammering above them and Noel could hear himself sobbing, could hear Vee calling on God, but he knew the whole thing was luck, all luck; it was like a boulder tumbling down a mountain, bouncing between impacts, randomly crushing or sparing. He heard the fourth bomb falling – a colossal splintering scream, like the sky being split in half – and the street lifted as if it were a sheet of plywood, and slammed down again.

Vee's neck seemed to expand and contract like a telescope; she lost her grip on Noel and fell to her knees. In an instant the world was swallowed by utter blackness, the air suddenly as thick as soup, peppery on the back of the throat so that she coughed, and coughed again, and swiped at her eyes with fingers that were instantly gritty, so that she knew that at least she wasn't blind, only blindfolded, and the thought was a drop of relief in a great basin of terror. The guns were hammering away, but distantly, as if swathed in blankets.

She climbed to her feet and flailed in the darkness and her fingertips brushed Noel's face. This time he flung himself at her, arms locked around her waist, and she clasped his head and waited, trying to see something, *anything*, that might give her some clue as to what they should do. They might be standing on the edge of a crater, for all she knew, there could be a corpse lying a yard away. Or a pile of them.

'Don't fret,' she found herself saying, mechanically. 'There, there.'

The growl of a motor car came from somewhere nearby, and

then a series of shouts. For a second or two a beam of light poked a foggy red hole through the darkness. 'Help!' she called, and then closed her mouth again, her tongue crusted with grit. Red grit, she thought; brick dust. This fog had been a house.

The glimpse of light somehow made the blindness even worse, and she started to inch forward, desperate to find an end to it. Noel moved crab-wise, still hanging on to her. There was more shouting, nearer now, and the crunch of a handbrake. Another torch-beam, swiping diagonally, briefly outlined a huge dark shape just ahead of her and she reached out and felt a metal surface, warm beneath her fingers – the bonnet of a parked van.

'Anyone there?' The dust seemed to soak up her words; it was like speaking into a cushion. Close by, she heard a sharp click.

There was no other warning, She turned her head and something wide and hard smacked her face and flung her into nowhere.

18

She was trying to find her purse, pawing through greasy heaps of clothes in a room full of rubbish.

Her cheek hurt.

She saw blood on a blanket.

She saw a man with hairy nostrils holding an oversized tea strainer above her face. 'Nice big breasts,' he said – she thought he said – 'and you'll soon be asleep.'

She saw an old woman thrashing her skinny arms and screaming for Mary.

Her cheek still hurt, a steady pulse of pain.

She saw tea in a thick green mug, a paper straw angled temptingly towards her mouth. She tried to sip and tea cascaded down her front.

There was a crash and she opened her eyes to find the world sharp and bright. An enamel bowl had been slammed on to the table beside her, and a nurse was pouring hot water into it from a jug.

'Can you manage to wash yourself, do you think, Mrs Overs?' asked the nurse.

'I'm not Mrs Overs,' said Vee, and the words came out as a string of vowels; her mouth wouldn't close properly and her cheek felt the size of a cottage-loaf. She raised a hand to her face and felt a wad of cloth and a bandage that encircled her head.

'You mustn't touch your dressing. If you want to ask anything you can write it down.'

The nurse extracted a tiny notebook from her pocket, together with a red pencil.

'I'll be back,' she said, 'after your wash.' She pulled a screen around the bed, and left Vee with a view of faded sunflowers.

She dabbed at herself with the flannel and memories came back in pieces. A letter handed to a bitch of a girl in a knitted hat. An empty wardrobe.

'Mrs Elias, it's morning,' called the nurse, from a couple of yards away.

'Morninaaaah.' The word stretched into a yawn. 'I had such a nice sleep.'

'I think a lot of people had such a nice sleep. There wasn't a raid last night.'

'No raid?'

'Not in London anyhow.'

'No raid! Did you hear that, Mrs Thomas?'

'What?'

'There was no raid in London last night.'

'No what?'

'Raid.'

'No bread?'

'No. No RAID.'

'Oh. May I have porridge then?'

'Morning, Mrs Connell. Did you have a nice sleep?'

'I didn't I'm afraid, nurse, I'm so used to the bombs now that it was much too quiet for me. I'm a bit funny that way.' There was a tinkle of self-deprecating laughter.

More pieces slotted into Vee's memory. A dropped torch. Shadows on a wall.

'Oh *Christ*!' The words came out as a blunt bellow, the sound of a cow giving birth. She pushed aside the bedclothes and tried to stand and found that she seemed to be on a merry-go-round, the floor rising and falling and the sunflowers revolving queasily. She dropped back on the bed, just as the nurse reappeared.

'What's wrong, Mrs Overs?'

'Where's Noel? Where is he?' The words were unintelligible, even to herself; she reached for the pencil and notebook.

I HAVE TO GO WHERE ARE MY CLOTHES?

'You can't possibly leave the hospital until Mr Feggerty says you can, and that won't be for another few days, I'm sure.'

I HAVE TO FIND SOMEONE. A BOY

Vee underlined the last word, and then jabbed at the letters with her pencil, looking up at the nurse, trying to will her into understanding the urgency of her request.

'Do you mean your nephew? The little boy with the ears?'

Vee nodded.

'He's come in to visit for the last two evenings. I expect he'll be back tonight. We don't usually let children in on their own, but he was very well behaved.'

She whisked away again and Vee lay back, limp with relief. The pencil clattered to the ground and she could no more have reached for it than flown a Spitfire.

It was the breakfast orderly who retrieved the pencil, and who answered a few basic questions before leaving Vee with a bowl of milk pudding. The spoonfuls slithered around an unfamiliar gap in her teeth.

She was in Ward 22 of Hampstead General Hospital, she'd broken her cheekbone and suffered a concussion and today was a Tuesday, which meant that she'd lost half a week.

'And the Eyeties are bombing Greece,' added the orderly,

collecting her tray; Vee had almost forgotten that there was a wider war. She felt for the dressing again and then cautiously explored the rest of her face; there was nothing missing, no holes, just a scabbed graze across her forehead.

After that, her thoughts seemed to come to a halt, and she jerked awake again to find the bed surrounded by doctors, her right cheek exposed to their view in a way that felt indecent.

'Depressed closed fracture of the right maxilla and contusion to right temporal region secondary to direct trauma,' announced a boy with spots and a moustache like a finely plucked eyebrow. 'Can you remember what happened to you, Mrs Overs?'

SOMETHING HIT ME

wrote Vee.

A BOMB

'Not a bomb, no. Keep watching my finger.' He traced a rapid cross in the air above her. 'And can you recite the alphabet for me? All right,' he added hastily, as she slushed and sprayed her way as far as G. 'That's enough. It's only the swelling that's preventing you from speaking clearly; it should improve over the next couple of days. Dressing back on now and stitches out on Friday, Sister.' And they were off, trundling a trolley full of notes towards the next bed while nurses fluttered behind like gulls following a tractor.

She was asleep when Noel arrived, and she opened her eyes to see him staring down at her from about six inches away, his expression tense.

'Are you awake?' he asked. 'I mean, properly awake?'

She nodded. He was wearing a man's coat with rolled-up

sleeves, and she reached out and felt the material. Wool.

'A woman at the tube station gave it to me. The nurse said you had concussion, which is when the brain gets shaken up in the skull. It causes clouded consciousness and memory loss. You kept opening your eyes yesterday but you weren't really seeing anything. What's six times nine?'

She mimed writing.

'Six times nine,' he repeated, handing her the notebook and pencil.

36 WHERE ARE YOU STAYING? WHAT ARE YOU EATING?

'That's not right, it's fifty-four. What's the capital of Sicily?' His voice was shrill, bullying; he was scared, she realized. She wrote:

AM NOT GOOD AT ARITHMETIC OR GEOGRAPHY. ASK ME HOW TO KNIT A SOCK.

'Oh.' He let out a long breath. 'I see what you mean. There's no point in giving me the sock answer, though. I wouldn't know if you were right.'

She pointed to a chair by the bed, and after a moment he sat down. 'I've been sleeping in Hampstead tube station,' he said. 'If you pretend you've been separated from your family then people give you food and things. During the day, I go to the library.'

YOU COULD GO TO YOUR UNC

'No,' he said, reading upside down.

THEY'RE NOT BAD PEOPLE

He folded his arms and looked out of the window. At the next bed, Mrs Connell's daughter was peeling an apple for her mother and complaining about the avarice of the greengrocer.

'Cup of tea, Mrs Overs?' asked the orderly.

'Yes, please.'

She waited until the trolley had been pushed away again and then picked up her pencil.

WHY ARE THEY CALLING ME THAT NAME?

'Because I told the ambulance driver you were my auntie Margery. I thought if we were related they'd let me go to the hospital with you, but they didn't. I think it's because they didn't want me telling anyone.'

'Telling what?' she mouthed.

'How you got hurt.'

She waited.

'It was the door,' said Noel. 'You got hit in the face by the ambulance door.'

She'd been thrown to the ground, taking Noel with her and he'd struggled to his knees in the black fog, shouting for help, hearing the groan of her breathing. The ambulance women had seemed more irritated than guilty, once it had been established that their victim was still alive. They'd loaded Vee into the back of the van and gone off to find more casualties and Noel had been handed over to a passing policeman.

'I came to visit you the next day. And the day after.'

'I know,' mouthed Vee.

She lifted her hand to her face and touched the dressing. Then she picked up the pencil again.

DOES IT LOOK BAD

He spoke reluctantly. 'There was a bit of a dent.'

'A dent?'

'Actually, the correct medical term is "depression". That's why they did the operation.'

'A dent.' So she'd look different for ever, she thought. Ugly. Her vision blurred.

'It doesn't matter,' Noel said. 'I'd honestly rather have a dent than ears like Etruscan jug handles.'

That almost made her smile; she reached out and gave his elbow a pat and he looked down at his arm as if she'd just thrown paint at it.

'I've brought a book with me,' he said. 'It occurred to me that when I'm not feeling tip-top I like being read to. Would you like that?'

She nodded. Not that she'd had any experience of it.

'It's an American detective story called *The Big Sleep*. I was looking for something that would hold the attention of an invalid and the librarian said it was a whip-crack read.'

He opened the book carefully. 'I shan't attempt the accent,' he added, and cleared his throat. It was a long time since he'd read aloud; at the end of the first page he looked up to see if Mattie was listening, and saw Vee jolt into place. She nodded again, encouragingly.

'Go on,' called Mrs Connell from the next bed, 'it's very good so far.'

'I think,' said Noel, 'that Philip Marlowe is assuming that Taylor had something to do with the death of Geiger.'

'How long since you cleaned your teeth?' asked Vee.

'I had an apple yesterday.'

'That's not what I asked. And when did you last wash your face?'

'Ages. They don't have the facilities on the underground and I didn't have any money for a toothbrush.'

They were waiting at the bus stop a hundred yards from the

hospital; in the daylight, Noel's skin had a greyish tinge, peppered with smuts. Vee yearned for a handkerchief to spit on.

'Of course it's possible,' said Noel, 'that Geiger was killed by someone he was blackmailing. Don't you think?'

Vee nodded absently. The wind stung her injured cheek. The large dressing had been removed early that morning, the stitches tweaked out and she'd seen her face in the washroom mirror. It had been both better and worse than she'd feared: bruising, no obvious dent, but an iodine-daubed operation scar like a thick-lipped, complacent smile just beneath her cheekbone.

'Lovely neat job,' one of the nurses had said, reapplying a smaller dressing. 'Try using lanolin daily.'

Though it seemed to Vee that what constituted a 'neat job' on someone's face would be considered an incompetent botch on a pair of trousers.

'So sorry you're going,' Mrs Connell had said. 'I wanted to hear the rest of the detective book. He's a card, your little nephew, isn't he?'

The card was currently looking up the road to see if the bus was coming. From this angle, Vee could see the back of his neck.

'Soon as we get home, I'm going to run you a bath,' said Vee. 'You can stay in it until you're the right colour again.'

'If we get the 46 south,' said Noel, 'we can take it as far as King's Cross, and then catch the train to St Albans. That way, you'll hardly have to walk at all.'

'Did you hear what I said about the bath?'

'Yes.'

'Just because you've managed on your own for a few days doesn't mean that you don't need me to look after you. I think that sometimes you forget how old you are.'

'I'm eleven.'

'You're ten.'

He shook his head. 'I was eleven the day before yesterday.'

It was ridiculous what made her cry these days; it was as if the blow from the ambulance door had unplugged something.

Noel was looking at her anxiously.

'I'll make you a birthday cake,' she said, wiping her eyes.

'Oh, I don't care about *birthdays*,' said Noel, dismissively. 'Don't worry about missing that. Mattie said that we should celebrate each glad moment as it comes.'

'I'll make you a glad moment cake, then. If I can get any eggs.'

When the bus came, a very old gentleman stood up to give Vee his seat, and she was glad to take it; bed-rest had made jellies of her legs. Noel stood in the aisle beside her, book in hand.

'Diversions taking place,' shouted the lady conductor. 'Don't thank us, thank Mr Goering.'

They passed a lorry being loaded up with rubble; next to it was a lamp-post bent almost in half, so that it looked like a giraffe peering in through the bus window.

'That's right where our bomb dropped,' said Noel. 'I remember seeing that lamp-post when the dust started to clear.'

None of the remaining houses in the street had any glass in the windows, or much in the way of roof slates, but there were still people living in them. One woman was scrubbing her doorstep, looking quite cheerful. Mrs Connell in the next bed at the hospital had informed Vee that it was good luck to have a bomb in your street, since the Germans never dropped two in the same place.

Beside her, Noel turned a page.

'I'm just glancing ahead,' he said. 'Getting the gist of it. It'll be easier to read aloud if I know roughly what's coming.'

'You'll have to return that to the library,' said Vee.

'I can post it.'

'Stamps have to be paid for.'

She closed her eyes for a minute or two and then opened them as the bus jogged over a pothole.

'Look,' said Noel. 'I bet that was the one before ours.'

'What are you talking about?' Outside the window she could see another hillock of fresh rubble in another windowless street.

'We heard four bombs dropped in a row, didn't we? Ours was the fourth. I'll bet this was where the third one landed. It's about a quarter of a mile away and there've been no raids in this bit of London since then.'

'He's right,' said the elderly gentleman standing beside him. 'The buggers dropped a stick of half-tonners going nor-nor-west, pardon my language.'

'Pardoned,' said Vee, closing her eyes again.

Noel laid a ruler across his mental map of North London, lined up the first two sites and, after some consideration, marked the next cross beside St Dominic's Priory. He felt guiltily pleased when the bus passed two friars exiting the church through a hole in the lady chapel wall. There was a crater in the playground of St Dominic's School next door, and a huge, leafless tree beside the road had snapped like a toothpick. The exposed wood was a sheaf of pale yellow splinters.

Noel shifted the imaginary ruler south-east.

'First one they dropped was the worst,' said the old gentleman. 'It hit a gas main, firefighters there till morning.'

'Diversion,' called the conductor. 'We will be diverting down Queen's Crescent and then Haverstock Hill.'

Noel worked out where the next mark would come, and frowned. The bus swung round a corner.

'Which street had the gas main?' asked Noel.

'Mafeking Road.'

Vee opened her eyes.

'What was that?'

'Mafeking Road. Blew up half the damn street,' said the old gentleman. 'Pardon my language.'

Vee nudged Noel. 'Ring the bell,' she said.

Where the solid, four-storey Victorian terrace had stood, there was only an undulating black wall, punched through with rectangles of sky.

A rope hung limply across the road. Noel stepped over it and walked towards number 23. Through the gap where the main front door had stood, he could see the scarlet berries of a rowan tree in the back garden. There was a frill of molten metal beside the doorstep; it took him a moment to realize that he was looking at the bootscraper.

'Wait for me,' said Vee. She caught up, and stood beside him as he looked down into the basement area. It was half-full of water, the surface scummed with ash and dotted with islets of charred wood. Only the top part of the window hole was visible and it framed not a pin-neat room but a dense mush of broken bricks.

'The floorboards burned through,' said a voice. Vee turned to see a girl of about twelve with a baby on her hip.

'It all fell in and they haven't got the people out yet and my cousin who's a fireman says they won't ever get anyone out because there'll be nothing left of them after the fire.' She shifted the baby on to the other hip. 'You're not supposed to go near it, in case it collapses.'

'So why are you here then?' asked Noel, savagely. He walked straight past her, away from the terrace, his face white.

'Don't mind him,' said Vee. 'He's had a shock. We both have.' Her cheek throbbed as if someone were rapping it with a drumstick. 'We knew the lady who lived in the basement of number twenty-three.'

'Oh.' The girl slid a curious look at Vee's face. 'And did you know the man as well?'

It took a moment for Vee to realize that the question was awry. 'What do you mean, *did*? Mr Overs wasn't down there. He was on duty. He'd started his shift.'

The girl was already shaking her head, her expression tense with superior knowledge. 'When the bomb went off, Mr Overs rushed back here and went in to try and rescue Mrs Overs.'

Yes, thought Vee, heavily, yes of course he did, that's exactly what he did; no power on earth could ever have stopped him.

She couldn't speak. She looked back at the window full of bricks. So they were both down there, poor sods, poor dull, devoted sods, and she would have been down there too, in that shoebox inferno, if Margery Overs hadn't been so . . . so . . . She shoved the uncharitable thought away and then flinched as a rat plopped into the basement lake and swam for the steps.

'Horrible,' she said, inadequately.

'Yes, it's very, very sad,' agreed the girl. The baby was wriggling, and she gave it her knuckle to suck. 'Did you get hurt in an air-raid too?'

'In a manner of speaking,' said Vee.

She found Noel sitting on a low wall just around the corner, and she sat down beside him.

'I'd better tell you,' she said, 'they're both gone. Your uncle went back in there to try and get your aunt.'

'They're not my aunt and uncle,' said Noel, automatically, his lips barely moving. He stared at his shoes for a full minute before speaking again. 'I have to tell you something. Something terrible.'

'Go on, then.'

'When I lived there I used to hope that I'd wake up in the morning and they'd be dead and Mattie would be alive again. That's what I hoped for.' He fiddled with one of his shoelaces and waited for a response. 'Don't you understand?' he asked, when there was none. 'I wished they'd die. I honestly did wish that, every single day, and now they're actually *dead*.' He looked round at Vee defiantly, as if hoping for a smack on the ear.

'Well, you can try and blame it on yourself if you like, but I think Hitler had something to do with it.'

He started to speak.

'No,' she said. 'You didn't make it happen. Lots of people are dying. Some of them are good and some of them are bad, some of them are loved and some of them never got a single speck of love while they were on this earth, but none of them are dead just because a ten-year-old didn't like them. *Eleven*,' she corrected quickly, before he could jump in. 'Goodness knows I've wished plenty of people dead in my time, and it never works. Never.'

That sounded wrong, she thought.

'Bad thoughts aren't the same as bad deeds,' she added, and that sounded better.

They sat in silence for a minute or two, but the wind was picking up and the air was full of black ash.

'Let's go,' said Vee. 'You'll have to help me up, I'm as weak as a kitten.'

He gave her his arm, and she kept hold of it, all the way to the bus stop.

PART THREE

19

'I feel as if I've been away for a month,' said Vee. 'I'd forgotten how clean it was here. And the air's nice and fresh.'

'It's the same as when you get back from a holiday,' said Noel. 'Though usually it works the other way around, doesn't it? Everything at home seems duller and smaller.'

'I wouldn't know, I've never been on a holiday.'

'What, never?'

'We had a chapel day trip to Saffron Walden, once. It was foggy.'

They were standing on the pavement outside St Albans station, oddly, mutually reluctant to step back into their life there. It was ten o'clock and the morning sky was the colour of cold cocoa, threatening snow.

'People are staring at me,' said Vee. 'What do I say if they ask? Where do I say we've been?'

'Visiting my relatives.'

'And one of them punched me?'

'You could tell the truth, say that you got injured in a raid.'

'No.' She didn't want to be a sensation; the spotlight made her panic. 'I'll say I fell over in the blackout. Heaven knows enough people do.'

And she recalled, suddenly, the thrilling snippet of local news that she'd overheard the week before – overheard and then forgotten in the scramble of events that had followed.

'What's the matter?' asked Noel.

'I've got to pop into the insurance office before we go home. I've just remembered something.'

They were passing Fleckney's Garage when Noel heard his surname called, and he looked up to see Mr Waring crossing the road, a crocodile of children trailing behind him.

'The wanderer returns! Mrs Sedge' – the teacher lifted his hat, paused momentarily when he saw her face, and then gave a little bow – 'I rejoice to see that the lost sheep has been gathered to the fold.'

'Yes, he's back,' she said, awkwardly. 'Needs feeding up a bit.'

'And when shall we be seeing him in the classroom?'

'Tomorrow,' said Noel, just as Vee said, 'Today.'

'*Today,*' she repeated, more firmly, giving him a look to remind him of his new, childish, status. 'I'll take your case and you go along with Mr Waring. I expect that he's doing something educational, aren't you, Mr Waring?'

'We're on our way to Brickett Wood for a lesson on edible fungus identification.'

'Well, there we are. Useful as well.'

She ignored Noel's pale glare; it would be much easier to sort out her business at the Firebrand office without him.

It didn't take long – in fact the whole procedure went so smoothly that she felt like composing a testimonial:

> *I insured my elderly neighbour at a shilling a week, and twenty-eight pounds and a florin has just landed safely in my purse, thanks to the efficient and honest services of this company. I'll certainly be recommending Firebrand Insurance to all my friends!*
> *Gratefully*
> *A housewife of England*

Old age had at last caught up with Miss Fillimore, who had

keeled over while walking her dog one evening, gone – according to the Coroner – between one breath and the next; a kindly death, especially compared to those poor souls in Kentish Town. The funeral had already taken place and Vee wasn't sorry she'd missed it; funerals always raised uneasy questions in her mind about the afterlife, and the difficult prospect of meeting those who'd gone before, particularly those whom God hath joined. When her own time came she didn't want to be ushered through the pearly gates only to find Samuel Sedge waiting for her with a song-sheet.

There had been forms to sign at Firebrand, and then a delay while the clerk went to fetch the key to the cash-box, but Vee had never had so sweet a wait. As she walked back to the flat, the bundle of money seemed to lighten the suitcase, rather than the reverse, and she spent it a few times in her head, first blowing the lot on a convalescent holiday in a spa hotel – her feet up on a chaise longue, a maid bringing her tea, Noel sitting in a nearby armchair with his nose in a book – and then changing her mind and buying a fawn cashmere coat for herself, and a brand-new bicycle for the boy. The next fantasy, a motor-tour of the Lake District, halted abruptly when she found that she couldn't open her own front door.

She inspected the key, in case it had sustained its own bomb damage during the week in London, and then she tried again. It wouldn't turn in the lock. She took a step back and looked at the door and noticed a pale crevice in the wood beside the jamb, where a long splinter had peeled away. There was a dent in one of the panels as well.

Abruptly, the door opened from the inside.

'Yes?' said a small, pale figure in a flannel dressing gown.

Vee couldn't speak at first, just flapped her mouth. 'That's my dressing gown,' she said, at last. 'What have you done to my door?'

'We had to change the keyhole.'

'What?'

'To get different keys.'

'You've changed the *lock*? What are you doing here anyway? It's my flat, I'm a legal tenant, I'll have the law on you.' She was pushing past the Austrian girl as she spoke, using the case as a battering ram, turning to shove her out into the street. Explanations could wait: there was a *foreigner* in her bloody flat, and one who'd kicked her way in, by the look of it, and was now shouting her head off and clinging on to the door and—

Vee registered, suddenly, exactly what it was that the girl was shouting.

'Donald!' called Hilde again.

Vee's head swivelled. At the top of the stairs, she saw her son. He was carrying a rifle.

Behind her, Hilde slid back inside the hall and closed the front door.

'This person has attacked me, Donald.'

'You've gone to Ireland,' said Vee.

'She has bended two of my fingers. They are very painful.'

'And I'm not a *person*!' shouted Vee, turning on the girl. 'I'm his *mother*. I pay the rent for this place and I'm telling you to get out.'

'No,' said Donald.

'What?' Vee turned her head again, too quickly, and this time the whole world turned with her and she found herself clutching the banister. 'You've got a gun,' she said, faintly, closing her eyes to quell the heave of the floor. She heard Hilde patter past her up the stairs.

'Are you hurt?' asked Donald; there was, possibly, a thin thread of concern in his voice.

'I got a concussion in the blackout, broke my cheekbone, had to have an operation, thank you for asking. This is my flat and I'm coming upstairs and I'm going to make myself a cup of tea so you'd better get that girl out of my way if you know what's good for you.'

'I do know what's good for me,' said Donald, in a peculiar tone of voice, and when Vee opened her eyes, Hilde was at his side, clutching his arm, looking down at Vee with those little black eyes.

'May I ask you take off your shoes,' she called down.

'Ask away,' said Vee. She dragged herself upstairs, and pushed past the pair of them on to the narrow landing.

Someone had hung a picture on the wall, a framed print of snow-covered mountains. Someone had tacked a fringe of beads on to the plain lampshade.

She opened the door to the kitchen and stared at the white tablecloth, the basket of raffia fruit, the vase of dried flowers, the easel – the *easel!* – by the window, slanted so that the morning light fell across a badly drawn tree. The curtains were tied back with ribbons. There were napkins on the table. In napkin rings.

'I will make the tea,' announced Hilde, bustling in. 'Sit, please.'

Vee started to argue, and then wearily pulled out a chair.

'I've only been away a week,' she said, to no one in particular. There was a scraping noise behind her and she looked round to see Hilde on her hands and knees with a dustpan and brush, sweeping the diagonal route that Vee had just taken to the table.

'Lemon or milk?' asked the girl.

'What?'

'With your tea. Lemon or milk?'

'And where are you proposing to get a lemon from? Mussolini dropping you a parcel?'

'I have a liddle dry peel from the last time I saw one.'

'Milk.'

Donald eased into Vee's field of vision. He propped the rifle in a corner and sat down at the other end of the table.

'What's going on then?' asked Vee, sharply, as if she was

speaking to a passing stranger rather than the fruit of her womb. 'Why are you still here? Why have you got a gun?'

'I joined the Home Guard.'

'Whatever for?'

'To get a firearm. Hilde had the idea.' He spoke her name with careful reverence, as if he'd get a cash prize for every mention.

The name in question was taking biscuits out of a tin barrel that Vee had never seen before, and arranging them on a plate.

'And was it her idea to move herself in?'

Donald looked shifty.

'It's a long story,' he said.

'I've got plenty of time,' said Vee. 'I'm not going anywhere – I *live* here, don't I? And before you start, isn't there someone else you should be asking about?'

There was a pause. Donald fingered his moustache.

'I saw Gran outside the Co-op, she was with Cousin Har—'

'I mean Noel! I mean the little boy you took to London and then lost.'

'Did you find him then?'

'Yes.'

'So that's all right.'

'No thanks to you.'

There wasn't a trace of guilt on his face, but there was something else – an expression, an *air*, that was unfamiliar. She couldn't quite put her finger on it.

'I thought I'd never see you again,' she said, the plaintive words out before she knew they were there.

'Something happened. We had to change the plan.'

'Donald?' It was Hilde speaking, holding out a tray to him. He stood up and went over and got it, Vee watching with astonishment.

'And now I will join you,' announced Hilde, taking a seat. She looked perfectly composed, sitting there in Vee's dressing gown, on Vee's chair, in Vee's kitchen. Vee herself swung round so she didn't have to look at her.

'What?' she said. 'What happened?'

'I can't say.'

'What, we're just going to sit here and have a little chin-wag about the sugar ration while a German pours me tea and wears my *clothes*?'

'Austrian.'

'And what sort of woman's still in a dressing gown in the middle of the morning?'

'This week I am on night shift at the factory,' said Hilde. 'I was almost in my bed when you came.'

'In *my* bed, almost in *my* bed.'

'Mum—'

'Would you like a Vanillekipferl?' Hilde seemed preternaturally calm, holding out the plate of biscuits.

'No.'

'I have baked them, but there is no vanilla or budder so they are very plain.'

'They're not the only ones,' said Vee with a venomous glance at her.

'No, Mum, you mustn't speak to Hilde like that.'

'I can speak to her how I like. This is my flat, my table, my—'

'I love her.' Donald uttered the threadbare old phrase as if it were newly stitched.

'What?'

'And she saved my life.'

Vee looked from one of them to the other, the large man (that was it, that was the expression she'd spotted: he looked like a *man*, his jaw as firm as Desperate Dan's) and the small, pale girl with her hair scraped back in an unbecoming bun, her eyes like currants on a dish.

'What do you mean?' she asked, feebly.

'We should tell her,' said Hilde. 'Because she has to know about the money.'

'What money?'

In the pause that followed, Vee found herself taking a biscuit. It wasn't bad. 'What money?' she asked again.

'*I* will tell,' said Hilde. 'I read the ledder you brought to me, Mrs Setch. Donald asked that I should talk to him about a matter that is Life or Death, so after my shift I came here, to this small flat and we spoke about these things for a long time, didn't we?'

She wheeled her gaze round to Donald, and he nodded. That afternoon, seated at the kitchen table, behind the drawn curtains, he had started to explain the whole bloody mess to her, and she had peeled away his lies like someone stripping wallpaper: the hush-hush job, the landlady, the nobby background, the London club – he had confessed to everything, exposed the unglamorous truth. And afterwards, when she'd asked for time to think, he had sat in misery and listened to her footsteps as she'd walked from room to room around the flat. She'd paused in his mother's room and he'd heard the squeak of the dressing-table mirror and had known she was looking at herself and he'd wished he could look at her too – wished he could stand behind her with his arms around her waist, gazing at their twin reflections.

Without her, he felt halved. A thought, tentative and unfamiliar, had wriggled up from some previously unvisited region of his brain: she deserved better than him.

'Then someone broke the door,' said Hilde.

He'd known it was death thundering up the stairs, and when the two men – the pallid one from Kensington, and a squat thug with hands like shovels – burst into the kitchen, he was still sitting on his chair, paralysed. In seconds, there was a razor at his throat, pressed to his Adam's apple so that he couldn't talk, or shout or even beg, and a warm thread crawled down his neck, and pooled in the notch above his breastbone; the world receded, so that he seemed to be looking through the wrong end of a telescope at two tiny men, discussing in conversational tones whether they should kill him in the bathtub or in a bedroom, and he had no thoughts left, only fear roaring around the inside of his skull like a stunt motorcycle.

And then Hilde had opened the kitchen door.

'What do you want?' she'd enquired, coldly. The pallid man had been looking out of the window; he swore and stepped towards her and she came to meet him, staring up at his pointed features like someone examining a large, ugly painting.

'What do you want?' she repeated. He moved uneasily, like a horse confronting a wasp.

'*We* ask the questions,' he said, 'not you. We'll take him with us,' he added, over his shoulder.

'Why? What do you get if you take him away?'

'Shut up. Sit there.'

She sat, and Donald felt the sting of the razor guiding him upwards and towards the door.

'Are you going to kill him?' asked Hilde.

'Shut up.'

'Do they pay you for this?'

'Shut *up*.'

'We can give you money. Donald has money, he has told me about his money. You could take his money and go away and I promise we would say nothing.'

The word 'money' seemed to hang in the air; the two men exchanged a swift, speculative glance.

'And then there would be no crime for the police to see,' added Hilde.

'What police?'

'I have just spoken out of the bedroom window to our neighbour who has a telephone, asking him to call the police. They will be here in a chiffy.'

'You're lying, you fucking foreign bitch.' But he strode to the window again and eyed the empty street. 'Get it then,' he said to Donald, 'get the money, let's see it.'

It was like a cold dream from the smallest hour of the night: footsteps and a blade just behind him, Donald knelt beside his bed and pulled out the shoebox, the illustration on the side showing a pair of tasselled loafers. He lifted the lid and a hand reached past him and extracted a roll of notes.

'How much is there?' asked the pallid man from the doorway.

There was a rustle and a muttered count. 'Maybe half a ton each. Bit more.'

The roll of notes reappeared in front of Donald's face.

'See this?' The roll waggled emphatically.

'Yes.'

'It's not enough. We leave with this, we'll be taking a few other things with us. Like your fucking *fingers*.' The last word was shouted so close to Donald's head that he jerked in shock. He started to gesture towards the Gladstone bag on top of the wardrobe, but Hilde was already speaking.

'There is more,' she said. 'I will show you.'

Donald stayed crouching, trying to work out what he was hearing – a door opening elsewhere in the flat, the squeak of a hinge. He dared to look round and saw the pallid man returning to the room, pushing something into the pocket of his coat as he walked, breaking step only to thrust his face into Donald's. 'I'm going to tell him,' he said, very close, very low, his breath smelling of bacon, 'that you'd done a flit and we couldn't find you. So from now on, you're the Invisible fucking Man, you're a cockroach under the carpet, we catch one more glimpse of you, you're finished and Eva Braun here's finished and they'll have to scoop you up in buckets before they can bury you.'

And both men were gone, hurrying down the stairs, clapping the front door shut, footsteps fading.

After a moment, Hilde appeared with a tea towel and knelt and dabbed at Donald's neck.

'A scratch, only,' she said.

He caught her hand and kissed it, and then laid it on his forehead like a cool benediction.

'Will you run away with me now?' he asked.

'No.'

'Please.'

'No. I have already run and run and I will not run any more.'

He closed his eyes in despair.

'I will stay, though,' she said. 'In this small flat. The rooms are not bad and the light is from the south-west.'

Vee had glanced between the couple as the story was recounted. She'd logged the tiny scab on Donald's neck, the pragmatism on Hilde's face, the soggy adoration on her son's.

'Whatever did you do to get in such trouble?' she asked, fretfully.

'I had a little business,' said Donald. 'Took me round and about.'

'Well you can't go round and about any more, can you?'

'I don't need to,' he said.

'Donald has a chob,' announced Hilde.

'What? Where?'

'In the bookshop.'

'The one downstairs?'

'Mr Clare needed an assistant.'

'What for? To clean his teeth for him?'

The insult was random, a time-filler as she tried to pull her thoughts together. 'So you're staying and she's staying. When were you going to ask me?'

'I didn't know when you were coming back.'

'You didn't wait long.'

'Hilde saved my life.'

'And spent all your money.'

'Yes, well . . .'

There was an odd pause. Hilde was sitting very upright, hands clasped in front of her.

'What?' asked Vee.

Donald cleared his throat.

'It wasn't just my money.'

It took a moment for the meaning to trickle through, and then Vee stood up so abruptly that her chair toppled over.

'You didn't,' she said.

There was no reply. She headed for her bedroom; it appeared untouched, spared the general redecoration, but she saw at once that the angle of the dressing-table mirrors was wrong, her bandaged face peering back at her in tilted triplicate. She lunged toward the left-hand mirror, swung it forward and stared at the hinge. Dangling from it was a frayed black thread.

She returned unsteadily to the kitchen doorway.

'You stole my savings.'

It was Hilde who answered. 'I had found the money by accident.'

'*Accident?*'

'Yes.'

'Do you think I'm soft in the head?'

'I had moved the mirror and something banged behind it and when I looked I saw a small bag hanging there.'

'And why did you move my mirror? Why did you need to do that?'

For the first time, the girl hesitated.

'I wanted to see my face,' she said. 'All of my face. The sides of it and the front of it.'

'Why?'

Hilde put a hand to her own cheek and pressed it, as if checking the freshness of a loaf. 'Because I wanted to know if I was more pretty than before. I wanted to know why

Donald was so much in love with a woman who looked like me.'

Donald made a choking noise. 'Not a woman,' he said. 'A lady.'

There was a brief silence.

'Oh, for crying out *loud*,' shouted Vee, derisively. 'This isn't a flipping stage play, I'm not going to start clapping. You swiped a hundred and seventeen pounds off me, you and this . . . this . . .' She struggled for a word to adequately describe Hilde; her son might think he'd bagged himself a member of the aristocracy but Vee knew a peasant when she saw one: all those airs and graces had been glued on, like beauty spots. She'd bet the whole bundle that Hilde had grown up on potato soup and an outdoor privy shared with half the village and any refinements had been filched from the place where she'd been employed as an under-housemaid. She opened her mouth to say as much – had the words 'If she's a lady then I'm Rin Tin Tin' ready to roll off her tongue – and then she saw that Hilde had leaned her head on Donald's shoulder, and he had put his right arm around her – gently, tenderly – and nobody had ever done that to Vee, not Harry Pedder (too busy unbuttoning her blouse), nor Samuel Sedge, who hadn't even had an arm on that side, and her rage was swept aside by a great gush of self-pity. Her throat closed, as if with a purse-string.

'Tea?' asked Hilde. 'Please sit.'

Vee sat.

'I knew,' said Hilde, pouring, 'that a good mother would of course spend all she has to save her child's life, so that is why I took the money. So now you have saved Donald with your savings and you can be very heppy. Another Vanillekipferl?'

Vee shook her head. 'What if those men come back?'

'I've got a gun now,' said Donald. 'Anyway, they think they've got all my money.'

Hilde flicked a glance at him.

'And they have,' added Donald. 'They have got all of it. So they won't be back.'

Vee looked from one of them to the other; she knew she was missing something but so much had been crammed into the last half hour that her head felt like a bolster.

'How can you be sure?' she asked. 'I won't be able to sleep at night, worrying. And there's Noel to think of, too. You can't have a child here with people waving guns around.'

'Who is Noel?'

The enquiry came from Hilde.

'The boy who lives here. The evacuee.'

The girl's face was a blank.

'*Noel*,' repeated Vee. 'Donald must have told you about him.'

'No. There is a child here?'

'Yes.'

'Where will he be sleeping?'

'I can make up a bed for him in the living room.'

'No, the living room is where Donald sleeps.'

'Oh.'

Hilde's face dropped in shock. 'Did you think I was sleeping in a bed with Donald?'

'Yes,' said Vee, recklessly.

'You think I'm a slud? I am not a slud. Until we are married I will not be in the bedroom with him.'

'*Married?*'

'We'll be getting married,' said Donald, 'as soon as Hilde's papers have been sorted out.'

Vee groped for the cup of tea, and took a gulp.

'Anything else you've forgotten to tell me?' she asked, weakly. 'Churchill hiding in the WC? New branch of Lyons opening in the parlour?'

'No, I think that is all,' said Hilde.

She was like a little iron bar, thought Vee.

'And now I must go to sleep,' added the girl, 'or I will not be able to help the war effort, which of course is what we all have to do. Goodnight.' She rose abruptly and left the kitchen, and Donald rose too and began to wash the cups, which in its way was as shocking as anything else that had happened that morning, and Vee drank her tea without tasting it and found herself remembering the previous time that she'd met Hilde.

'Did she get the other letter?' she asked.

'What other letter?'

'When I gave her your note she was expecting another letter. From abroad.'

'Oh.' Donald turned, a tea towel in his hand. 'She's looking out for a letter from her family.'

'They've not been in touch?'

'No.'

'Why not?'

'Because they got taken away and they're all dead, most likely. She doesn't talk about it.'

He hung the tea towel on a hook that certainly hadn't been there a week ago. 'I've got to get off to work now,' he said.

'All right,' said Vee. 'I won't stop you.'

She watched him tiptoe into Hilde's room, and return with a tie and a jacket. Was he taller than before? Or maybe he was just standing straighter, as if braced by something. By a little iron bar, possibly, tempered in some unimaginable fire.

She must have dozed for a while, sitting at the kitchen table, because when she next sipped her tea it was stone cold. I have twenty-eight pounds in the world, she thought. She stood, and her body felt strangely light, all ballast lost, as if a nudge from a sharp elbow might send her floating out of the window. And once out there, off she'd go again on the same old journey, bumping along with the breeze, blown from one temporary perch to another, nothing to show for the last twenty years, life slipping through her fingers like sand. VERA SEDGE, it would read on her headstone, NO LONGER AT THIS ADDRESS.

She took a mouthful of cold tea. Noel would be back soon: she had to pull herself together and come up with a plan for tonight and another for tomorrow; dear God, she had to come up with a plan for the next few *years* because what on earth would happen to an evacuee with no family and nowhere permanent to live? He could end up in a children's home: football matches and community singing and a future in the forces – round holes for the squarest possible peg. Her hands were clammy at the thought.

She went to the bathroom and splashed her eyes, and then studied her face in the mirror. The bruise was spreading; the whole area from her half-closed eyelid to her chin was a puffy palette of sunset hues.

You wouldn't, she thought, look at someone with an injury like that and think 'door'; you'd think of something huge. You'd think a house had fallen on her. You'd think she'd been dug out of the ruins, lucky to survive.

You'd think she'd come back from the dead.

Halfway through English dictation, Harvey Madeley passed Noel a note.

Were have you been did you run of to give your spy riport to the Germans.

Noel corrected the grammar and spelling, wrote *None of your business, you utter ignoramus* at the bottom and handed it back. At playtime, Madeley came over, gave him a Chinese burn and then punched him in the stomach.

Noel's wrist was still hurting when school ended, and he lingered in the playground until Harvey's fat arse disappeared round the corner. It wasn't until he crossed the road that he saw Vee, waiting outside the Co-op. She still had his suitcase and it had been joined by a large, shabby holdall with a broken zip.

'Good morning at school?' she asked.

'No. What's the matter?' She looked somehow dazed, her eyes flicking like a punch-drunk boxer's.

'I've had some surprises.'

'What do you mean?'

'The flat's a bit full now. My son's moved his fa—' She hesitated; never had the phrase 'fancy woman' seemed less applicable. 'My son's moved his fiancée in.'

'Oh. Can't you tell him to move her out again?'

'No.'

'Why not?'

'She's a piece of work. What's wrong with your wrist?'

'Someone gave me a Chinese burn.'

'You should have clocked him one.'

'He'd have beaten me senseless. Why didn't you clock Donald's fiancée one?'

Vee imagined the whirl of fists, teeth, nails.

'Ditto,' she said.

A lorry rumbled past, canvas flapping at the back to reveal a double row of soldiers, swaying in their sleep.

'So do I have to go somewhere else now?' asked Noel; there was no expression in his voice, but his face looked oddly stiff.

'I told you,' said Vee, sharply, 'that I was going to look after you. We're both going somewhere else.' She saw his face relax again.

'I told you,' she repeated, more gently. 'I wasn't lying.'

He nodded, diffidently. 'So where are we going?'

'How would you feel if we left St Albans?'

'I'd cheer,' he said, instantly.

'Good.'

'I'd hang bunting. I'd hire a brass band. I'd get one of those sky-writing aeroplanes to leave a message.' He pictured the words GOODBYE AND GET STUFFED MADELEY hanging in mile-high smoke above the city. 'I'd commission a statue of me hawking out of the train window as we left.'

Laughter caught in Vee's throat; it was painful, like a swallowed bone.

'What's the matter?' asked Noel.

'Nothing,' she said, dabbing her eyes.

'You can be in the statue too,' he said.

'Doing what?'

'Waving graciously with a handkerchief over your nose, like the queen when she's driven through a slum.'

'You have to listen,' she said, trying to steady herself. 'This is serious. I've had half an idea but I need your brains for the other half. We have to work out where we're going to live and . . . and some other things as well. Complicated things.'

Noel cocked his head, waiting.

'It's not . . .' she picked a careful path through the words. 'It's not the sort of plan that you'd want to end up explaining in court.'

Noel felt a stir of excitement. 'You mean it's legally wrong but morally right?'

There was a short pause.

'Yes,' said Vee, with just a touch of uncertainty. 'Want to hear it?'

5th March 1941

Dear Mr Churchill

I'm sorry not to have dropped you a line since before Christmas, though you couldn't really call it Christmas, we had mutton followed by a box of fruit jellies that my second husband went all the way to Watford to buy. He has been unwell with shingles which he caught when fire-watching at the Conservative Club, so for him to go all the way from Harpenden to Watford was very kind, and it wasn't his fault that the box was water-damaged and we couldn't eat them.

Our minister (Methodist) said it was a chance to return to the true meaning of Christmas, but I know for a fact that his wife won two oranges and a tinned turkey roll in a raffle.

I won't keep you long as I am very busy as I'm sure are you.

1. *I have been told by an old neighbour from St Albans that all those saucepans that were collected for making Spitfires last year are still in a big pile in that scrap-metal yard I told you about because they were selling stolen spoons. We're told on the wireless to boil down pigs heads and make jam etc but how can anyone do that when the only pan left in their second husband's kitchen is a great heavy iron pot like their own grandmother used in the days before electricity. I don't have the strength in my arms to even lift it so will have to carry on buying jam in the shops if I can get any. And the railings are the same, my neighbour says there's a great heap of them next to the pans. I wrote to the Ministry of Supply about it but they said anything to do with metal was the Ministry of Works so I wrote to the Ministry of Works but I had no reply which is why I'm writing to you.*

2. *My second husband says well done about Abyssinia, but he says you need to pull your socks up about Greece. He was in Greece in the last war and he says you should know that they're a tricky bunch with no loyalty, and also malaria.*

That's all for now, except I think the lack of pans is bad for morale and since it is against the law to Undermine Morale I think it could be a police matter. Speaking of which, my daughter Vera has not been seen or heard of since November and neither has her evacuee. The constable at the station said there is no evidence of a crime so won't do anything about it which is just typical.

Yours faithfully

Flora Brunton (note married name)

20

During raids, they sat in the cellar, wrapped in blankets, and the war was reduced to the odd muffled thump. By the light of a hurricane lamp, Noel read aloud from a succession of Agatha Christie novels and Vee pictured every scene as happening in their current house, guests dropping dead in the bamboo-papered drawing room, Hercule Poirot picking his way down the lane, spats dusted with sand.

The house was dreadfully cold. They carried a Chinese screen down from the first-floor back bathroom and curled it around the kitchen hearth. During the day, Noel sat as close to the grate as possible and worked at his lessons. He had refused to go to school, even if they could find one still open.

'How will you learn if you don't go to school?'

'You can set me essays and areas of study the way that Mattie used to. I can get books out of the library.'

'What sort of essays?'

'Ones with a question mark in the title. Like "What is Freedom?" or "Is the Child the Father of the Man?" Discuss.'

'Discuss?'

'Yes. That's what you have to do in essays.'

'And how do I mark something like that?'

'Mattie didn't give marks, she just wrote comments.'

'Yes, but . . .' Vee tried to think of another argument, but the truth was that she didn't mind having him around during the day. She was still trying to get used to being Margery Overs; it was like wearing an old-fashioned jacket tailored for someone of an entirely different shape.

'I can't be noticeable,' she said. 'I have to look like your guardian.'

'You can't.'

'You know what I mean. I can't risk anyone asking questions. I have to be——'

'Unobtrusive.'

'Yes.'

It meant not arguing in shops, it meant walking at a measured pace instead of hurtling from one task to another, it meant not fidgeting in queues, or jumping into others' conversation or letting out long, irritated sighs, or barking with fury when the greengrocer leaned on the scales so that she ended up paying for a pound and a half of carrots and part of his elbow. It meant keeping her voice low and reasonable. By the time she got home, she had indigestion from all the unsaid remarks.

'Try this for an essay title,' she said to Noel. '"Who Profits Most from the War? Nazis or Shopkeepers?" Discuss.'

They'd been there a month when there was a rap at the door.

'Only a man selling firewood,' said Vee, returning to the kitchen. 'It gave me a fright, hearing the knocker. Thought it was our marching orders.'

Noel looked up, eyes vague, mind still on the page. 'What do you mean?'

'We can't stay for ever, can we? It was a good idea to start off here, but people are getting bombed out, the landlord could cram this place with lodgers; he's bound to turn up sooner or later.'

'But there isn't a landlord,' said Noel, as if stating the obvious. 'It belonged to Mattie.'

'You mean she *owned* it?'

'Yes.'

'What, all of it?'

'Yes. How could she only have owned *some* of it?'

'If she had a mortgage, Mr Knife.'

'Well, she didn't have a mortgage. She bought it for sixteen hundred pounds in 1922.'

'So who does it belong to now?'

Noel boggled at her as if she'd just asked him how to spell the word 'bun'.

'It belongs to me, of course.'

'You?'

He nodded. 'I'm the sole beneficiary. I actually went along with Mattie when she signed her will. The solicitor's quite a nice man, he looks rather the way that I imagine Mr Wemmick would look. You know – Jaggers' clerk,' he added, when Vee stayed silent. 'In *Great Expectations*.'

She had to drink half a cup of tea before she could speak again, although what she really wanted was a large gin.

'I suppose there'll be papers and things to sort out,' she said, more to herself than to Noel. 'No hurry, though.'

After the war would do, she thought. Sufficient unto the day was the evil thereof. And the good.

While Noel worked at his books, she cleaned the house, room by room, taking her time about it. What she couldn't get over was the number of cherishable objects: china eggs that a damp cloth restored to brilliance; antique mirrors that reflected a softened, grey-green world; paintings – actual paintings, not prints. Every room contained something that she wanted to stroke, or hold.

That's what money got you, she thought: things that you wanted to touch.

The kitchen was less cherishable, the stove a dangerous antique, the larder full of mould and mouse droppings.

'What?' asked Noel, when she screamed.

'A dead mouse, I think.' She'd reached into a bread-crock right at the back of the larder and her fingertips had touched something soft. She brought the crock out into the light and tipped it on to a newspaper. A heavy cloth-wrapped bundle dropped out.

'Oh,' said Noel, standing up so fast that his pen bounced across the room. 'I know what that is. I'd forgotten about it.'

She let him open it. The cloth was a silk scarf, patterned with peacock feathers; inside was a tangle of jewellery, brooch pins protruding like booby-traps, a long rope of seed pearls binding the whole clump immovably together. It took the rest of the afternoon to untangle; Noel gave up after half an hour and slid back to his books but Vee sat on beside the window, gently teasing the elements apart. There were handfuls of rings, a garnet choker, a jet mourning brooch, a necklace that glittered coldly and shouted money. And then there was a medal, the ribbon a twist of green and purple, the silver disc bearing two illegible words. She scratched at the tarnish with a thumbnail and read:

MATILDA SIMPKIN

'Your godmother's,' she said, holding it up for Noel to see. 'And there's one of those Holloway brooches as well, with the portcullis. And the safety pin with the chip of stone.'

She stood up to get the pleats out of her back, and then went to fill the kettle. When she returned, Noel had laid the suffragette medals out next to each other on the window seat, like a display in a museum case.

'They're all blackened,' he said.

'We can polish them with lemon juice. If we can get some.'

CROOKED HEART

'Mattie was very proud of them.'

'I'm sure she was,' said Vee.

He waited for the barb that came stitched to every comment that Vee made about Mattie, and when it didn't come he felt a curious sensation, like a key turning in his chest. It was almost like happiness, and so unexpected that he wanted, in some obscure way, to thank her.

'I know that Mattie didn't ever have to worry about working, or being able to pay for things,' he offered, awkwardly.

'Even so,' said Vee, 'I couldn't have done what she did. Do you know, I've just remembered that vinegar's good for cleaning silver, and we've got some of that.'

The pins came up nicely.

'I can't remember the last time I had fish and chips,' said Vee.

'I found out where Mrs Gifford is,' said Noel. 'When you were in the hospital, I copied out a list of asylums at the library, and I went to a telephone box and rang every number until I found her.'

She'd long since ceased to be surprised at his competence. 'So where is she?'

'Doulton Grange.'

'Near Hatton in Hertfordshire?'

'Yes. Do you know it?'

She nodded. Oh yes, she knew it: Samuel Sedge lying mute on a bed while she sat beside him, chattering with bright desperation.

'Could we go there?' asked Noel.

'It wouldn't be very nice. They're not nice places.'

'I'd like to go.'

'She might not even be talking. I don't suppose she'll recognize you.'

'I don't mind.'

'And it's not as if we ever got her pins back for her, is it?'

'No, I know. But now I could give her these instead.'

'*These?* But don't you want to keep them?'

'Yes, I do, but I'd rather give them to Mrs Gifford.'

He looked at her, his expression mulish, and she could tell that he'd made up his mind, and that if she refused to take him, he'd find a way to get there by himself – would walk, or thumb a lift, or commandeer a passing tank – and it occurred to her that their life together would likely contain many such moments, Noel being what he was.

She sighed. 'All right then, if you must. But we'll have to find out the visiting hours.' Her memory shrank from those awful journeys, the bus crawling along country lanes, the long, dreary walk from the lodge gates up to the hospital, the dread she felt on the way there, the exhaustion on the way back.

'I still have the asylum's number,' said Noel. 'I can use the telephone box on Pond Street. I'll go now.' Vee watched him put on his shoes, and stirred herself.

'I'll come with you. We need salt.'

There was a queue for the telephone. Noel occupied the time by mentally reciting 'The Charge of the Light Brigade', and then watching a troupe of Girl Guides who were ambling past, carrying a banner that read

IS YOUR JOURNEY REALLY NECESSARY?
WE'RE WALKING TO
SAVE FUEL!!!

Behind them, a taxi, two buses and an army lorry inched up the road, the taxi-driver shouting abuse out of the window.

Vee was watching as well, her eyes on the taxi; it was giving her an idea.

'Two o'clock till three o'clock on the second and fourth Tuesdays of the month,' said Noel, emerging from the phone box.

'I need to make a call too,' said Vee. She closed the door

firmly on him, so that he couldn't hear what she said to the operator; she was put through with surprising speed.

'Fleckney's Garage.' In the background, someone was using a grinder.

'Could I speak to Mr Pedder, please?'

'Oh my God, you again? But I told you—'

'Oh hello, Harry, this isn't a very good line – I didn't recognize your voice.'

'I can't talk to you now. Or later.'

'No, don't call off. I'll only try again tomorrow. I might accidentally get your wife next time.'

'But—' He was practically spluttering with panic. 'Wait.' There was a pause, and the sound of a door shutting. The snarl of the grinder disappeared and she could hear Harry's footsteps returning to the desk.

'I told you that I didn't want to hear from you again.'

'Yes, well, something's cropped up.'

'Christ, I had to move bloody heaven and earth to get you that signature.'

'I thought you just had to tell the magistrate you wouldn't give him any more black-market petrol.'

'Don't say it.'

'Unless he signed my new identity card.'

'*Don't say it.* You don't know who's listening.'

'All right. Anyway, it's nothing to do with the signature; that all went through very nicely, thank you. It's only a little thing this time.'

'Please, Vee, just leave me alone.'

'I will after this. I promise. It's only a small favour . . .'

She was smiling when she left the telephone box. Noel looked at her curiously.

'Wait and see,' she said, before he could ask. 'It's a surprise.'

21

The station was called Bramley Halt, and once the train had juddered off into the distance, only Vee and Noel were left standing on the platform. A crowd of sparrows twittered viciously in the bushes beside the footbridge.

'Adelstrop,' said Noel.

'What's that then?'

'A poem about an express train stopping at a remote rural station on a hot afternoon, and no one gets on or off and the writer looks out of the window and sees meadowsweet and haycocks dry, no whit less still and lonely fair than the high cloudlets in the sky.'

'That would have been in summer, though.'

'Late June, the poem says.'

'This time of year, he'd have had to write about muck spreaders.'

Noel snorted. 'There are high cloudlets, though.'

'That's true.' She tipped her head back to look at the sky, a milky blue dappled with white. 'It's a nice enough day.'

They crossed the bridge and came out into a high-hedged lane, and Harry Pedder was there already, standing glumly beside a shining green motor car.

'It's a Bentley!' said Noel. 'A Bentley Speed Six!'

Harry nodded, grudgingly. 'The 1933 model. Didn't know he was coming too,' he added, in Vee's direction.

'We stick together,' she said, serenely. Harry opened the passenger door, and she didn't climb in straight away, but took a moment to enjoy the sensation of being waited on. The interior of the car was cream, and smelled of leather polish.

'Come on, come on,' muttered Harry, 'before somebody sees us.'

The seat was delicately sprung, and the dashboard a walnut veneer that shone like a rinsed plate. She'd once been given a lift in the back seat of the Methodist minister's Austin, but there was no comparison between that bruising journey, spent wedged between two hundred hymn books and a tea-urn, and her current glide between the hedgerows.

'I wasn't expecting such a nice motor car,' said Vee. 'Thank you.'

Harry nodded, tightly. 'I've got to deliver it on afterwards, so don't think I'm doing it just for you.'

'I meant what I said,' said Vee. 'This'll be the last thing I ask of you. It's just that we had to visit the hospital and I couldn't quite face the walk.'

Harry grunted.

'How's business?' asked Vee.

'It's all government regulations, something new every week, one flaming headache after another.'

'And the family? Children all well?'

He gave her a look and she smiled demurely.

'Only asking.'

'Well don't.'

'I had a ride in a Bugatti once,' piped Noel, from the back.

They travelled in silence for a while, and twice Vee saw Harry steal a glance at her face.

'What's the matter?' she said. 'Looking at my scar?'

'It's not so bad,' he said. 'Thought it would be a lot worse underneath all those bandages. Gave me a hell of a shock when you turned up at the garage looking like the curse of the mummy with him in tow. Who is he, anyway?'

'My nephew,' she said, blandly.

'Doesn't seem right to mix up a child in all this.'

'All what?'

'Your schemes. There are names for what you did,' he added, censoriously. 'Blackmail and forgery.'

'As a matter of fact, it was his idea,' said Vee. 'He asked if there was anyone official I had the goods on.'

'Had the what?'

'It's an American phrase. We'd been reading a detective book by a Mr Raymond Chandler. So I thought of you, Harry, and your connections and your yard full of red petrol. Ooh look, Noel – lambs!' She watched a field of sheep whisk past. Ahead, the extravagant roof-scape of Doulton Grange Asylum – all cupolas and dormers and twisted chimneys – was showing above the treetops.

'Nearly there,' she said.

Noel had half-expected a scene out of a Hogarth print – cell after cell of lunatics dressed as Napoleon or Julius Caesar, deranged laughter echoing along the corridors; instead, he and Vee were shown into a cream-painted day room where the main noise was the sizzle of a poorly tuned wireless. Beneath the static, the sound of a dance-band flared and receded, as if someone were opening and shutting a door.

A number of small tables were scattered around the room, with two or three people sitting at each; it looked rather like a whist drive, except that there were no cards and no one appeared to be having fun. A man at the nearest table was knitting, the needles held about an inch in front of his face, a narrow khaki snake drooping between them.

'Occupational therapy,' said Vee. 'They used to teach them

how to make fireside fans out of waxed paper, but I suppose knitting's more useful.'

Noel was scanning the room.

'Or sometimes they'd have to glue seashells on to boxes, but I don't suppose you can get the shells now.' The place was plucking at her nerves. 'Or the glue,' she added. 'Or the boxes.'

'Mrs Gifford's over by the window,' said Noel; he recognized her profile, beaky and spare, her jaw moving as she talked to the woman beside her.

'Go on then,' said Vee.

He hesitated, fingering the cloth pouch in his pocket, sudden panic drying his mouth, because whether Mrs Gifford welcomed his gift or threw it out of the window, it was the end of something – the quest completed, the curtain drawn – and he didn't know, couldn't imagine, what would come afterwards.

'Do you want me along with you?' asked Vee.

'Yes. No.'

'Which is it?'

'No. I'd rather see her on my own.'

'All right then. I'll wait here.' She sounded relieved.

He took a couple of breaths, as if about to duck underwater, and then walked across the room and Mrs Gifford's voice came out to meet him, a purling stream of reminiscence into which he was instantly incorporated: '. . . she gave us a cheese as large as a cartwheel and Ada suggested we roll it down the hill only we had to borrow the Hadleys' donkey cart to get it up there and here's young Hadley now, have you finished your prep?'

'Yes,' said Noel. She was tidier than when he'd seen her last, her hair neatly plaited, her clothes ill-fitting but clean; she smelled of carbolic.

'I don't have any eggs,' complained the other woman at the table, shrivelled in shawls. 'If we had eggs I could show you how to make the perfect Victoria . . .'

'We threw eggs at the Member for Haverford West, I was

always a crack shot, Lena Fitzackerly said I could have bowled for Surrey. I expect you're awfully hungry after cricket practice, I shall ring for tea and sugared buns. Do take a seat . . .'

'. . . sift the flour. You have to sift it . . .'

'. . . the gardener will be here directly, I simply must compliment him on the rhododendrons, did you ever see blooms like it? I believe they call that colour *cerise* . . .'

Noel sat, and the two conversations flowed onward, twin currents mingling and then diverging, Mrs Gifford animated, the other woman talking grimly at the tabletop, imparting a lifetime of kitchen skills to a small section of oilcloth.

'Do you remember me, Mrs Gifford?' asked Noel. Her gaze dabbed at him and then bounced off again.

'Of course, you're Gloria Kennedy's little nephew, I last saw you in your petticoats on the lawn outside the Woodfields' house—'

'No, it was last September.'

'And it was a particularly lovely autumn, we had baskets and baskets of damsons.'

'I had a collecting box and you gave me a lot of money. You were living in an upstairs room in Chetwynd Street and the first time you invited us in' – he raised his voice over hers – 'the first time you invited us in you were wearing a Hunger Strike medal.'

There was a hitch in Mrs Gifford's speech, the stream burbling over a snag. She talked on, but her eyes darted towards Noel again, following his movements as he took the cloth pouch from his pocket.

'And the reason I knew it was a Hunger Strike medal,' he said, feeling around inside the bag, 'was because my godmother had one too.'

He clinked the silver disc on to the table, citation uppermost, and Mrs Gifford peered at it, her speech briefly petering out before suddenly resuming.

'Ah yes, Matilda Simpkin, though of course we called her Mattie.'

Noel's head jerked back. Hearing the name out loud was like being smacked with a pillow – a buffet both shocking and pleasurable.

'Mattie Simpkin,' said Mrs Gifford again. 'Did you know that she could whistle and hum at the same time?'

He nodded, though he didn't dare speak, didn't dare *breathe* in case he broke the tiny thread of memory. Mrs Gifford's eyes held his, grey-green and quite sensible.

'We'd all sing "Bread and Roses" in our cells after lights out: "As we come marching, marching, we bring the greater days", and then Mattie Simpkin would whistle and hum the chorus and I'd lean my head against the water pipes so I could hear her.'

'You should always have cold hands for pastry,' said the other woman, 'and warm hands for bread and you must put the butter on ice for at least half an hour before making pastry.'

Mrs Gifford's gaze shifted. 'There was a skating party at Lancing last week,' she remarked, 'and Agnes Calder went through the ice clear up to her hips.'

She was gone again, and it was as if he'd just glimpsed Mattie round the edge of a closing door; Mattie, present and correct, Mattie splendid, solid, brave and loud. He picked up the medal and grasped it so tightly that the edge dug into his palm and then he dropped it back into the pouch and held it out to Mrs Gifford.

'This is for you,' he said.

She took it from him without apparent interest, tucked it into the pocket of her cardigan and carried on talking, and Noel stood up, his legs feeling clumsy and cold. He turned to see Vee coming across the room towards him and he realized, with a strange sort of shock, that he was pleased to see her.

'All done?'

He nodded. 'She knew Mattie, she remembered her.'

'That's good. Can we go now? This place gives me the whinwans.'

He turned the word over in his head as they walked back along the corridor.

'What are "whinwans"?'

'Have you never heard that word before?'

'No.'

'That's a first. I suppose it means the creeps.'

'What's its origin?'

'I've no idea, it's just what people say round here. Tell you what, that can be your next bit of homework.'

'The etymology of "whinwan"?'

She nodded. 'Discuss.' She gave him a sidelong glance. 'You're smiling.'

'I do smile sometimes.'

'Not often enough.'

She let him sit in the front seat of the Bentley on the way back to the station.

22

The bombing stopped in May, though it took weeks for them to lose the habit of nightly fear, to straighten up, like grass after the roller has been shifted.

June was bright and warm, day after day of brilliant skies, and Vee began to feel restless. She found herself staring at the Red Cross collector outside the Co-op, envying the jolly rattle of coins into the box; it took an effort to shove the thought away.

She was bored, she decided.

'I might put a card in the newsagent's window,' she said to Noel.

'Why?'

'Clothing alteration and fancy work. Do you think that's the sort of thing your Auntie Margery might do?'

'I don't see why not.' He was weighing flour, frowning at the scales, a recipe for potato pie propped against the colander. He was good at cooking, she'd discovered; moreover, he actually *enjoyed* it. One day he might make someone an unusually useful husband, though she suspected he'd end up in bachelor quarters in an Oxford college, being waited on.

'The telephone's working again now,' she said. 'Mostly, anyway. I could put our number.'

'All right.'

'The only thing is . . .' She paused until he turned to look at her. There was a white smudge on his chin.

'What?'

'You might be the one to answer it. And then you'd have to say, "I'll just go and get my aunt." Or you'd have to sing out for me if I was upstairs, or in the garden, or in the kitchen. Wouldn't you?'

He waited for her to start making sense.

'You don't call me anything,' she said. 'You don't have a name for me. You don't even say "Aunt".'

'Don't I?'

'You must have noticed.'

He shook his head.

'Well, do you think you could try? There are going to be times when we have to talk to other people. How about "Auntie"? Or "Auntie Margery"?' Though she could hear the lack of conviction in her own voice; she didn't feel like an auntie or a Margery.

'I just used Mattie's first name. Can't I do that?'

Vee sighed. 'All right then, though people will find it odd. Maybe you could shorten it a bit. Marge sounds better than Margery.'

He went back to his pastry-making and Vee found a stub of pencil and the back of a sheet of drawer-liner and started to work on her advertisement.

'How many fs in "professional"?'

'One. You know you said I could call you Marge?'

'Yes.'

'What if I shortened it even more?'

'To what?'

'Mar.'

She looked round, but his back was to her, his ears silhouetted against the window. A puff of flour ballooned up from the bowl.

'Mar,' she repeated, tasting the word, letting it melt on her tongue like a sugar-lump. 'I don't mind that. I've been called worse.'

Acknowledgements

I'd never have finished *Crooked Heart* without the friendship, support and advice of Kate Anthony and Gaby Chiappe, the two writers to whom it's dedicated. Thanks too to Georgia Garrett (as always) and to Bill Scott-Kerr, who, despite having to wait years and years and *years* for this book, remained unfailingly patient and encouraging. And finally, thanks to the *Herts Advertiser* and *St Albans Times* (now defunct) for being the source of much inspiration.

Lissa Evans has written books for both adults and children, including *Their Finest Hour and a Half*, longlisted for the Orange Prize, and *Small Change for Stuart*, shortlisted for the Carnegie Medal and the Costa Book Award.